THE
OPENING

a novel

Tim McWhorter

Manta Press

Cover Design by Tim McWhorter
Author Photo by Julie A. McWhorter
Copyright © 2021 by Manta Press

Published by Manta Press
Pickerington, OH 43147

The Opening
ISBN: 978-1-7357289-4-0 (paperback)
ISBN: 978-1-7357289-5-7 (eBook)

Printed in the United States of America

Author's Note

Hey, before we get started, just wanted to put this out there: suicide sucks. If you ever feel you're at that point, please reach out. Get help.

Someone is always available and ready to listen.

National Suicide Prevention Lifeline
800-273-8255

PROLOGUE

A crowd had gathered.

Some were tourists, in town for only a week, soaking up as much sand and surf as they could before returning to the concrete jungle for another year. Residents of Angler Bay filled in the gaps. He knew many of the pained faces staring up at him—anxiously eager to do something—poised to stop what could never be undone. Maybe it was the acrid fumes that kept their feet rooted in place. Fear of getting caught in the fray. He only hoped they kept their distance.

"Don't do it, Floyd!" one of them shouted.

"It's not worth it!" cried another.

He heard the pleas and ignored them.

He raised the red gas can above his head, draining every last drop before tossing it aside. The container clanged end over end down the concrete steps. It came to a stop on the sidewalk, looking up at those brave enough to stand witness. The next few moments were certain to be horrific. Moments they would never forget, the image burnt into their brains.

Floyd coughed as fuel streamed down his face and stung his eyes. The fumes constricted his throat. He choked on the absence of fresh air. His lungs burned with a lack of clean oxygen. Breathing became a struggle as he reached into his pocket for the second half of the equation.

He pulled out the lighter.

"Somebody get help!"

"Somebody call Helen!"

He held the lighter—a scuffed black Zippo he'd had since Korea—down and away from his body. He didn't want to see it. Seeing it might bring back memories, obstacles he'd overcome in the past. The dented and paint-chipped lid, having once saved him from the point of a bayonet, might cause him to second guess.

Meanwhile, the pleas kept coming.

"Somebody, please! Do something!"

He turned his back to the crowd and looked upon the doors of The Chamberlain Theater. *His* theater. A grim, silver chain snaked through the long, gothic-styled handles. The two ends converged at a padlock, which sealed the entrance. Taped to the glass, a simple, white sheet of paper. The bank's letterhead across the top, as much as the chains, barred him from entering the premises. He'd owned the theater for over forty years. A lifetime. He remembered the day they installed the heavy, custom-built wood doors, which opened to the auditorium. The morning the marquee sign arrived, polished and majestic, strapped to the back of a flatbed truck. From that day forward, The Chamberlain Theater was no longer an afterthought, sought only when rain had washed out the summer sun and surf. It became the anchor of the town center.

These memories, the bank couldn't have. He'd be taking them to hell with him.

Gasoline dripped from his nose, his chin. It pooled at his feet.

Good memories became harder to come by as time wore on. Thanks in part to an economy in the toilet, and bills that never stopped coming, even after the customers had. He'd spent countless afternoons alone in his office, brainstorming ways to bring in more business. He'd failed at every turn. And when the bank's patience had reached an end, they'd foreclosed and taken the only thing he'd ever had in the world. The bastards may as well have filled the gas can and placed it in his hands.

He wiped his face with his shoulder, coughed into it.

An hour ago, he'd kissed his wife's cheek while she slept beneath the roof he could no longer provide. He was too proud, too ashamed to see his failure reflected in her emerald green eyes. He'd fed the cat, scratched behind her ears the way she liked, then quietly closed the door behind him.

If he was honest, losing the theater wasn't the only reason he stood outside its walls, soaked to the bone with gasoline. There was that other thing. Good or bad, he'd done what he'd done. If he could, he'd take the whole building down to hell with him. Then its secrets would never be discovered. Nobody would find out what he'd done. The mistakes he'd made.

He shook his head.

He raised the lighter to his chin.

Sensing the end was near, the crowd's chorus of pleas swelled. Cries of his name filled the crisp morning air. And as a lone brave soul, unable to stand idle any longer, charged up the steps, Floyd took one last stagnant breath.

He closed his eyes.

My turn now...

He spun the flint.

Act One

ONE

Nick popped a blue Xanax and let it dissolve on his tongue.

It was opening night. The smell of fresh buttered popcorn hung in the air. Money was being exchanged for tickets. And moviegoers were filtering into the newly-remodeled lobby in numbers like The Chamberlain Theater hadn't seen in years.

In his father's words, Nick should be as happy as a tornado in a trailer park.

Yet, his father was no longer around, and the walls were closing in around him. At least that's how it felt. The curtain wasn't due to raise for another hour, and already, Nick's undershirt clung to him like a clammy second skin. The night was almost too important. The stage, too big. His mind looped through the list of businesses he'd started and had subsequently failed at. The do-it-yourself frozen yogurt shop he'd whimsically called "Fro-Yo-Self." The video store / pizza shop where patrons could order a pizza, then search for a DVD while they waited. Seems he was always chasing a new take on an old favorite. Would this new type of movie theater be the one to elevate him above the title of failed businessman? Or, because it was the biggest, costliest venture yet, would The Chamberlain Theater serve as the crown jewel atop an already hulking coronet of failures?

Nick popped another Xanax for good measure.

The light music floating above the lobby's gathering crowd played calming notes in his mind. People were talking, laughing. Their numbers continued to grow. Currently, there were no fires to put out.

So far, so good.

Standing at the lobby's edge, Nick was hesitant to look in Amber's direction. The box office had only been open a few minutes, and already she'd needed assistance with the register twice, despite claiming extensive experience on her application. *She'll get it*, Nick assured himself. She had to, and not just because he woefully dreaded the hiring process. Replacing Amber at this point would be difficult. Like any community, Angler Bay was full of teens in need of a seasonal job, but it seemed few of them wanted to work at The Chamberlain Theater. The fact he'd only received a handful of applications told Nick most were steering clear of the place. A building this old, rumors of the theater being haunted were inevitable. The previous owner torching himself on the front steps only served to add more fuel to an already growing fire. No pun intended.

Nick sucked it up and looked in Amber's direction. When she looked back his way, he gave her a thumbs up in the hopes of getting one in return. When he got one, he let out a cautious sigh of relief.

The good vibes didn't last.

"Looking good, Nick."

Shit. Nick's heart settled into his already queasy stomach.

Though the voice had come from behind him, Nick knew who it belonged to. If there had been any question at all, the meaty hand that clamped onto his shoulder gave it away.

Nick turned, ducked out of the grasp, and reached to take the man's large hand in his own. "Mayor Blackwood."

The mayor of Angler Bay wasn't particularly tall, but at six-foot two, he towered over Nick. The man also had a good hundred pounds on him. Whoever said that no man was an island unto himself, had never met Jonas Blackwood. The guy was his own damn continent, with an ego to match. His hand devoured Nick's the way a great white swallows a baby seal.

"Glad you could make it." Sweat trickled down the back of Nick's neck as he watched the mayor take in the new lobby: the fresh crimson paint on the walls; the shiny mirrored glass of the new concession counter; the gold floor-length drapes that created the illusion of window coverings, even though they cloaked nothing but drywall behind them. Situated between the glitzy, neon pink interior of the Starlight Twistee Cone, and a collection of dumpsters in the world's least-used alleyway, there was no need for windows in The Chamberlain's lobby. Or, anywhere else in the theater, for that matter.

"Ain't no way I'd miss opening night." The mayor had a wicked twinkle in his glassy eyes. His cheeks were red. His sloppy smile spoke of merriment and Tanqueray, telling Nick he'd most likely just come from one of his famous four-course dinners: a steak and three gin and tonics. "Hell, I feel like she's as much my baby as yours."

And there it was.

Nick bristled before mustering his best attempt at a cordial smile. "Well, it was your hands that pulled the strings, Mayor. Wouldn't be much of an opening night without all your help."

Ever since Nick had purchased The Chamberlain, the mayor hadn't let him forget that it was his doing that made it happen. It was apparently the mayor that pressured the bank to hold the theater's previous owner to terms, to stop allowing him more time on his payments. It was the mayor who wanted to see the theater start making money for the town, and not the other way around. Nick sometimes wondered if he'd always feel indebted to the guy, no matter how long he owned the theater. Only upside was that it provided another shoulder for the guilt about the way it had all gone down.

Poor old bastard.

Nick shrugged it off. He wasn't letting the Mayor, nor the ghost of the theater's previous owner, get under his skin tonight. Not on opening night. It wasn't like Nick was responsible for the livelihood of nearly four thousand people. That was the mayor's cross to bear.

"Well, shit. I appreciate that, Nick." With a wink and a grin, revealing teeth that were no stranger to fine cigars, the mayor took his leave. He sauntered over to the concessions counter and began taking stock of the offerings.

Nick wiped his hand on his pants leg, all too happy to be rid of the mayor. The guy could eat his weight in popcorn and candy for all Nick cared. Just as long as it kept him out of Nick's hair.

Fanning air into his collar, Nick scanned the room's growing population.

From across the lobby, he once again checked Amber's status. The line at the ticket counter had all but disappeared. The young woman smiled and gave another unprompted thumbs up. The smile soothed a bit of the fire in Nick's belly. The smile was a welcome alternative to the furrowed brow and frenzied eyes from earlier. A moment later, when the window was clear of customers, he weaved his way through the crowd.

"Hey, Mr. Fallon!" Amber chirped when he approached. "What's up?"

Nick pulled a crumpled paper towel from his pocket and wiped sweat from his forehead. "You see Manny come through, yet?"

The engineer had worked for Nick since the day after he'd closed on The Chamberlain. Not only was Manny the first employee he'd brought onboard, but Manny had helped oversee the engineering involved in transforming the old, lackluster theater into a high-tech movie house. He was smart, knew his way around electronics, and was one of the few people Nick had been able to count on throughout the theater's makeover. Manny had never failed to show up for work, had never let Nick down, unlike most of the contractors he'd hired. So, the fact he hadn't seen him yet that evening added more stress to Nick's opening night anxiety.

"Nope." Amber took a look around, as if Nick hadn't thought of doing so. "No, sir, I haven't."

Nick checked his watch for the third time in ten minutes. "Well, if you see Manny before I do, please tell him I'm looking for him."

"Will do." Amber smiled and feigned a salute. Then her smile disappeared. "Oh, yeah. Speaking of looking for someone, that reporter came in a few minutes ago. You know, from *The Standard?*"

The perspiration under Nick's collar turned cold.

* * *

Nori Park gently closed the heavy wooden door behind her.

Being an investigative reporter in a town where little needed investigating, she found excitement in her job where she could. Tonight, that meant being the first to check out the new theater with the troubled past, which was about as interesting as things got in the sleepy town of Angler Bay.

After college, she'd shot for the big city. Like most in her field, Nori was drawn by the prospects of pulling back the curtain on political corruption, corporate wrongdoing, organized crime. Ultimately, she'd fallen short, landing at a small-town newspaper along the North Carolina coast. Despite the lack of any real excitement to report, the trade-off wasn't without its benefits: she got to spend her down time at the beach. She'd even taken a handful of surfing lessons last summer. All in all, Angler Bay wasn't a bad place for a kid from the gritty streets of Seoul, South Korea to end up.

The auditorium greeted Nori with the combined scents of fresh paint, newly stretched vinyl, and just the slightest hint of old smoke hovering above it all. Other than the smoke, everything smelled new, looked new. Everything had a shine. She'd been to the old theater once before, a disastrous first date three years back. The Chamberlain had been run down, but still possessed a quaintness and character amid its peeling paint and soda-stained carpeting. A historic place where one could almost feel its history. It was said that Eisenhower had once attended a function at The Chamberlain, had sat in that very room.

But never in seats like these, Nori observed.

She ran her hand along one of the slick seat backs. These seats were plush, clean, and word had it, high-tech. They were nothing like the creaky, velvet-covered antiques she remembered being so uncomfortable.

Nori grabbed an end seat in the back row and tried it out. The cushion gave some, cradling her butt perfectly. She leaned back, her head against the cushioned rest. The back seemed a little too upright, and the armrests a little thin. Otherwise, the new seats would make for a fairly enjoyable movie-watching experience.

Don't get too comfortable, she told herself. *You're here to work, remember?*

Nori rose to her feet. After pulling an iPad from her bag, she slung the satchel over her shoulder. She started down the sloping center aisle toward the giant silver screen down front, eyes scouring her surroundings. Row after row of the red and black seats spread out in perfectly curved lines. Overhead, various black boxes hung from the ceiling, strategically placed. They weren't speakers. Those were easy to spot hanging along the front and edges of the large room. The black boxes either had pipes or thin tubing running to and between them. She raised the iPad and snapped a few photos.

"Interesting."

TWO

"Seriously?" Nick lacked the skill needed in keeping disappointment from his voice. "Amber, I asked you to let me know *the moment* she arrived."

Amber met Nick's chagrin with a pained look of her own.

The tension in Nick's set jaw lifted. He took a deep breath.

"Okay, so. She got here a few minutes ago?" he continued. "Can you define *a few minutes*?"

"I don't know," Amber shrugged. "Ten? Maybe twenty?"

Nick took a deep breath and urged the Xanax to quit screwing around and kick in already.

"Any idea where she might be now?" He looked around the lobby, fearing the worst. Had the reporter grown tired of waiting for him and left? A golden opportunity would be lost if she had. Nick was counting on the publicity an article in the local newspaper would generate. He searched the growing throng of gatherers. He didn't see the reporter anywhere. And there were few places the reporter could hide.

A dull ache sprouted behind his eyes.

"Maybe," Amber said, eyes glued to the floor, "she's checking out the auditorium?"

Shit.

Nick spun on his heels. *Shit! Shit! Shit!* He considered

reminding Amber of his number one rule for the evening: that no one was to enter the auditorium before it was time. But it was potentially too late for reminders. For now, he' have to rest his hopes on the word *potentially*.

*   *   *

With the wooden doors closed behind him, the peaceful calm of the auditorium replaced the chaos of the lobby.

Nick allowed himself a moment. He closed his eyes, willing away the headache that was now scratching and clawing its way to life behind them. He took a deep breath, counted to five. He let it out slow. Opening his eyes, Nick took a few steps down the sloping center aisle.

At first glance, he saw no signs of Ms. Nori Park. For the reporter to help spread the word about the new and improved Chamberlain Theater, a good impression on his part was a must. Not being available to greet her on arrival was not a step in the right direction. On a night that demanded perfection, Nick wondered if he was the right man for the job.

He scanned the rows of newly installed red vinyl seats, an exciting and integral addition to the auditorium's landscape. Their ability to rock, toss, and cajole the moviegoer at precise moments was a crucial component of the 4D experience. Nick could hardly wait for someone to give them a try. Someone other than himself, Manny, and the crew that installed them.

It didn't appear that someone would be Ms. Park. As far as Nick could tell, she wasn't seated among them. The aisles leading down to the front of the auditorium were just as empty. Perhaps the reporter hadn't come this way after all.

Nick took a painstakingly deep breath and let it out slowly.

It took the weight of every opening night responsibility to keep Nick from simply grabbing one of the seats, kicking back and allowing himself to drown in a sea of memories. It was times like this, when he was alone in the auditorium, that he missed his parents most. His father, especially. Nick couldn't begin to count how many Sunday afternoons he and his father had spent hunkered down, enveloped in the magical world of a darkened movie theater, popcorn in one hand, soda in the other. Some dads were football guys. Some were into music. Nick's dad was a certified, true blue movie buff. If Nick were honest, when the opportunity to own his very own movie theater arose, the idea appealed just as much to the son in him as the businessman. He only wished his father was still around to see it. The 4D experience would have knocked his multi-colored socks off.

Nick chuckled and looked to the ceiling rafters. "Miss ya, Pop."

He was about to walk back up the aisle and return to the lobby, when a final glance around stopped him. A flash of movement down front caused Nick to take a double-take. Were his eyes screwing with him? Was that? He chuckled. It was. In the front row, an ass clad in black slacks rose into the air. Nick started making his way down the center aisle.

When he reached the bottom and came upon the rest of what he assumed was Ms. Park, Nick subtly cleared his throat. "Miss Park?"

A head popped up where the ass had been. The owner of both bolted upright, her long russet ponytail swinging though the air. The young woman displayed all of the grace of a child-thief caught stealing cigarettes from her mother's purse.

"Mr. uh, Fallon. Hi." The young woman reached out her hand. Then, just as quickly, pulled it back, as if the action was somehow out of sequence. With an awkward grin, she bent and retrieved her satchel from beside her feet. Only when the canvas bag was securely slung over her shoulder did she once again offer her hand.

"We finally meet." Nick took her hand and gently shook it. "But, please, call me Nick."

The reporter smiled, nodded.

"Okay, Nick," she said, already enjoying an expeditious recovery. "But only if you call me Nori. Miss Park is a reminder that I am still unmarried, thus my mother is still without grandchildren. It's hard enough keeping her voice out of my head. I sometimes worry it's stuck there permanently."

Nick smiled. "Understood."

First impressions being what they were, the supposedly hard and tough reporter didn't seem anything like the mayor had described. His nickname of "ball-buster" didn't quite fit the bill. In fact, the young lady seemed rather nice. Her smile appeared to be genuine. It lent a look of pleasant courteousness to her handsome face. A face some might even consider 'alluring'--

Whoa, Nick urged. *Slow down, cowboy.*

Taking a step back, Nick erased all intimate thoughts from his mind. It didn't help that he hadn't had a date in over a year. First things first. He spread his arms wide.

"So, what do you think of the new and improved Chamberlain Theater? I see you were familiarizing yourself with our state-of-the-art, fully-interactive seats."

"Oh." Nori tugged at her ear. "Yeah, sorry."

Nick smiled on the inside. Tugging her ear was something his grandmother used to do. And just like that, Nick decided that he liked this Nori Park person.

"Not at all," he said. "Please, have a look around."

Even as he suggested it, Nick realized there really wasn't much to see. Unless you dug deep under its slick façade, The Chamberlain looked very much like any other movie theater. With the possible exception of the seats. To the untrained eye, they appeared bulkier and sat higher than standard seats.

"Are you familiar with 4D cinema?"

Nori shook her head, glancing around the expansive room. "I have to be honest, Mr....um, sorry, Nick. I'd never heard of 4D before this. Around here, we haven't seen too many 3D movies come our way, let alone 4D."

"Well, here at The Chamberlain, we're gonna skip right past 3D and go straight to four. Do not pass go, do not collect two hundred dollars." Nick smiled, paused an adequate amount of time for the reference to sink in. When the silence became awkward, he patted the top of the nearest seat. "So...uh...please, make yourself comfortable."

Nori accepted the invitation, taking the seat she'd been looking under the hood of earlier. Satchel in her lap, she clasped her hands over it and leaned back. She wore the crooked grin of someone mildly excited, yet unsure of what they were getting themselves into.

"Now," Nick said, once she appeared settled, "I can't actually start the film, but I can give you a small sample of how it all works. The kind of experience our moviegoers are in for."

"Sounds great."

Nick tilted his head forward in an abbreviated bow.

"If you'll excuse me."

Nick made his way up the aisle and through the doors to the hallway, questioning himself the whole way. Was he being charming enough? Too charming? Was he coming across as too eager for a good review? He didn't know, and ultimately, he couldn't worry about it.

Where was Manny?

Nick could only hope that the reason he hadn't seen his engineer was because he was in the control room, running through last minute preparations.

*   *   *

As soon as Nick entered the control room, Manny met him with a toothy thumbs up.

"Way to go, Nick! She's way more attractive than the ladies you normally date. If you dated, I mean. I can imagine."

Nick shook his head, immediately downplaying any suggestion of interest in the reporter. Sure, Nori was attractive. And admittedly, his status in the relationship department teetered on the verge of nonexistent. His Friday and Saturday nights were usually spent at home. He ate more than his share of dinners in front of the television. However, his relationship with the reporter was strictly business. Had to be. There was no way Nick was going to muddy the waters and risk a bad review based more on how noisily he ate chicken wings than how he operated his theater.

"It's not what you think, Manny."

"Yeah, but it's not *not* what I think, right?" Manny tilted his head, eyeing Nick over the top of his black hipster frames. His over-exaggerated wink and mischievous smile told Nick he simply wasn't getting it. Manny was a brilliant engineer. Not to mention one hell of a poker player. But Nick sometimes found him a little too carefree with his thoughts. The tendency to overshare was a Millennial trademark. Nick blamed social media.

"Miss Park is here on behalf of the media—"

"Nori," Manny interrupted. "She asked you to call her Nori."

"Right," he said. "Nori's here on be—" *Wait a second.* Nick's expression contorted into a full-face furrow. "So, what, you were eavesdropping on us, too?"

Manny merely shrugged.

Nick shook his head, but there wasn't much admonishment behind it. He tried to be upset with Manny for listening in on his private conversation with Nori. *Should* be upset. Whether it was the excitement of opening night, or the headache that was starting to suck his energy, Nick just wasn't feeling it.

"Anyway," he said, recalling where his original thoughts were heading, "I want to show *Nori* a little of what we have to offer. Can you give her a taste?"

"Love to."

Manny pushed his glasses further up the bridge of his nose. He turned toward a touchscreen the size of an iPad, and tilted it toward him. The screen glowed a light blue. A large red and white Raxon Technologies logo hovered in the middle. Square icons, the size of postage stamps, lined the bottom of the screen. According to Manny, the system was surprisingly easy to operate. Nick wouldn't know. He had yet to try to learn the system. That was what he paid Manny for.

"What do you wanna throw at her first?" the engineer asked. "A little wind? Rain? A blast of stink?"

Nick pulled at his collar, then rubbed his temples with his thumbs as he considered all available options. "How about we just start with the seats."

Nick watched Manny's smile turn upside down.

"For starters," Nick encouraged.

Pouting like a child a fraction of his age, Manny turned to the screen. He intertwined his fingers and turned them inside out. He cracked his knuckles the way a classical pianist might when sitting down at the ebonies and ivories. After studying the screen for a moment, Manny said, "Let's give her posterior a little jolt, shall we?"

As Nick stepped around the control panel and peered through the tiny window overlooking the auditorium, two things happened: first, he heard Manny tap the screen; and secondly, the top of Nori Park's head popped up above the seat back. Her shriek of surprise exploded through the control room. Nick buckled. It was as if the reporter was there beside him, instead of a hundred feet away on the other side of an insulated wall.

Nick turned to his engineer. "Seriously, dude. Turn off the

house mics."

Manny offered a wry smile as he complied.

With another tap to the screen, all of the seats in the theater reclined sharply backward. Nori's hands instinctively shot out and grabbed the armrests, just as Nick knew they would. The sensation of falling always produced the same predictable reaction. It was as inevitable as tears at a funeral. Nick smiled. He couldn't wait to watch an entire theater full of moviegoers have the same unilateral reaction.

He checked his watch. Forty minutes till showtime.

"What next?" Manny asked, a childlike eagerness in his voice. "Can I at least hit her with the mist?"

Nick gave it some thought. As eager as he was to impress the reporter with the theater's bag of tricks, he also felt the need to make her wait. He preferred she experience all that the new Chamberlain had to offer at the same time as the rest of the town.

"Sorry. I know what I said, but I think that's enough." Nick patted his engineer on the shoulder and turned to leave. "The first rule of entertainment, Manny. Always leave the audience wanting more."

THREE

When Nick met Nori outside the theater doors, he could tell the reporter was working hard to conceal a smile.

"Interesting seats, Nick. But I hope there's more to this 4D experience than the shaking and softcore groping of moviegoers." As she spoke, Nori's fingers danced across the screen of her iPad. "So? Is there more?"

Nick clasped his hands behind his back. "Well, of course there is, Ms. Park—"

"Nori."

Nick nodded his apology. "Of course, there is, Nori. But, wouldn't it be more fun to experience the rest of The Chamberlain's secrets along with everyone else?" Nick looked once again at his watch. "Which won't be much longer."

The reporter stopped tapping. "I still have a few questions if you have time."

Nick sighed internally. If only Nori was alone in vying for his attention at the moment. In addition to everything else he had going on; his headache was also demanding equal representation. Not to mention the haze creeping up the edges of his field of vision. He simply didn't have time. All of them would have to wait.

"As you can imagine, Nori, tonight's a very busy night." He

paused, allowing the furor growing in the lobby to emphasize his point. "But if you'd like to walk with me…"

"Sure," Nori said, pointing to the auditorium doors, "but real quick, did you notice, it kinda smelled like smoke in there?"

Nick nodded. He'd expected this. The auditorium did have a faint smoky smell from time to time. Like burnt wood or paper. From what or where, no one knew. And it was only on occasion, never constant. His contractor had cleared the auditorium of painters the first time he'd detected it. Nick called in not one, not two, but three electricians to check the wiring. Every search came up empty. As unsettling as the smell of smoke could be, especially in an enclosed space like a theater, it had been determined that there was no danger. Nothing was burning, nothing was on fire. Where it originated, what brought it out, these were questions nobody could answer. Apparently, there wasn't anything that could be done about The Chamberlain's unusual smell of smoke.

Except to hope it went away at some point.

"It comes and goes. As of yet, no one has determined why. But I assure you, after several thorough investigations, The Chamberlain Theater has earned a seal of approval. It is completely safe." Nick turned to the lobby, directed Nori toward it with a raised hand. "Shall we?"

Opening night at The Chamberlain had intensified while he was away. The number of dressed-up townsfolk congregating in the lobby, complimentary glasses of champagne in hand, had doubled. A modest line had reformed outside. And what had started as a low murmur among the crowd had now grown to a tempest that nearly drowned out the music Nick was piping in. The lobby was electric.

Despite his condition, Nick flushed with satisfaction. Everything was actually going well.

Nori cleared her throat.

"Can you tell me about the films you'll be showing here at The Chamberlain?"

Nick exchanged a smile and nod with a passing well-wisher and the elegant woman accompanying him. The man looked familiar, but Nick couldn't place him. Possibly someone from the bank. The mayor had introduced him to so many suits over the past year, they were like minnows in a seine net. Nick had a hard time telling one from the other.

"Initially, I'm offering three films, all developed specifically to run in accordance with our 4D capabilities." Nick continued to nod and dole out smiles as he snaked his way through the crowd, Nori Park in tow. "One is a family-oriented film that takes the audience on an adventure around the globe, exploring the wonders of nature. The audience will feel the stifling heat of the desert, as well as the chill of the arctic. When we reach the rainforests, well, let's just say that the dampness you'll feel on your skin won't be sweat."

"The black boxes!" Nori interrupted. "The ones hanging from the ceiling."

Nick spun on his heels. "Exactly! It's a stunning ride, and the kids will eat it up. Perfect summer matinee fare." Nick turned and continued making his way through the crowd. "The other two films, well, they're more adult oriented, specifically the one we'll be showing tonight. It's a murder mystery with a lot of tension and more than a few scares." As he spoke, a cloud floated through Nick's vision. He stopped for a moment and rubbed his eyes. Perhaps he'd spun around too quickly a moment ago. "Do you scare easily, Nori?"

"Afraid not," she chuckled. "My father is a big horror buff with questionable parenting skills. He recruited me as his watch buddy at an early age. So, if you hope to scare me tonight, Nick, you have your work cut out for you."

Nick smiled, though it was growing increasingly painful to

do so.

"Challenge accepted."

"Nick!"

From across the room, one of his employees waved his hand wildly, in an obvious attempt to get Nick's attention. With an apology, Nick excused himself and made his way to the concession counter.

"Can't find the straws anywhere, Boss." John-David emphasized his plight with empty hands raised in the air.

In addition to the complimentary champagne, The Chamberlain was offering a full complement of movie theater concessions for opening night. That included a soda machine that offered as many flavor combinations as one's imagination could conjure. There were the basics: Coke, Diet Coke, Sprite. And then there were combinations only a demented mind would conjure up: grape cream soda, orange root beer, pomegranate ginger ale. You name it, the machine could make it. Though it would be easier to drink with straws.

Nick fished in his pocket. He pulled out a cluster of keys. Holding the keyring at arm's length, he began searching for one silver key in particular. He blinked his eyes twice, squeezed them shut a second time before eventually reopening them. Once he found the right key, he isolated it, and handed the keyring to John-David.

"Check the storage room," Nick said, fighting back a grimace. "I know I ordered them."

With a respectful smile, the young man with alternating strips of black and purple hair took the keys and started making his way through the crowd.

Nick scanned the counter. "How's everything else look, Zach?"

"Real good, Boss." The other young man working the concession counter was John-David's twin brother, identical

minus the purple streaks in his black hair. It was the only way
Nick could tell them apart. Zach was putting the finishing
touches on a pyramid display, alternating boxes of Raisinets, Sno-
Caps and Goobers. "Everything's pretty much set up. But, no
one's really buying anything."

"That's alright," Nick said, glancing around. "We're just glad
they're here."

Nick checked his watch again. It was becoming a habit, and
not a good one. Showtime couldn't come soon enough. He
rapped his knuckles on the glass countertop. With one more
quick inspection of the concession counter – napkins in the
dispenser? Check. Fresh popcorn popping? Check. Sweat
breaking out on his forehead? Check. – Nick turned and bumped
directly into Nori.

"Those two look awfully familiar." Her head was down,
fingertips once again doing a number on her iPad. "They
wouldn't happen to be…"

"Zachary and John-David Blackwood," Nick said. She didn't
have to finish her thought. He knew exactly where it was
heading. He nodded, though not enthusiastically. "The mayor's
nephews."

Nori's head popped up. "Yes!" Her eyes were wide, alert
with the scent of a scoop. "But I thought they were both in
jail…"

And here it comes.

Nick's stomach tightened. He'd heard the rumors, the talk
concerning the mayor's delinquent, yet hard working nephews.
Heard how the police in Angler Bay tended to look the other way
because of their last name. It was a small town, after all. Nick
also knew that questions regarding their hiring were bound to
come up once people learned of their employment at the theater.
He'd armed himself with the best answers he could come up
with. Only now didn't feel like the right time to mount a defense.

He'd hoped to at least get through opening night first.

"Work release," he said, and hoped to leave it at that.

Nori's eyes narrowed. She studied Nick's face. Her eager fingers hovered above the iPad's screen like circling vultures over a carcass.

"And did hiring them have anything to do with returning a favor or…?"

"Um…"

Luckily for Nick, a large contingent of Angler Bay's city council entered the lobby together. Feigning distraction, he plausibly ignored Nori's inquiry. There was entirely too much riding on the evening—and Nori's review—to get caught up in controversy.

Not to mention the fact his vision was coming and going in waves of pixelated clouds. His skull felt like it was about to crack and split apart from the pressure mounting behind his eyes.

"Ladies and gentlemen." Nick busied himself, shaking every hand he could find, kissing every cheek thrust his way. "Welcome to the historic Chamberlain Theater. Or, should I say, the new and improved Chamberlain Theater."

Heads turned this way and that. Everyone craned their necks to take in the lobby's new décor. Smiles broadened the faces of some. Several remained pensive, appearing wary of being there in the first place. Nick could see it in their eyes: the theater's recent history running through their minds like a scrapbook full of newspaper articles. When he'd first embarked on this venture, he knew that history was a hurdle he would have to overcome. Self-immolation of a beloved member of the community wasn't something a small town soon forgot.

Nick raised both his hands and his voice as he addressed the room.

"For those of you who have been here before, I'm sure you'll notice the many updates we've made. Including an entirely new concession counter with more drink options than you could dream up." Nods of approval accompanied most of the gazes. The more they looked around, the more the apprehensive among the group seemed to warm to the idea of being there. "But I assure you, the updates don't stop here in the lobby. I think you'll find much to like in the auditorium, where the most significant changes were made. Not to mention, the most money spent."

Nick waited for the small laughter to die out before he continued. "We'll start seating in about twenty minutes, so feel free to look around. And please, help yourself to some champagne."

After a few more congratulatory handshakes, Nick found himself without an audience, though not alone. He was surprised, and maybe a little disappointed, that the reporter insisted on sticking around. He had hoped to lose her and her probing questions somewhere along the way, then catch back up with her after the movie when she'd undoubtedly have more immediate things to ask about. Apparently, she wasn't going to be so easily dismissed. Nick filed that information away for future reference.

"So, would now be a good time to answer some questions, Mr. Fallon?"

Nick's heart sank like a stone.

Aw, shit.

The reporter had fallen back on addressing him as 'Mr. Fallon' instead of Nick. And it didn't sound like a misstep on her part. A bad sign for sure. Was it because he hadn't been forthcoming in regards to her question about the Blackwood twins? Had he done something else? Something he wasn't even aware of? He didn't know, and the category 5 hurricane brewing in his head wasn't about to let up long enough for him to find out.

"I'm sorry, Ms. Park, but I have some last-minute business

to attend to before we open the doors." *Ms. Park. Shit.* Their relationship was apparently back on formal ground. Nick reminded himself to tread lightly. A good review, while still within reach, may very well be teetering on the precipice. "Any chance we could resume this interview a bit later? After the show, perhaps?"

He didn't wait for a response. The coward in him couldn't get away fast enough. Nick weaved his way through the crowd, heading in the direction of his office down the hall. Once he felt he was safely out of Ms. Park's view, he altered course. His office promised last minute interruptions, and therefore, wouldn't provide the solitude he sought. He needed to be alone for a few minutes before the movie began. Circling back around, Nick made his way toward the auditorium doors. A quiet theater all to himself was the best place Nick could imagine to ride out the next twenty minutes.

And this fucking headache.

FOUR

When the house lights went down at 8:00 pm, The Chamberlain Theater was only a few seats shy of capacity. Considering that Nick's lean marketing budget was word-of-mouth dependent, he was certainly pleased. A sellout would have been optimal. Not to mention how good it would have looked for the piece Nori Park was writing. But a near sellout was a victory in itself. Who cared if almost half of the tickets had been comped? Given the theater's recent history, most townsfolk were reluctant to even step foot on the premises. Nick wasn't about to disparage those who had braved their fears, lured by free admission or not.

When the lights faded, so did the chatter inside the auditorium. A hushed anticipation befell the room. Darkness reigned. Those who hadn't yet put on their black-framed 3D glasses did so now.

From his end seat in the back row, the butterflies nesting in Nick's stomach took flight. He imagined it was the same feeling a painter or sculptor felt when they were about to reveal their work to the world. The only difference was that, with the exception of writing a bunch of checks, Nick had little to do with making The Chamberlain the state-of-the-art masterpiece it was. He'd never so much as gotten his hands dirty.

That hardly tempered his excitement.

What did begin to quell his excitement, however, was realizing that the lights had been down for a full two minutes, and the movie had yet to begin.

Two became two and a half.

Nick wasn't the only one to notice. Around the room, murmurs and idle chatter crept back into the fray. The noise level slowly elevated. Pin-drop silence was soon replaced by a soft din as everyone grew uncomfortable sitting in the dark. The only light in the room was the glowing red exit sign down front. It cast an eerily crimson glow over its corner of the auditorium.

Subtle waves of nervous nausea rippled in Nick's stomach.

Two and a half minutes turned into three, three into four. And as darkness continued to embrace the room, whispered musings turned to heightened grumbles. A shout from down front. The not so flowery language urged the movie to start. Another voice seconded the motion. The cursing seemed a little out of character given the nature of the event. Nick blamed the free-flowing champagne. It might prove to have been a bad idea if credits didn't start rolling soon.

He'd gone thirty-two years having never picked up a musical instrument, but Nick was soon playing the kick drum with his foot. He looked at his watch. The tiny hands proved out of reach in the dark. He was about to get up and see what the hell was taking Manny so long when a beam of light suddenly pierced the pitch.

The large screen down front lit up in a brilliant white. A buzz tickled the air. Seconds later, the screen once again went black before ferrying in the opening credits. Names and responsibilities crawled across the screen in misty white lettering. From somewhere off screen, the breathy panting of a young woman seeped into the auditorium. Strategically-placed speakers soon filled the room with an almost tangible adrenaline.

While the rest of the audience tensed with apprehension, Nick actually relaxed. He smiled, settling deeper into his seat. A year in the making, and the new Chamberlain's first official showing was finally underway…

The credits end and the screen evolves into a starry night. A light fog lingers around the edges. The camera pans down, and slowly, a stretch of woods comes into view. A muddy path weaves its way through moonlit trees and brush. The source of the panting bursts onto the path from behind a clump of shrubs. A young woman, clad in a white tank and cut-off jean shorts. Her traversing of the path resembles more of a series of stumbles than a run. Her tank top is torn and flutters from one shoulder, her hair is long, dark, and matted. Flecks of mud and dead leaves cling to her bare legs.

She appears alone.

The woods are thick with the unknown.

When the woman casts a glance behind her, her eyes widen. Her pace quickens and her breaths come more rapidly. Steam and fearful whimpers escape her trembling lips. She slips. She falls. When she hits the ground, the seats in the theater tremble. Murmurs bubble up from the audience. Sprawled out, the woman turns and looks behind her. For the first time, the catalyst of her fear is revealed.

A towering man, his face lost in the shadow of a grey hoodie.

The woman's scream echoes through the trees, reverberating through the auditorium.

She begins crawling on her hands and knees. Tears streaming down her face, her pursuer closes the distance. From behind, he lifts his soiled boot to the woman's backside. He shoves her face first into the mud. She sprawls. He pins her down, a knee straddled to each side.

The woman whimpers, too out of breath to scream, too weak from exhaustion to fight.

The camera cuts away. Silhouetted against a crescent moon, a long, carving knife rises into the night sky. It hovers long enough for the audience to gasp and the desperate woman to mutter a single phrase…

"Please, no…"
The knife arcs downward.
The screen goes black.

The audience screams from the poke in the back. It is subtle. It is perfectly timed. It is all part of the 4D seat experience.

The screen explodes with light as the sound of tires on gravel roars from the surrounding speakers. A jeep full of teenagers, top down, driving dangerously fast up a wooded mountain road. Their music is upbeat and loud. So are their spirits. An empty beer can soars out the back.

Inside the theater, screams of shock devolved into nervous laughter and chatter. The audience let out a collective sigh of relief. And Nick couldn't help but smile, thinking how quickly word of The Chamberlain Theater was going to spread.

*   *   *

The first sign that something was wrong came moments later.

On the screen, two of the teens stood inside a cabin, gearing up to head out into the stormy night. A third teen had gone out to the Jeep for a cell phone charger and never returned. The teens opened the cabin door. A fierce wind whipped at their jackets.

At the same time, a blast of wind swept through the auditorium. Six powerful fans, strategically concealed, transformed the room into a storm-riddled forest.

Murmurs followed.

Nick smiled. *Here we go.*

Aware of what was coming, he braced for it. The audience, however, was unprepared. When the teens stepped out into the rain, fine mist began to fall from the auditorium's rafters. The mist was meant to be brief, light and not enough to get the audience more than the slightest bit damp.

Within seconds, however, the first scream erupted.

Others soon followed.

The mist continued to fall.

The wind continued to whip.

A foul odor permeated the room, bringing Nick upright in his seat. A thin film covered his black-framed 3D glasses. The movie screen, and everything else in the room, was suddenly tinted in a deep red.

Nick tore the glasses from his face. Something was seriously wrong. Water was clear. What spewed from the overhead misters was not. Neither was the liquid covering his lenses, and everything around him.

Shouts and screams soon formed a chorus. The overwhelming stench of iron overtook the auditorium as the mist continued to rain down.

"The fuck?" someone shouted.

"My God!" cried another.

By the time Nick realized the misting pumps had sprayed blood onto the audience instead of simple H20, everyone else had realized it, too.

Cries of disbelief joined the mist in filling the air. Some cried out in anger, others in terror. All were born of shock. People rose from their seats, their once-pristine suits and dresses awash in red.

Chaos was erupting, faster than Nick could react. He too found himself on his feet, and just as quickly, the center of attention.

Nick raised his hands to the crowd that had quickly gathered around him.

"Everyone, please, remain calm."

Not a soul listened. Initial shock subsided, immediately replaced with panic.

"I assure you," Nick shouted, shuffling backward toward the door, "it's just a malfunction of some sort. Maybe a prank. But I promise you there is no danger. Everyone please remain calm. I repeat, there is no danger!"

Nick wiped blood from his lips, preventing it from seeping into his mouth just in time.

Shielding her head with her satchel, Nori Park joined Nick at the back of the room. A hundred of her closest friends trailed closely behind. "If this is a prank, Nick, or some sort of publicity stunt, I'm going on record to say it's pretty screwed up."

Row after row of blood-drenched theatergoers spilled into the center aisle. In a scene straight out of a George Romero movie, they eked their way toward Nick and the exit doors, all cloaked in blood, all slipping and sliding through its muck. A grotesque mob had assembled before his eyes, growing angrier and more panicked by the second. Any chance of quelling the situation before it spiraled out of control was quickly slipping away.

"Please, let us out!"

Other voices echoed the sentiment, though not all were as polite. The sounds of people spitting the metallic-tasting blood from their mouths could be heard throughout the auditorium. Somewhere down front, some poor soul retched violently. Soon another followed. The sound turned Nick's stomach. He could only pray the retching didn't set off a chain reaction.

He turned and grabbed the door handle. The plan was to get everyone out, take stock of the malfunction afterward. The door, however, wasn't on board.

It wouldn't open. Wouldn't even budge. Grabbing hold of both handles and giving them a tug didn't improve the situation. The other door was also locked. Spitting both blood and expletives from his mouth, Nick jerked the handles back and forth. He shook the doors violently. The fact they wouldn't open both bewildered and frightened him. *How? Who? Why?*

"Manny!" Nick looked to the projection window. Where was his engineer? The streak of faint blue light remained connected to the screen down front. The beam spotlighted falling red flecks. "Manny! Unlock the doors!"

Gasps all around.

"The doors are locked?" The frantic voice came from behind Nick. "You locked us in? What the--"

Nick spun, faced the crowd.

"No! no!" he shouted. "They're not supposed to be locked." His heart raced. His mind reeled with potential scenarios as to why the doors might be locked. None of them were good. None were logical. "I don't know *who* locked them," he admitted. "Or, why."

Nick dug into his pocket for his set of keys. His pocket was empty. He checked other pockets. The only thing he found was an empty baggy that used to contain four oval-shaped blue pills. And then he remembered: he'd given his keys to John-David. He'd been so eager to sidestep Ms. Park minutes later, that he'd sidestepped John-David as well. He'd forgotten all about his keys.

Nick blocked out the chaos enough to try and assess the situation.

Blood continued to rain from the ceiling.

The movie continued to play. On screen, the two teens trudged along a muddy path, clutching jackets tight around their collars, shouting their friend's name over the din of falling rain. The screen flashed a brilliant white. Lightning lit the stormy night.

In the auditorium, a flash from an overhead strobe coincided perfectly. Thunder crashed through the speakers, further fraying

Nick's nerves. He turned back to the control room window.

"Manny!"

Still no response. Nick wiped metallic-smelling rain from his eyes. Tried to, at least. The blood only smeared, leaving behind a slick residue.

Where the hell was his engineer? How could Manny not see what was going on in the auditorium? And who the fuck had locked the doors?

Nick's attention drifted back to the screen where the teenagers' story continued to play out. Realizing everything that was to come dropped a sick ball of lead in the pit of his stomach.

FIVE

"Let me through, God dammit!"

Nick's heart took a nose-dive. The voice was unmistakable and the last thing he needed at the moment.

"Let me through!"

The first commotion gave birth to a second, internal commotion. A parting of the crowd made its way up the center aisle, heading straight for Nick. Even in the midst of their own distress, people couldn't get out of the man's way fast enough. It was as if the headless horseman was plowing his way through the sea of people. As the commotion inched its way closer, Nick took a deep breath, readying himself for the confrontation boring down on him.

"Let me through!"

The crowd before Nick split in half, spitting the mayor out at his feet.

"Damn it, Fallon!" roared Blackwood. "What's the meaning of this?"

Another disoriented flash of light. Everyone, Nick included, braced themselves for what naturally followed. He quickly covered his ears. Nearby patrons who were paying attention, mirrored the move. For those too slow to act, the exploding thunder sheered the air, piercing eardrums.

The room shook from the massive display of power.

Fissures crawled up the walls. The floor rose up, tremoring violently. Legs buckled and people fell. Above the crowd, rows of suspended lights swayed back and forth.

Eyes turned skyward.

Nick held his breath.

Miraculously, the lights held.

Once the moment had passed, and the thunder had faded, the audience pounced. A great throng of people rushed forward, pinning the mayor against Nick and Nick against the doors. Panic was the new order of business. The crowd threatened to overtake Nick, their alarm growing into something with a harder edge, something with teeth. The Chamberlain's 4D experience had gone bad, and its patrons had had enough. Opening night was officially over.

"Everyone, please!" Nick screeched, fighting to breathe. The speed with which the mob's anger intensified startled him. Matters were spiraling out of control. He'd been too caught off guard, too ill-equipped to stop it.

"Please stay calm!" he shouted, as he worked to free his arms. An elbow dug deep into his sternum. He tried to slink away from it, but there was nowhere to go. His back was already lodged against the door. "Anyone try the emergency exit down front?"

Not a single voice responded. Screams and animalistic cries were the film's new soundtrack. The noise level in the room was deafening, and Nick's shouts barely rose above it. He could hardly breathe, crushed by the weight of hysteria. Nick clawed his way up onto his toes and checked the progress at the emergency exit. People were gathering down front. Gathering, but not exiting. The door remained closed. Nick could only assume that someone had tried to open it. Tried and failed.

"Fallon, I swear!" The mayor grabbed Nick by the lapels of his sport coat. Nick felt himself being lifted up, his back against the door. "Let me out of this fucking theater!"

Grasping the mayor's thick arms, Nick tried wrenching the man's powerful hands free. His attempt was feeble. His grip was weak. The man's skin was too slick with gore.

"Mayor!" Nick shouted, adrenalin fueling his courage. "If I could, I would! Now let me go!"

The mayor's eyes brimmed with brutality. His nostrils flared. His lips straight-lined. Nick sensed it was everything the man could do to keep from snapping Nick's skinny neck. Nick readied his fists in response, prepared to fight his way free. Then, just as suddenly as he'd grabbed him up, the mayor let go of Nick's jacket, dropping his feet back onto the floor.

Without explanation, the mayor spun and erupted. A madman set loose. One by one, he shoved people to the side, brutally clearing out space all around him. Had someone pushed him from behind? Was the guy claustrophobic? Had the stress of seeing the town's salvation bathed in blood sent him over the edge? Nick didn't know, and he didn't care. He was thankful for the space and the distraction. He had room to breathe.

As he sucked in some badly-needed air, Nick sensed a presence creep up beside him. Fists poised and ready to swing if need be, he turned to it. Nori Park greeted him with eyes wide. Nick sent some of his tension away with an exhaustive exhale. As much as he'd tried to avoid her, the reporter was a sight for desperate eyes. When her hand snaked around his arm and found his, Nick's heart swelled. He knew the gesture, knew the empathetic motive behind it. It was more for his benefit than any security she sought.

And it was a godsend.

"Deep breaths," she said. Nori's soothing brown eyes bore into Nick's. Her gaze held his captive. "These people need you to stay calm."

Nick nodded, not yet ready to give up the connection. He

took a deep breath as instructed. The benefits were immediate. His pulse slowed. His breathing steadied. The anvil of bedlam surrounding him was momentarily cast off his shoulders. When he could finally tear his eyes from Nori's, he closed them for just a beat.

Deep breathes.

Reopening his eyes, he looked out over the mass of people with more calm and clarity than before.

Patrons still gathered at the emergency exit. Others continued to push and shove their way up the aisle toward Nick and the doors. Caught between the two factions, a huddled mass made up the majority, gripped by shock. They'd filtered into the middle of the room and now stood there, unsure of their best option. As if there was one.

Crimson rain continued to shower.

Having no other alternative, the film continued to play.

A high-pitched scream shredded the speakers. Collectively, the room's attention was drawn to the screen in time to see a table lamp brought crashing down upon the head of one of the teens.

Inside the auditorium, things went from bad to worse.

The entire overhead lighting system suddenly came to life. Riggings began swaying back and forth. It was as if a giant hand worked the bars like the strings of a marionette. One after another, bolts started to sheer. And one after another, riggings came careening down. Patrons scrambled, attempting to escape the falling debris. There was nowhere to go. Screams joined together, melding into one mass of static white noise.

Nick looked on helplessly as a man shoved his wife out of the path of an untethered rigging. The long steel bar swung downward, just missing the woman. It caught the man, swiping him across the face. The metal took skin, muscle and bone as souvenirs. The man collapsed in a heap. His wife's anguish was lost among the white noise.

But, not on Nick.

He clutched his stomach, hoping to keep his dinner down.

All throughout the room, light riggings swung and light riggings fell. A handful of patrons looked up and were immediately punished for their actions. Screams and shouts of despair once again erupted as fractured metal and shattered glass ruined eyes and changed lives forever. The auditorium soon bloomed with an unworldly pandemonium. The ability to discern the blood coming from the misters from the blood of the innocent had been stripped away. There was no escaping the red liquid. Those who tried slipped and fell, joining bodies already littering the concrete floor.

Nick gasped as the crowd parted before him.

A man rushed up the center aisle. Toby Gesture, Angler Bay's School Superintendent, came at Nick with a three-foot section of light fixture raised high above his head. Nick ducked away just as the man in what may have once been a grey suit coat passed him by. Only then did Nick realize the man hadn't been headhunting him. Toby swung the piece of steel downward like an axe, crashing the metal bar against one of the wooden doors. The strike made a loud report, but if it made even a scratch, it wasn't visible in the dim light. A second strike proved just as fruitless; the heavy, wooden doors too formidable. Toby's efforts were admirable, but did nothing to release the crowd from its prison.

As the last of the riggings served their fatal blow, a woman approached Nick. Her hair was blonde, soaked in red and stuck to her face. Her dress was ripped and barely hanging on. A deep gash had opened her up from her shoulder to her collarbone. Muscle and tissue showed through. If blood loss wasn't an issue yet, it soon would be. Despite her condition and the surrounding chaos, she appeared calmer than anyone in her position should.

A sad smile even tugged at the corners of her mouth.

Nick wasn't a doctor, but he diagnosed her condition immediately: the woman was in shock.

"Excuse me, sir." Her voice remained as temperate as if she were asking a waiter about the day's specials. "Is there any way out of the theater besides these doors and the emergency exit down front? Any other exits at all? I...I would like to leave now."

Nick could muster only a blank stare. The irony of her mentioning the 'emergency exit' wasn't lost on him. The Chamberlain's emergency exit wasn't allowing people to exit during an emergency. He looked around, tried to process through the chaos. Tried to come up with some semblance of an answer for a woman who probably needed it more than most. There simply wasn't one. The Chamberlain was, and always had been, a movie theater. It wasn't like a performing arts theater. There were no gangways or catwalks overhead. No backstage areas or hallways. Just one large room with three doors and a—

Nick's eyes lit up.

He craned his neck, turning his attention from the injured woman to the pane of glass through which the film continued to play. His gears started to grind. Hope pried its way into his chest. For the first time since the misters started spewing blood, a plan was developing in Nick's mind. An honest to goodness, 'holy shit, let's do this' plan.

The window to the control room was the size of a small microwave and at least fifteen feet off the ground. Still, it was a way out. If they could somehow get someone up to it, albeit a small someone, the glass could be broken and that someone could crawl through. Then all the person would have to do would be to exit the control room and unlock the auditorium doors from the outside. What they might find inside that tiny control room was anyone's guess. Nick had a doomsday imagination, and it had already conjured visions of Manny sprawled on the floor in a pool of his own blood. What other explanation could there be for his engineer's absence? And quite frankly, it was the only excuse Nick would accept at this point.

Nick searched the crowd and found Nori Park comforting a man and woman nearby. He immediately started sizing her up. She was the definition of petite. Narrow shoulders, slender waist, and if she stood even five two, he would be surprised. Nori would easily fit through the window. If only there was a way to get her up to it.

When Nick met Nori's glance over the crowd, he wasted no time beckoning the reporter over.

"Nick, we need to get these people out of here," Nori said, after pushing her way through the crowd. "Tell me you have a plan."

"I have a plan." Nick bit his lower lip. "But you might not like it."

SIX

"What are we waiting for?"

Once Nick had detailed his plan, more specifically, her role in it, Nori hadn't hesitated. She hadn't questioned if there were other options. She hadn't even glanced up at the window to see what she was up against. She simply took a deep breath and nodded. "Let's do it."

Nick returned the nod and addressed the crowd.

"Everyone! Can I have your attention?" He found he didn't need to shout as loud as before. No need to kill his throat. The screams had died down. Only sobs of despair and pain could be heard during the film's quiet moments. Nick made his way through the crowd, sidestepping bodies and puddles of blood. He did his best to ignore both, but he'd have better luck ignoring trees in a forest. "We have a plan, but we're gonna need some help."

Nick grabbed a couple of large men by the arms.

"Okay, fellas. It's like this."

Nick laid out his plan while the men exchanged glances. When he was done, they took a moment to silently pass judgment on his idea, even though he hadn't asked their opinion. The men ultimately nodded and began removing their jackets.

A long black lighting rig stretched across four rows of nearby seat backs. One large metal post ran the length of the fixture, while smaller bars shot out to the sides every so often, effectively creating a ladder with its rungs on the outside.

"Excuse us. Coming through."

Between the three of them, Nick and the two men easily transported the section of rigging to the back of the theater. They wedged one end of the long pole under the back of a seat, and rested the other end against the wall beneath the window. The top of the rig fell short of the window by a few feet. It would have to do. Not only was it the longest section they had, it only needed to get her close.

"Is it gonna hold?" Nori asked.

Nick looked the structure up and down, taking an unqualified measure of its strength.

"Should. We'll hold it. Make sure it doesn't go anywhere. Oh, and…"

Nick made his way to the doors and searched the floor for the piece of metal with which Toby had attacked them. Scooping up the steel bar, Nick returned to the ladder.

"When you get up there," he said, wielding the piece of metal, "I'll toss this up to you. Just make sure you clear out all the glass around the frame so you don't get all shredded."

Nori looked up at the window, her bottom lip tucked between her teeth. Nick wondered what was going through her mind. As the architect of the plan, he was pretty sure he had the easy job. He was also sure they both knew it.

"Ready?"

It was like she flipped a switch. When Nori turned back to Nick, any hint of trepidation had left her face. A calm determination had taken over. She took a deep breath.

"This is all gonna make for one hell of a story."

And she was right. Opening night at The Chamberlain Theater had turned into one hell of a story. The publicity would be even bigger than he had hoped. Unfortunately, it wouldn't be the type of publicity he was looking for. He'd heard the phrase, *"there's no such thing as bad publicity"* a million times. It was business mantra 101. But, gazing out over bodies, parts, and the throng of blood-soaked and desperate people looking to him for deliverance, Nick couldn't envision how any of this could get a positive spin.

The first jutting cross bar hit Nori about mid-thigh. It was too high for her to reach on her own, so Nick helped her get a leg up with his interlocked fingers. The crossbar gave a little under her weight. Nick held his breath. Doubt entered the picture and he started second-guessing himself. Who the hell was he to determine whether or not the bars would hold her? Who the hell was he to be looked upon as an authority on anything?

Nori gingerly tested her weight on the first bar. When the piece of steel proved worthy, she climbed up onto the second one. The other cross bars were spaced more favorably, and Nori took them one at a time with relative assurance as Nick and another man held the fixture firmly against the wall.

The loud revving of an engine filled the auditorium.

Heart in his throat, Nick turned to the screen.

The teenagers' jeep careened down a jagged embankment, straight toward a flooded creek bed. Simulating the bumpy ride, the plush theater seats started to rumble, shake, and pitch from side to side. If anyone had been seated in the plush new seats, they would have felt like they were seated in a jeep careening down an embankment instead of a movie theater. Since everyone was either on their feet or on the floor, it proved a wasted display of the theater's power.

"Nick!"

The shout dragged Nick's attention back to Nori.

She had reached the halfway point, and now clutched the steel pole against her chest. The rocking of the seat was causing the makeshift ladder to move. It was no longer wedged beneath the seat. It was no longer stable. Making matters worse, Nori's weight made it top heavy. The pole shifted about. It lurched. It threatened to topple.

"Shit!"

Wrapping his arms around the steel bar, Nick put all of his weight against it. The man who had been helping had disappeared, assumedly in a panic. Nick cursed him under his breath, saving some admonishment for himself. He'd proven just as unreliable. He'd allowed himself to be distracted by the wonder of two hundred and fifty blood-drenched theater seats, all shifting about violently. In doing so, he'd let go of the ladder. Just like he'd promised not to.

It was a misstep. One made worse by the fact that the seats should have stopped rocking by then. On the screen, the jeep had already flipped and lay submerged in the creek bed. The only wheel rising above the surface spun freely. Still, the theater seats jerked about frenetically, causing the entire auditorium to tremble.

If Nick didn't know better, he'd think The Chamberlain itself was trying to shake the ladder out from under Nori.

"Keep going!" Nick shouted. The steel beam tried its best to wrench itself free. His palms seared with a burning sensation. The pain sharpened as the metal's edges sliced through his hands and forearms. He fought for control. He couldn't let go, despite the pain. Not again. Nick wasn't about to fail Nori a second time. "I got it!"

Blood trickled down Nick's wrists and arms. It was his own, and it was fresh.

After a meeting of gazes and a nod of encouragement from Nick, Nori once again started to climb. This time, she didn't stop until she'd reached the last cross beam. Nick relaxed minutely. His initial assessment had been wrong. Not only was Nori high enough to reach the window, but if she raised up on the balls of her feet, she'd probably be able to look through it.

Nori looked down. In the first sign of nerves she'd shown, she hesitated. She locked her arms around the steel pole and rested her forehead against the wall just below the window.

"Come on, Nori." Nick knew she couldn't hear him. If he'd wanted her to, he wouldn't have said it under his breath. Was it the height? It appeared so, but he couldn't tell for sure. "You got this."

Nori looked down and met Nick's stare. Her eyes gleamed with resolution. It was all there: fear, anxiety, regret in accepting the task in the first place. Nick hoped she wasn't backing down. He hoped she was merely delaying the inevitable.

"You can do it, Nori!" Releasing a hand from the ladder, Nick bent and retrieved Toby's steel bar. He stood ready to toss it to her whenever she was ready for it, his heart beating fast enough for the both of them.

Nori nodded. After another moment's hesitation and a collective breath, she rose up on the balls of her feet. She peered through the pane of glass.

The window exploded.

The blast sent piercing shards of glass outward. Tiny crystals arced through the air and rained down on everything below. The makeshift ladder blew backward, taking Nori Park with it. Steel ripped itself from Nick's grip. The long metal bar took on the appearance of a tree falling in the woods. It toppled, crashing down upon the backs of seats. Metal sliced through vinyl, tore away foam. When it met the seat's steel frame skeleton, the rigging stopped abruptly, shedding a lifeless Nori like a baby bird. The dark void between the seats was all too eager to swallow her up.

Nick's heart stopped. He used his bloody arms to cover his head. Sharp beads of glass stung his skin, yet his mind remained focused on Nori.

The explosion in the control room ignited a chain reaction. A second explosion ripped the auditorium doors off of their hinges. The two slabs of oak took on the role of missile, sailing through the air, mowing down anyone unfortunate enough to be in their path. Thankfully, most didn't see it coming. Their corpses were spared the painful knowledge of how they'd died.

Those in the crowd who were still alive erupted. Wails of pent-up anguish and relief echoed throughout the room as the mob rushed the open doorway and spilled out into the lobby.

Nick did just the opposite. He worked against the grain, parting his way through the oncoming melee. Nori had fallen hard, landing somewhere between two rows of seats. He feared the worst. The concrete floor, as is its nature, would have provided little cushion. And the blast...

"Nori!"

Nick searched among the seats, unsure which row had claimed her. One after another revealed nothing but visceral debris—bodies, both intact and not—painted in slick crimson. Nori was nowhere among them. There was no sign of the reporter anywhere. Had she somehow slipped past him? Escaped with the crowd without him noticing? Was she even capable of doing so after such a horrific fall?

Nick suddenly realized he was the last one remaining. He'd spent so long enveloped by chaos, the ensuing silence proved haunting. Everywhere he looked, irony littered the auditorium. He shared the room with many of Angler Bay's most esteemed citizens, and yet not a one had breath enough to make a sound.

With his strength and search exhausted, Nick slowly made his way up the blood and glass-strewn aisle toward the awaiting doorway.

SEVEN

Stepping through the doorway was like stepping back in time.

The lobby swarmed with people. Nick recognized many, having just been trapped with them while the world he knew turned to shit. Only something was amiss. Nobody looked the worse for wear. Nobody looked as if they had been through the same harrowing ordeal as Nick. Smiles graced faces. Glasses of champagne were in varying states of being emptied. Suits and dresses, stained with blood only moments ago, were crisp, clean, and elegant as the moment they were taken off the hanger. And all throughout the room, laughter and a sense of festive anticipation filled the air.

It was opening night as intended.

Bewildered, Nick took a step back.

"Hey, boss!" Manny jogged down the steps from the control room, approaching from the side. "Don'tcha think it's about time—" His question and stride were both cut short.

From somewhere in the room, a sharp gasp started the festive vibe's downward spiral.   Laughter slowly died. A hush rode a wave through the lobby. All eyes turned toward Nick; all grew wide when they saw him. Champagne flutes fell away from lips. Hands rushed to cover mouths. Some arrived in time to quell oncoming gasps. Some didn't.

Even Nori, who had been talking to the mayor's nephews, iPad in hand, stopped mid-question when she saw Nick. The sour expression on her face melted into one of concern.

Meanwhile, Nick's mouth could have caught flies. The strength in his legs weakened. His mind began to race.

What...

Nick turned back to the auditorium, the scene of the worst carnage he'd ever witnessed. He gasped. He took a step back. His psyche suffered another blow.

The auditorium was free of blood, was no longer bathed in it. The seats, their vinyl already a nice Imperial red, showed no other shades of the color. No bodies littered the aisle way. No body *parts*. Even the light fixtures, which had caused irreparable damage to life and limb only minutes before, hung suspended from the ceiling where they belonged. The only evidence of destruction of any kind was the glistening of broken glass just inside the doorway.

Nick turned back to the gawking crowd, caught somewhere between the past and present, reality and anti-anxiety-fueled hallucination. He became acutely aware of pain lashing both of his arms. Looking down answered one question, but created so many others. Rivulets of blood trailed down each arm. The slick red substance coated his hands and fingers. It dripped onto the freshly-polished tile floor. Two small puddles were forming. Within seconds, they had converged into one large pool that surrounded the soles of his black dress oxfords.

It was with that image seared into their minds that startled patrons began shuffling toward the lobby's exit. And it was at that moment that Nick's future, and that of The Chamberlain Theater, changed forever.

*   *   *

The scene inside the theater's lobby looked to Nick like the end of an action movie. Die Hard, or one of any number of Liam Neeson films where a loved one is wronged and vengeance must be dealt swiftly. Red and blue lights swirled on the street. They shimmered through the theater's glass front, reflected on its interior walls. Angler Bay PD milled about, the detectives taking statements from anyone brave enough to stick around. Medics in dark blue windbreakers saw to Nick as he sat perched atop a concession case full of untouched buttered popcorn and uncorked bottles of champagne.

The credits were rolling on a shit show, and Nick was finding himself the unfortunate star.

The cuts on his arms had been bandaged and forgotten. It was the bump on the back of Nick's head that gave the medics the most concern. Fainting on a tile floor, as it turned out, was a dangerous endeavor. Not to mention, a painful one. Everyone within earshot urged him to seek further medical treatment at the hospital. Nick shook them all off, assuring everyone he was fine. The headache and wooziness weren't ailments a couple of Advil and a glass of bourbon couldn't cure.

Blood was found on one of the four-foot-long wall sconces mounted just inside the auditorium's doors. Glass littered the floor. By the looks of things, Nick had somehow wrapped his arms around the decorative light and held on for dear life. Why or for what purpose, nobody knew. And Nick couldn't explain. Or, didn't want to. That's the thing about hallucinations as the result of taking too many pills. Doctors are wary to prescribe more. Still, he'd been made to promise to check in with his physician the following day.

Eventually, the last of the well-dressed crowd dispersed. While some headed home, eager to slip out of uncomfortable neckties and girdles, others left for after-parties that Nick was no longer invited to. There were no festivities in store for him that night. Not anymore. In the matter of an hour, Nick had gone from town savior to the most talked about man in Angler Bay. And not in a good way.

As patrons filed out, the expressions on many of their faces told Nick they would not be coming back. Pitiful looks of derision emphasized that fact. He'd been given one chance, and he'd shit the proverbial bed. One opinion in particular was echoed numerous times: perhaps The Chamberlain should have just remained closed. Nobody mentioned the theater's previous owner by name. Nobody had to.

When even the police and medics had vacated the premises, the only soul left hanging around was the mayor. If Nick thought that Blackwood had lagged behind out of concern for his medical condition, he was quickly proven wrong. With a hand on Nick's shoulder, the mayor simply looked him in the eye and asked when the theater would be up and running.

Nick could only shake his head in wonder as he walked toward his office down the hall, leaving the mayor alone in the lobby.

Was the guy for real?

Nick didn't know. But then, the mayor's motives weren't the only things Nick was having difficulty in deciding what was and was not real.

Act Two

EIGHT

They'd been at it for over an hour when the owner of the gourmet food shop with the supposedly haunted basement excused herself to check the status of a catering order. As she ascended the steps leading up from the cold, dank basement, the husband-and-wife paranormal team known as F.A.U.S.T. exchanged a look.

"Anything?" Börne asked.

Claudia exhaled deeply. "Sorry, *meine Liebe*. I'm not feeling anything down here." Closing her eyes, she again rested her hand on the masonry wall in question. Black, child-sized handprints blanketed the old bricks, their origin unknown, their age just as much a mystery. After a moment, she looked back at Börne and shook her head. "Nothing."

Börne nodded and kicked at a nearby cardboard box filled with what appeared to be Christmas decorations. *Scheisse!* And to think, this one had had potential. Strange handprints *and* strange sounds? He should be used to it by now. More often than not, their investigations ended this way. In the more than ten years he and Claudia had been researching the paranormal, they had actually acquired very little substantial evidence. Nothing that 'proved' the existence of ghosts or spirits, even though he and his wife were both full-fledged believers. For her part, Claudia was very much in tune with the spiritual world, had been since long before they'd met. If there were spirits around, she'd connect with them. They were just running into fewer and fewer spirits lately. And too many individuals who'd watched enough paranormal television shows to start believing they had a haunting on their hands any time something out of the ordinary took place.

Most of them didn't.

Börne and Claudia's careers had suffered for it. Their support had taken a hit. They'd refused to utilize some of the tricks other paranormal teams with less integrity used on their fake television shows. Which was a big reason why F.A.U.S.T.'s cable show had been cancelled after just two seasons. Viewers didn't want speculation, no matter how educated the guess. They tuned in to see results. Evidence. Proof. Their ratings slumped. So, when he and Claudia decided not to take the network up on their offer to 'conjure' a few spirits with the help of their production team, their plug was pulled. Now they produced their own videos and uploaded them to their YouTube channel, letting their handful of true fans decide for themselves which haunts may or may not be real.

Despite it all, Börne's hopes remained high at the start of every new job. He had to stay optimistic. Otherwise, what was the point?

Börne walked to the foot of the stairs and looked up. He could hear their host talking on the phone. By the sound of it, somebody wasn't having a good day.

"Could be awhile," he said, turning back to Claudia. "Wanna, you know…" He smiled and raised his eyebrows a couple of times.

Claudia chuckled and surveyed the drab basement. "Not quite the setting girls fantasize about. Besides—"

The clomping of footsteps on the stairs cut her thoughts short. As the footsteps grew louder, Börne turned to Claudia with a shrug.

"Guess it's a good thing you turned me down."

The woman emerged at the foot of the steps.

"Why is it so damn hard for people to follow simple orders?" she asked. She used her thumbs to type something on her cell phone before sliding it into the front pocket of a pristine green apron. "So, you two. What do you have for me?"

Börne looked first to Claudia, gauging whether they were both on the same page. When his partner nodded, he turned back to the shop owner.

"Well, I'm sorry to say," he said, "we're not finding any evidence of the paranormal down here. Could very likely be a water pipe or your HVAC system that's making your noise. As for the handprints—"

"A water pipe?" The woman wore a scowl as she split her time between Börne and Claudia. "You think the noise we hear coming from down here is a damn water pipe?"

"I'm sorry," Claudia said, shrugging. "I'm not connecting with anything or anyone down here."

Börne began gathering and stowing the few pieces of equipment he had trucked down to the basement. Most of his equipment remained in the car out front. No use bringing it all down until they knew there was a need for it. And more due to their host's attitude than the fact they weren't having any luck summoning spirits, their work here was done.

As Claudia headed toward the stairs, the woman's irritation showed through, "Guess I'll try somebody else. Someone better."

"With all due respect, ma'am," Börne said, passing the woman on his way to the stairs, "there is no one better."

NINE

Nick stood on The Chamberlain's front steps. While scrolling through Google's list of local ghost hunters on his phone, he managed to keep an eye on the young man twirling the colorful, arrow-shaped sign down on the sidewalk. The words 'now open' were emblazoned across the piece of cardboard. After the kid dropped the sign for the sixth time, Nick sighed out loud. He couldn't help but wonder who had come up with such a ridiculous job in the first place. Who had decided that twirling an advertisement was a skill worthy of getting paid money for? The more Nick thought about it, the more he realized: if anyone was the boob in this scenario, it was him. He was the one shelling out almost ten bucks an hour for the kid's 'services.'

He had to do something. It had been nearly six weeks since the nightmarish opening night and business at The Chamberlain had been almost nonexistent. Word around town was there was something either seriously wrong with the theater, or seriously wrong with its owner. Had the stress of remodeling and reopening the theater been too much for him? Had he flipped his wig that night and taken all those pills in the hopes of ending it all? These were just a few of the theories going around.

For his part, Nick didn't remember much of anything from opening night, so he didn't have a theory of his own.

The rumors spread like a virus, reaching all corners of the state and beyond, mutating as they went. Like a children's game of Telephone. Occasionally a rumor would make its way back to Nick while he sat in a bar or stood in line at the bank. He had somehow become everything from the unfortunate owner of a haunted theater, to an out-of-control drug addict, to a deranged cult leader intent on recruiting young people for his full moon sacrifices.

The opening night article Miss Park had run in the newspaper had been less than flattering and hadn't helped matters.

And when strange things actually started manifesting at the theater within weeks of opening—bursting light bulbs, uncooperative seats that would toss patrons to the floor, the ever-present stench of stale smoke—Nick's opening night episode was relabeled. It was no longer the hallucinatory result of taking too many Xanax. Nick's visions were now premonitions of things to come. The Chamberlain was quickly earning the reputation of being cursed. When word hit the Internet, accounts of The Chamberlain's phenomena began popping up on blogs and websites catering to fans of the paranormal. Subsequently, only two groups of people were buying a ticket these days: thrill seekers; and vacationers looking to get out of the heat, unaware of the theater's growing reputation. And there were few of both. It was as if a warning was included on the signs welcoming visitors to Angler Bay. Most nights, Nick showed films to mere handfuls of people. If he was lucky.

And if there was one thing Nick was not when it came to business, it was lucky.

He had to do something.

Despite the small numbers, paranormal-enthusiasts in search of their own personal Chamberlain story rarely walked away empty handed. It was as if the theater had taken on a personality all its own, and not one with a sunny disposition. Even those seeking phenomena sometimes got more than they bargained for. Bumps, bruises, minor cuts. The seats sometimes shook so hard, patrons would find themselves ass-up on the concrete floor. The exploding light bulbs would rain slivers of glass that easily found their way into eyes, ears and hair. A handful of customers had required minor medical attention, causing Nick to spend many nights lying awake in bed, expecting to either be sued or shut down. Neither ever happened. Nick continued to grapple with whether or not that was a godsend or curse.

He had to do something.

Which was why he currently found himself in the market for a ghost hunter.

His search for "ghost hunters near me" had initially been a shot in the dark. More for a laugh than anything. He didn't expect any listings to actually come up. And while none of the entries looked all that professional or instilled much confidence, he was surprised to find that there were enough to constitute an actual list. Though very few were what he'd consider to be 'near him.'

The kid on the sidewalk attempted to spin the signboard behind his back and failed.

Nick continued to scroll, doing his best to ignore the debacle on the sidewalk. He was about to retreat into the theater's cool air when he recognized a familiar face coming up the sidewalk. The large man sported a light grey suit, dark sunglasses, and used a folded newspaper to fan himself from the afternoon heat. As he approached The Chamberlain's steps, he took them two at a time.

A dark cloud passed in front of the sun. Nick's mood soured. He tried to put on a happy face. He more than likely failed.

"Afternoon, Mayor."

"Nick." The mayor's face was glum.

"Too nice of a day to look so down, ain't it?"

On the sidewalk, the cardboard sign once again twirled through the air, bounced out of the kid's hands, then hit the ground. When the wind blew the sign, tumbling into the gutter, Nick bit his bottom lip.

Fuck my life.

"Too nice of a day, huh?" Even as the mayor fanned himself, the sweat beads on his forehead multiplied. "Tell that to those blood-thirsty sonsabitches in city council. Nick, I'm telling ya, I just came from a meeting, and if we don't turn this damn theater around, we're both as good as the Titanic. S.U.N.K."

"And here I thought it was too hot for icebergs."

The mayor fake sniggered. "I ain't kidding around, Nick. You better embrace one fact: the whole reason you're still in business after your little fiasco is because I laid my ass on the line for you. You and this damned theater were supposed to save us all, remember?"

Nick remembered. Though by his recollection, he only wanted to open the theater of his own ambition. Make his way in the world, blah, blah, blah. The whole 'saving the town' idea was the mayor's, and for Nick, well, that would be great if it happened. He liked Angler Bay, would love to be part of a revitalization. But, saving his business, his livelihood, his dream was his first priority. And quite possibly, his last chance. Blackwood calling his ambition into question made the devil's sweat break out under Nick's collar.

"Now, the way I see it," the mayor said, pointing the newspaper toward the theater, "you either start promoting the hell out of what's going on in there, start bringing in the freaks who are into that kinda shit, or clean up the mess and start running a viable movie theater where families can come and shell out their hard-earned vacation dollars. Vis-à-vis, the original plan."

Nick held his tongue, silently counted to ten. What was the boiling point of blood, anyway? To say that his relationship with the mayor had become strained over the past few weeks was like saying cats and dogs didn't always see eye to eye.

"You don't have to remind me of the importance here, Mayor." Nick envisioned himself punching Blackwood in the teeth, sending the guy somersaulting down the steps to the sidewalk. He smiled a little inside. "But there's more to what's going on in there than a 'mess' that can simply be cleaned up."

The mayor snapped Nick in the chest with the folded-up newspaper.

"Look at the numbers, Nick." The mayor turned away and started down the steps. "A fuckin' mess is exactly what we've got here."

Nick nearly smirked at the mayor's use of "we," like they were in it together or something. If that were the case, then why did he feel all the weight was on his shoulders? "Think I'm gonna call someone," he said. "There are these shows on TV—"

Blackwood stopped halfway down the steps. "Hey, you gotta make a call, then make a call. Make five of 'em. Make as many as it damn well takes."

"Problem is, I'm not finding anyone local."

"No one local? Shit, I got all kinds of local. What do you need?"

"I need someone to come out and investigate, figure out what's going on in there. According to the paranormal articles I've read—"

"Ghostbusters?" The mayor full-on chuckled. "You shittin' me, Fallon? That's what you're looking for?"

Nick looked away, his mood now soured beyond saving, despite the ideal weather.

"Hey," the mayor continued, turning away. "Do, what ya

gotta do. I mean, shit. Who am I to judge? I'm only the dumb bastard who gifted you this golden hen."

As the mayor strolled down the steps toward the sidewalk, Nick hoped the sign would get away from the kid one more time and smack Blackwood upside the head. Maybe take out an eye.

No such luck.

*   *   *

As the credits rolled on the evening's final showing, Nick chucked a tub of buttered popcorn into the trashcan. He was glad he'd only made one tub's worth, which was pathetic in and of itself. But these were the tricks of the trade when it came to running a theater that too often showed its films to a room full of empty seats. You make one tub of popcorn. If it sells, you make another. If it doesn't, you don't lose as much money. And on the off chance someone requested two tubs, well then, he would worry about that trifling dilemma if and when it happened.

Now that he was The Chamberlain's sole employee, all of the tasks fell on Nick's shoulders, even the mundane duties like cleaning out the popcorn popper. Nobody wanted to work at the theater. Help was hard enough to find before opening night. Since then, any and all want ads he'd placed had gone unanswered. Even Manny had taken his engineering talents elsewhere, citing the fact that he didn't want to do the mundane jobs, either.

But Nick wasn't that naïve. There was more to his engineer leaving than a fear of popcorn.

When the auditorium doors opened, the evening's only four customers spilled out into the lobby. The teenagers, two young men dressed in black from head to toe, and their equally bleak-looking girlfriends, started making their way through the lobby.

One of the young men wore a dark grey skullcap, despite the summer heat. All four flaunted black and grey ink everywhere skin showed, and none of them would make it through a metal detector without setting it off.

They were society's fringe, and Nick was grateful to have them.

"Hey, bra," said the skullcap, with three silver rings in his eyebrow and two in his lip. "We want our money back."

Nick cringed.

Here we go.

He was getting used to refund requests when those unaware of the theater's growing reputation were caught off guard by the occurrences. Most of the time, Nick would put up a fight, try to convince the unhappy customers that it was all part of the show. But there were some things, like an exploding exit sign that sent plastic shrapnel into the audience that couldn't be explained as such. Nick could only shrug his shoulders at that point. Easy come, easy go.

That didn't mean it wasn't getting old.

"Yeah, man." The other young lad was a good half a foot shorter than his girlfriend. That didn't stop him from walking with his arm cocked up, draped around her neck. It looked awkward. It looked ridiculous. It looked like he was hanging on for dear life. "Nothin' happened."

Nick choked on his own saliva. "Nothing happened?"

The two young men shook their heads in unison, as if they shared a brain. The young ladies never lifted their eyes from their cell phones, clad in pink spider web cases. No irony there.

"So, no mist?" Nick asked. "No wind? What about the seats? Did they move around?"

"We got all that man." The kid shrugged. "It was cute."

"So…" Nick cocked an eyebrow. *Wait a second.* Did they really want their money back *because* nothing out of the ordinary happened? Not possible. "You're kidding me, right? You paid for a movie, and now you want a refund because a movie was all you got?"

"We didn't pay for the movie, yo." The taller kid spoke with his tattooed hands, emphasizing every other word with a gesture. "Could give two shits about the movie. We paid to see some sick shit go down. All we got was a butt massage and some wind in our hair—"

Nick nodded to skull cap. "And you felt left out, am I right?"

The young man ignored the cut and kept talking.

"We wanted to see some ghost-type shit. Like everyone is talkin' about online. And like he said, ain't nothin' happened."

"Yeah, man. Fuckin' lame."

Nick was no genius. He didn't have to be to realize he wasn't going to win over these two jerkoffs. He would have had better luck trying to convince Jason Voorhees to stop killing sexually active camp counselors. He'd refund their money alright. Nick simply couldn't believe it had come to this. How ridiculous the situation at the theater had gotten.

"Come on." Nick walked over to the ticket booth, followed close behind by the fearsome foursome. A minute later, he counted out their money and laid it on the counter. "There ya go. Thirty-two dollars. Can I assume the Twizzlers and Slushies were to your satisfaction? Or, will you be needing a refund for those, too?"

"Nah, man," skullcap said, scooping up the cash. "They was alright."

Nick watched the four teens exit through the front door. As he followed behind, he couldn't help but chuckle through the awkwardness. Maybe he should just close the theater and open up a candy shop. The sweet stuff was the only thing he was making a profit on. Nobody ever returned their box of Whoppers because they *didn't* find stale pieces inside.

As Nick turned the lock on the door, a young woman's ghostly face appeared in the glass. Nick jumped, nearly losing control of his bladder. *Holy shit!* Recovering, he couldn't help but chuckle again and shake his head. If he was that easily frightened, then he was definitely the wrong owner for The Chamberlain.

The girl rapped on the glass.

Nick turned the lock back and opened the door.

"Change your mind about the Twizzlers?"

The young lady was cute. Her impish smile and diamond-studded dimples were both brighter when she wasn't staring down at her phone. Catching another glimpse of her date standing on the sidewalk, Nick determined she could do decidedly better.

"You know what would be cool, man?" she said before popping her gum. "If you called these guys."

The young lady opened her white denim vest, revealing a black t-shirt underneath. Emblazoned on the shirt was the image of a woman: pale-skinned, flowing auburn-red hair, dressed in a long black gown with a blood red parasol resting on her shoulder; and a man: equally pale, spikey blond hair, also dressed predominantly in black save for a white frilly shirt and a vest the color of a good cabernet. A grey and white wolf sat obediently at the man's feet. In the background sat a long, black hearse. It was apparently nighttime in the photo, because a larger than life-sized moon hung over their shoulders. The letters F.A.U.S.T. glowed beneath the scene in neon yellow letters.

"Faust." Nick remembered the name from his Lit courses in college. Faust was a character in German folklore who sold his soul to the devil in exchange for knowledge. Cool story, but Nick didn't see the connection. "Why would I call them?"

"They investigate places like this," she said. "Haunted places." The raised eyebrows and the way her statement lifted at the end like a question told Nick she couldn't believe he hadn't heard of F.A.U.S.T. Like they were a household name or something.

"Ghost hunters?"

The girl now popped her gum even as she spoke. "They explore haunted places, film it, and post the videos online. Even had their own TV show. They're, like, famous. Maybe they can make this ghost thing work for ya. Or get rid of it, if that's what you want."

Nick looked at the photo on her shirt again. "They look like ghosts themselves."

The girl let out a sigh and allowed her jacket to fall back over her shirt.

"Never know, might be good for publicity, nothin' else." The girl looked around the theater lobby, then back at Nick. "Looks like you could use some of that, old man."

With a boisterous pop of her gum and middle finger in Nick's direction, she was gone.

Old man?

Locking the door behind her, Nick fought the urge to return the finger.

TEN

Nick's kitchen doubled as a home office. With stacks of paper everywhere, the table saw more use as a desk, and three of the four chairs gathered more dust than butts. He hadn't been in town long enough to make any real friends, he told himself. He also used the excuse that he'd been too busy with the new business. The excuses depended on the day and his mood. Only thing he knew for sure was that, as things regressed at The Chamberlain, the likelihood of his making friends would more than likely remain on the same trajectory.

Nick downed the swill at the bottom of beer number five and set the bottle beside numbers one through four. He'd never been much of a beer drinker, but some unseen magnet in The Sand Dollar Carryout's neon sign had pulled his car into the lot on his way home that night. It had been a long day. And having recently sworn off Xanax—some might call it being scared straight—Nick had to fill the void with something. The humidity in the summer night's air had suggested that a cold beer would go down nicely.

It hadn't been wrong.

Now, with his laptop open on the table, the members of F.A.U.S.T. stared back at him.

Börne and Claudia Forrester. A husband-and-wife ghost

hunting team who were, as described, relatively famous. At least in the world of paranormal research. Nick perused the home page of their website, finding YouTube video after YouTube video of the Finding Apparitions and Uninvited Spirits Team. More affectionately known as F.A.U.S.T. Each of the videos had been viewed at least fifty-thousand times. Nick had heard the term "internet star" before, but hadn't known what it meant until now.

The website was simple. Photos of dusty old televisions, screens full of static. An antique doll slumped in a rocker, the passing of time and shadows causing the child's plaything to appear dark and sinister in the black and white photos. Grainy images of old houses and what looked to be either an abandoned hospital or insane asylum. Nick wasn't sure which and didn't really care. The building was creepy either way. And coming from a guy whose theater had become spirit central as of late, that was saying something. A string of crimson words scrolled across the screen, telling him to 'enter if he dared.' It was the only color on the page, unless shades of grey and black were considered 'colors.'

Nick yawned and twisted the top off the last remaining beer. He was beyond drunk. Another twelve ounces of pale ale in his belly would ensure a hangover in the morning. But he felt obligated. It just seemed wrong to drink its five buddies, but not beer number six. He flicked the metal cap across the table where it joined the others. Nick took a long drink, winced, then turned his attention back to the screen.

He blinked. He opened his eyes wide. He pulled his lower lids down with his fingers, all with the goal of getting them to focus.

He let go and blinked a couple more times.

The word 'ENTER' hovered in the middle of the screen, fading in and out like a ghost. Was it him? Or, were the letters blurry as all hell? Nick maneuvered the arrow to the center of the screen and waited for the prompt to fade back in. It took its sweet time. Nick's head swam. He could feel himself fading in and out. Growing impatient, he resorted to repeatedly clicking the mouse until the word reappeared behind it.

"Gotcha!" he exclaimed when it finally appeared.

The screen went dark.

When it came back on seconds later, an image of a beautiful woman with sultry, long red hair graced the screen. Her eyes blazed a wild green as they peered deep into Nick's soul. Beside her, a toe-headed man leaned against a hearse. Both were dressed in black, both looked as dour as they possibly could.

It took a few seconds for Nick to put two and two together: it was the same couple as on the young lady's t-shirt.

The couple known as F.A.U.S.T.

After clicking through a few more gritty videos showing Börne and Claudia Forrester creeping around old decrepit buildings, always at night and sometimes in night vision green, Nick felt he had seen enough to make a decision. If anyone could help with the disturbances at The Chamberlain, it was these two. Plus, he really needed to get to bed. Morning was guaranteed to be a ball buster. The longer he put off sleep, the worse it would be. He would blame The Sand Dollar and its damn neon sign.

Before shutting down his computer, however, Nick scrolled the mouse to the top of the screen, took a deep breath, and clicked on the link that said 'CONTACT.'

*   *   *

Börne Forrester set down his black bag filled with video equipment and stretched his back out. It had been a long night of climbing rickety stairs, lugging equipment, and capturing nothing of real importance to show for it. The old Porter farmhouse had been a bust. And damned if it hadn't started out so promising. The property's backstory checked all the right boxes: a multi-generational homestead; folks described as quiet who kept primarily to themselves; rumors of incest and marital rape dating back to the turn of the century; the death of a young girl at the hands of her schizophrenic step-mother. The decrepit, old building had all of the makings of a classic haunting.

Yet, once again, they'd captured nothing. Not on film and not on audio.

Tapping the space bar on his keyboard, Börne woke the computer. The motor started to hum. While he waited for the screen to come alive, he dropped into the wheeled chair in front of what amounted to his desk. The office was makeshift, set up in an alcove of their dining room with a short counter that could realistically be used for little else. It was an odd architectural aspect of their Chicago home, something you wouldn't see in any houses back home in Germany, but it served a purpose. Answering fan mail and editing countless hours of video footage didn't require much space.

Sauntering into the room, Claudia Forrester ran a hand over her husband's shoulder, up his neck and through his blond hair. An open bottle of wine sat breathing on the table. She set a pair of crystal and pewter wine glasses beside the bottle. Pulling out one of the dinette chairs, she dropped down into it. She released her feet and a sigh of relief when she drew the silver zipper down the length of her calf. Her new pair of spike stiletto stretch boots with the 7" heel were sexy as heck, and played a huge role in her personae, but comfortable they were not. Claudia kicked her bare feet up onto the chair beside her. She crossed one bare ankle over the other and flexed her toes.

"Well, that was more fun than anyone should ever have." Sarcasm stained Claudia's words as she reached for the tall, green bottle. Tilting it sideways, she poured the ruby-red *Spätburgunder* into one of the glasses. She didn't stop until the glass was full, well past the standard stopping point. "Not sure this bottle's enough to drown out this evening, but it's a start." She slid the glass of wine across the table toward Börne, then went about pouring a glass of her own.

Börne scrolled through two days-worth of new emails, none of which piqued his interest. At least none that couldn't wait until morning. He spun his chair away from the desk and took up the glass of wine.

"To what are we drinking?" he asked, kneading his wife's foot with his free hand.

Claudia ran her fingertip around the rim of the glass.

"How about the simple fact this evening is over."

Börne's lips curled into a wicked smile. He let go of Claudia's foot and slid his hand up her leg. "Who said it was over?"

Claudia leaned down, looked at Börne from behind hooded eyes, and placed her lips within reach.

"Prost," she whispered.

Börne closed the distance and kissed his wife fully. Pulling away, he clinked his glass with hers.

"Prost."

He had just sat back and taken a sip of wine when the computer binged. A new email. His attention shifted across the room to the monitor.

"Leave it," Claudia said.

Börne took another sip before setting down his glass.

He shrugged.

"Force of habit." He rolled his chair back over to the desk. After clicking on the subject line, he began perusing the latest email.

"Worth interrupting the moment for?" Claudia asked, unbuttoning the top two buttons on her dress. Tipping her head back, she reduced the amount of wine in her glass by a third.

"Maybe." When Börne was done reading the email, he scrolled back up and read it again. "Interesting, at least."

Claudia dipped her nose into her glass, savored the hint of cherry. "You going to share?"

Börne spun around so that he faced her. "How would you feel about a trip to the beach?"

Claudia laughed. She held dear her alabaster skin. Protected it. Her image was nothing without it.

"Do I look like someone who enjoys spending time at the beach?"

"Okay, then," Börne said, his smile returning. "How about a dark and creepy movie theater?"

ELEVEN

Thirty-three.

That was how many tickets The Chamberlain sold over the next week. Not even a fourth of the theater had they all shown up at once. And the smart money would bet that even those numbers wouldn't continue.

Part of the reason they were as high as they were was due to the busload of cosplayers from a horror convention being held in nearby Wilmington. They all piled in on a Friday evening, all dressed in horror getup. It was Nick's first experience with cosplay, and he'd admittedly been impressed. Every subgenre of horror had been represented. There was a Jason, a Freddy, all manners of aliens and demons, and not one, but two very seductive vampiresses. Flesh-eating zombies made appearances in one version or another, some more realistic than others. One unfortunate soul even left a severed arm behind in the men's restroom. Nick still kept the prop under the concession counter, but doubted anyone would be coming for it.

So it was, that Nick wondered if the convention was still going on the following Tuesday morning when two apparent cosplayers knocked on The Chamberlain's glass door an hour before the first scheduled showing.

"Sorry," he said, poking his head out the door. "The first

show isn't until one. Doors don't open 'til 12:30." Nick looked the pair up and down, then gave them a thumbs up. "Great costumes, though."

The woman looked at the man. The man looked at her. They both looked back at Nick.

"We are looking for Nick Fallon." The man's accent was heavy, thick with European influence. Austrian, maybe German. He tilted his head forward. He slid his dark, red-lensed sunglasses down the slope of his nose to reveal icy blue eyes. "Would you know where we could find him?"

It was Nick's turn to look from one to the other. There was something vaguely familiar about the twosome. The woman's flowing red hair. Her skin, pale as a cloud. Both clad in black from head to toe despite the summer heat. Nick knew them from somewhere. He couldn't settle on where. Then it hit him, and he shook his head. How drunk had he been that night?

"Wait. F.A.U.S.T., right?" Nick found himself pointing at the two, literally wagging his finger at them. He caught himself and self-consciously pulled his hand back. He slid it into his front pocket. "Sorry. But you are, right? You're the ghost hunters."

The man and woman exchanged another glance, this time with visible scowls, as if something in Nick's declaration had caused them pain.

"We are F.A.U.S.T., yes." The woman nodded. "I am Claudia Forrester and this is my husband, Börne." The woman's voice was sultry, an octave deeper than most. "But, ghost hunters, we are not. We are paranormal investigators. Ghost hunters are frat boys who measure their testosterone levels by stumbling around abandoned warehouses, using cell phone cameras to *capture* things they want you to believe they see and hear. I'm afraid we don't do any of that. May we come in anyway?"

Nick stood, mouth agape, blocking the doorway. It was as if

manners were something he'd never been taught. His mother, *God rest her soul*, would be ashamed.

"Shit. Absolutely." Nick stepped aside, holding the door so the two could enter. Once they had passed through the doorway, Nick caught a glimpse of the street. A freshly-waxed black hearse sat out front, attracting a small crowd. One man cupped his hands around his face, trying to peer through the darkly tinted windows. Nick shook his head. It was as if the circus had come to town. He closed and locked the door before his two guests could draw the gawkers' attention his way. Turning to said guests, Nick smiled and spread his arms wide. "Welcome to The Chamberlain Theater."

Both nodded their appreciation before turning away.

Claudia wandered further into the lobby, the sound of her high-heeled boots echoing throughout the quiet lobby. She quickly turned her focus to the ceiling. With her head tilted back, her flowing auburn hair cascaded all the way down to her black, leather-clad rear end. She ambled slowly about the room, eyes glued to the ceiling. Concentration hardened her face as she peered into every nook and cranny. It was as if she were looking into the lobby's soul.

Nick joined the woman in looked up at the ceiling. All he saw were white, decorative ceiling tiles, sections of silver ductwork intersecting here and there, and two large fans that were currently keeping the lobby about fifteen degrees cooler than the outside.

Nick sidled up to the concession counter, leaned against it, and crossed his arms over his chest.

"What's she doing?" he asked, keeping his voice low.

The husband, Börne, hovered nearby. "Getting a sense of their temperament."

Nick's brow wrinkled. "Their?"

Börne nodded. He pulled a pewter pocket watch from a slit in his vest, then replaced it seconds later. "The spirits."

Nick's attention returned to the ceiling.

"Really? You think there are spirits here?"

Börne slid his sunglasses up onto his head, nestled them in his spiky blond hair.

"If they're here," he said, nodding, "she'll find them."

Nick frowned. "But…here in the lobby? Nothing's ever—"

His thought was cut short by the sound of one of the auditorium doors opening. The wooden door let out just enough of a squeal to alert Nick and the Forresters to its movement. Everyone stopped what they were doing and turned in the direction of the auditorium.

Seconds later, a bright light illuminated what they could see of the auditorium through the open door. Music began to play through the auditorium's speakers. All in all, it seemed as if the auditorium itself was trying to capture their attention, maybe lure them in.

"Anyone else here?" Börne asked, now standing beside Nick.

Nick stared at the door, dumbfounded, and simply shook his head.

"Excellent." Claudia's booming voice echoed throughout the empty lobby, startling Nick. "When can we start?"

Nick turned to Claudia. Though he was relatively certain she'd asked the question of him, her eyes were alert and focused on her husband. Börne returned her gaze with eyebrows raised.

"Um…The first show of the day is in less than an hour, if you'd like to sit in," Nick offered.

Claudia thought about it. At least it looked to Nick like she was considering it. Her mind appeared hard at work on something. She drew in her bottom lip. She checked on the auditorium's open door, then gave the lobby another once over. She shook her head.

"I don't think so." Claudia sauntered over to the counter. She gave a modified bow in Nick's direction. "But, thank you all the same." She pulled her sunglasses out of her fiery mane and placed them back over her eyes. "Tonight, though, you shall be closed, yes? We will return around ten o'clock. I assume that works for you?"

Nick was about to answer that yes, due to a city ordinance restricting how late downtown businesses could remain open, ten o'clock would indeed work for him. But he just as quickly deemed it unnecessary. Claudia had started toward the door without waiting for an answer. She really wasn't looking for one. Returning a nod from Börne, who had also replaced his sunglasses, Nick followed the husband-and-wife team to the front door and out onto the steps.

"See you guys at ten, then?"

Claudia tossed a queen's wave over her shoulder as the Forresters glided down the concrete steps toward the sidewalk and their awaiting hearse.

Nick assumed that meant they were indeed on for ten o'clock, then he cautioned himself. He could already tell that making assumptions with these two would most likely not serve him well.

They hadn't even asked to see the auditorium.

*　*　*

After signing a few autographs and kindly dispersing the crowd that had gathered around the hearse, Börne unlocked the passenger door and opened it wide.

"That didn't take much convincing."

Claudia stepped up to the car, but stopped short of getting in. She turned and looked up at The Chamberlain Theater's marquee. The façade was old, grey stone in need of a good power washing. The tall, red letters were showing their age in spots. Its glass doors and ticket booth window, however, gleamed in the sunlight, making mirrors of both.

"Let's just say I got a feeling," she said, turning and climbing into the passenger seat. "This one'll be worth the trip."

Börne shut the car door, then nodded and waved to the few lingering onlookers as he made his way around the front of the hearse.

"Yeah?" he said once he'd climbed behind the wheel and shut his door. "You mean, I did good this time?" He started the car's engine and pulled away from the curb in the direction of their hotel.

"You did good, my dear." Claudia rested her hand on Börne's thigh. "Though after the Wrigleyville debacle, the bar's been set pretty low."

Börne snickered. "I'll never live that one down, will I?"

Claudia smiled. She closed her eyes and rested the back of her head against the headrest. "Not as long as I'm around."

TWELVE

Nori Park clicked on the 'send' icon and sat back in her chair. After several starts and stops, her latest article was finally on its way to her editor for review. The mayor and city council were butting heads on budgetary matters. Specifically, how to pay for a much-needed sand dune restoration project. It wasn't Black Lives Matter. It wasn't #MeToo. It wasn't anything particularly exciting or even noteworthy to most. But someone had to keep the townsfolk—at least the few who cared—apprised of what was going on in their town. No matter how mundane those matters may be. And, for better or worse, that someone was her.

The sky through the newsroom windows had been blue when she'd started her article. She'd watched it morph into a rich orange, then purple, and finally a deep black. One by one, the tiny offices along Nori's corridor had also gone dark. About an hour ago, a dull ache had settled in her lower back. She'd been sitting too long. Her rumbling stomach reminded her that her social life wasn't the only thing she'd been neglecting. But, that's how it went when she was up against a deadline. All non-essentials were eligible for sacrifice.

Nori picked up her cell phone and checked the time. *9:23.* Mrs. Chang, the owner of the Chinese restaurant near her apartment, shut down her woks at 10:00, sometimes earlier if business was slow. Nori needed to get moving if she was going to make her date with the couch, a glass of white wine and a steaming bowl of shrimp lo meine. It wasn't the food of her homeland, but it was a close second. She also wanted to squeeze in at least a couple of hours of Netflix before shuffling off to bed. She was tired of plugging her ears when people in the office started talking about the latest episode of the shows she liked. She was about four episodes behind everyone else and needed to fix that.

Nori closed her email and briefly brought up the Reuters news website one last time. It seemed things were happening all over. Turkey was waking to another terrorist bombing. A nightclub shooting in Texas. Wildfires in California. All big stories, all terrible events for anyone involved. Anyone, that is, except those in the media. A necessary evil, bad news put food on their tables, gas in their cars. It covered the rising costs of healthcare. And nobody on Nori's side made any apologies for it, no matter how much they were judged and sometimes derided for it.

There were times she dreamed of being in the thick of things, reporting on the stories the entire country, if not the world, were tuning in for. However, because that kind of work could take an emotional toll, there were also times she was thankful she wasn't.

Then there were times when she just felt lost. Neither thankful, nor preoccupied with what could be. Lately, Nori was simply bored. So much so, the tendrils of indecision were infiltrating her thoughts, consuming them. She had three options really: remain relatively content with the quiet life and equally uninteresting job; move somewhere more exciting where reportable things actually happened; or find a new profession altogether. No one option outshined the others, for varying reasons. Each had its pros and cons. She knew her parents' preference. Short of moving back home with them to South Korea, they would be content for her to stay right where she was, living life out of harm's way. To them, boring meant safe. To Nori, it simply meant boring.

"Hey, Park!"

Callie Lipton, Nori's best friend and the newspaper's junior editor, popped her head in the door of the newsroom. Hailing from New York City, Nori often wondered about the career choice Callie had made. Moving away from arguably the biggest, most news-active city in the world, she'd settled in little old Angler Bay, North Carolina, home to beautiful sand and surf and little else. Heck, they'd only recently gotten a Starbucks. Callie claimed to welcome the peace, the slow-paced lifestyle. For the first fifteen years of her career, Callie lived through and reported on everything the Big Apple could throw at her. Survived it, as she liked to tell it. Now she relished her position as Number Two at the Angler Bay Standard, the sleepiest rag on Earth. All newspapers had the occasional slow news day. For The Standard, it was like one long, never-ending slow news day.

Mr. Dingle's wayward cats were bigger celebrities around town than the Kardashians.

"Jason and I are heading over to The Galley for drinks and a late dinner," Callie said. "Apparently, he's in the mood for oysters. So, you know what that means."

Callie's wink and smile told Nori everything she needed to know about the Liptons. More specifically, how they'd be spending their evening once they got home. Nori and Callie had had more than one conversation about Jason, his oysters and how they affected his libido. Not only was it more information than Nori needed to know, but also the reason she had to hold in her smirk every time she saw him.

"Think I'll take a raincheck." Nori glanced at the time before shutting down her computer. "You kids have fun, though."

"Oh, you know we will," Another wink and smile. "Maybe this weekend?"

"As long as aliens don't invade our little town, or anything else interesting enough to keep me glued to my desk."

"Cool!" Callie said. "Jason's talking about taking out the boat, cruise up the coast. If it goes anything like usual, he'll fish, and I'll lay in the sun drinking mango hard seltzers until he gets frustrated with not catching anything and we come home. It's a whole thing. You're definitely coming along this time."

"Sounds like an offer I'd be crazy to refuse." Nori rose from her chair and started gathering her things. "My doctor's been hounding me to work more mango hard seltzers into my diet, anyway. Works out perfectly."

"Awesome!" Callie flashed her signature smile. A model's smile. A movie star's smile. It was always Nori's belief that Callie should be making headlines, not just reporting them. "Talk more tomorrow?"

Nori's answer was a simple nod.

Callie lightly danced her fingertips on the doorframe before vanishing.

Slinging her satchel up onto her shoulder, Nori swiped her cell and keys.

Callie reappeared in the doorway. "Hey!"

Startled, Nori jumped and dropped her keys on the floor. "Shit, Callie!"

"Sorry." Callie chuckled. "Almost forgot, though. Heard some chatter this afternoon that might interest you. Sounds like there's something going on over at The Chamberlain."

THIRTEEN

It had been an unusually quiet day at the theater. Even by The Chamberlain's standards. Nick hadn't sold a single ticket. Hadn't bothered to show a film. One woman did poke her head into the lobby, but only to inquire about using the restroom. Nick couldn't even interest her in a snack for the road. Losing money on this latest business venture was becoming a full-time job. An occupation he was all too familiar with, and unfortunately, getting good at. So far, he had managed to ignore the phone calls from his accountant. Unless he had a rich uncle, who'd kicked the bucket and left Nick his fortune, she wasn't calling to pass along good news. He didn't return her texts, nor open her emails. Avoiding one's accountant certainly wasn't the best way to run a business. But then, could owning a theater that never saw asses in its seats really be considered "running a business?"

For at least the fifth time that day, Nick wondered if calling in the paranormal investigators would actually make a difference. Did he even believe in ghosts? It was a question he'd never considered until he'd been forced to recently. He still didn't have an answer, couldn't explain the things that were happening in the auditorium. Ultimately, he'd decided to let them take a look, do whatever it was they did, and see what they had to say. It really couldn't hurt either way. Nothing else, perhaps he'd get some publicity out of the whole thing.

It was 9:55, and Nick was sitting on the concession counter munching his way through his second bag of Twizzlers when he saw the members of F.A.U.S.T. walking up the front steps. Bathed in the harsh light from the overhead marquee, their pale features appeared even more opaque against the night. Nick hopped down from his perch and met them at the door.

"Good evening, Mr. Fallon."

Nick nodded to Claudia, then Börne as they passed through the doorway. "Good evening."

Nick closed the door behind them, his attention instantly drawn to Claudia. He couldn't help it. Her transformation practically commanded it. The black leather pants and boots from earlier in the day were gone. Her black top, too. It had all been swapped for a long, flowing white gown that trailed like a shadow in her wake as she floated across the lobby floor. The dress concealed her feet. She didn't walk across the floor. She glided as she made her way around the lobby, once again familiarizing herself with the nearly century-old room.

Mesmerized, Nick couldn't tear his eyes away.

"I could use a hand."

Nick started at the voice beside him. "Sorry?"

"My equipment," Börne said. "From the car? I could use some help bringing it all in." Börne seemed annoyed, causing Nick to wonder if he hadn't been staring at the man's wife a little too long. Or, too admiringly.

"Right. Sure."

He followed Börne out, leaving Claudia staring off into space. For the first time since they'd arrived, Nick noticed that Börne was also dressed more elaborately than he'd been that morning. Black was still the order of the day, from his top hat to his boots. He draped himself in a long black frock with silver buttons down the front and tails that hit behind the knees. Only his ruffled white dress shirt and burgundy red vest stood apart from the black of everything else. To Nick, the guy looked like a gothic superhero. He had no doubt the two would draw attention wherever they went in Angler Bay.

In contrast, Nick felt more than a little underdressed in his khakis, light blue button down, and sensible loafers.

"So, do they always hang out near the ceiling?" Nick asked, as they descended the steps to the street.

"What do you mean?" Börne asked.

"She's always looking up at the ceiling," Nick explained. "This morning you said she was gauging the temperament of spirits. So, I was wondering if they typically hang out up there?"

Börne shrugged as he swung open the rear door of the hearse. "Not usually."

"But she is looking for spirits…"

"Could be." When Börne looked up at Nick for the first time since stepping outside, a smirk pulled at the corner of his mouth. He winked. "Could be that my wife studied gothic architecture at university and just likes old buildings."

Two trips to the car.

Four black cases, a laptop bag, and a duffle bag.

By the time they were done, a mini pyramid of paranormal research and video equipment had been erected in front of the concession stand. Apparently the Forresters weren't ones to travel light. Or waste time. Börne immediately began rooting through his duffle bag. Claudia ventured down the hallway toward Nick's office and storage room.

And Nick just stood there, hands in his pockets, caught somewhere between anticipation and skepticism.

"So." Börne pulled out a laptop, flipped it open, and started tapping away at the keyboard. "We did some research. Your theater has some very interesting history, Mr. Fallon. One incident in particular stood out. I mean, *way* out. Like a nun at a gentleman's club. Tell us what you know about Floyd Cropper."

The couple's roles had apparently switched since their visit earlier in the day. This morning, Claudia had pretty much been the only one of the two investigators that spoke. With the exception of a brief exchange between he and Nick, Börne may as well have been a mute who'd had his tongue removed. Now, though, Börne seemed to be running the show. The F.A.U.S.T. team had been there ten minutes, and Claudia had yet to utter a single word.

"I'm sorry," Nick said, remembering that a question had been asked. "Who?"

Börne repeated the name.

Even after hearing it aloud a second time, it still didn't ring Nick's bell. *Floyd Cropper.* Seemed like he'd heard the name before, somewhere, but he had no idea who it belonged to. His lack of poker face must have betrayed his ignorance, because Claudia finally spoke. And when she did, Nick felt like a lecture was forthcoming and he should be taking notes.

"In all the years since The Chamberlain has been in existence," Claudia said, returning to the lobby, "Angler Bay has seen only three tragic deaths. What I would consider to be tragic, at least. Deaths above and beyond a simple car crash here or there. Two young boys, ages ten and twelve. Took their boat out one night and were never seen again. They presumably drowned or were washed out to sea. Never found the boat, either."

Nick nodded. "The mayor's boys."

"I'm sorry?"

Nick looked up at Claudia. "Stephen and Mitchel Blackwood. They were the mayor's sons. Though, he wasn't the mayor yet. This was back in the eighties, I think. Story goes it was Mitchel's little rowboat. Got it for his birthday. Apparently, they couldn't wait 'til morning like they were told, so they snuck out at night to try out the boat." Nick shrugged. "And, like you said, were never seen nor heard from again."

"Damn," Börne said. "That's enough to kill a man."

"Or, make him mean," Nick said.

Börne nodded. "Or, that."

"There's still a debate around town," Nick continued. "Some people say that losing his sons is what made the mayor the way he is. Others argue that the way he is, is why he lost his sons."

Claudia looked at Nick, brow furrowed. "I don't follow."

"Rumor is," Nick continued, "Blackwood was pretty hard on the boys. Would knock 'em around some. Especially when he'd been drinking, I guess. Some swear that the boys didn't drown at all. They actually ran away."

"And what do you believe, Mr. Fallon?" Claudia asked.

Nick shrugged. "Don't know. It was all before I got here. And I've learned first-hand how rumors work in a small town like this. Stick around long enough, and I'm sure you'll hear one or two about me and The Chamberlain."

"Which brings me to your town's third tragedy," Claudia said. "The Chamberlain's previous owner."

"Floyd Cropper," Börne re-iterated, pointing out front. "The old man who started a fire out on those steps, using himself as kindling."

"Oh." Nick exaggerated his nod, trying hard to sell it. "*That* Floyd Cropper." He felt foolish. He continued to nod slowly, a piss poor attempt at stalling. Nick felt like he should offer more, but what could he say really? He knew little of the theater's previous owner. No more than what Börne had just shared. Mr. Cropper had lost the property, and subsequently set himself on fire in protest. Right or wrong, that's all Nick knew. All he cared to know. Self-preservation and all that.

"Seems to me," Börne said, looking up from his laptop, "Floyd Cropper would be a good place to start the conversation,

Mr. Fallon. You know, about what's going on in your theater."

"Please, call me Nick. And do you really think so?"

Claudia approached the counter.

"Makes sense, doesn't it? The man had nothing, Nick. No family, other than his wife. No kids. No grandkids. By all accounts, the theater was all Floyd Cropper had. Then he lost it."

"Literally *and* figuratively," Börne interjects.

"He's so crushed over the loss of his beloved theater," Claudia continues, "that he kills himself in a particularly violent manner just outside the front door. Seems to me, that's exactly the type of spirit that would want to stick around and cause problems for the next owner. It's practically text book."

What was it about Claudia—*her accent?*—that made her so alluring? Not to mention, distracting?

"Uh, yeah," Nick said, clearing the queries from his mind. "I guess you're—"

A sharp rap on the glass door stalled Nick's thought.

Everyone jumped, startled, including the two who dealt with scary things for a living.

Nick immediately joined Claudia and Börne in a chuckle. At least he had an excuse. He wasn't used to all this ghost talk. Still, they hadn't even started yet. Something told him he better get used to it all real quick.

Don't be such a chickenshit, Nick.

But a moment later, when Nick saw who was pressing their face against the glass, he knew he had cause for worry.

"Shit," he whispered. With a deep sigh, he addressed the husband-and-wife team of F.A.U.S.T. "Excuse me."

He strolled to the front door, taking his time. The taste of Ms. Nori Park's unflattering opening night article crept up the back of his throat like acid reflux. There were a hundred reasons why the reporter might be knocking on his door, but only one of those reasons made sense.

She pulled away from the glass—hands still cupped around her eyes—as Nick approached.

"Can I help you?" Nick held the door open a mere six inches. It was enough to be able to look the journalist in the eyes. He wasn't about to give her space enough to slip through.

"Aw, don't be like that, Nick." As she addressed him, Nori's eyes were everywhere but on Nick. She weaved side to side, up and down, trying to see past him. "You're not still upset about the article, are you?"

Nick's jaw came unhinged. "Seriously? That article is part of the reason there's no one here this evening."

"Oh, there's someone here, alright." Nori finally stopped evading him and met Nick's gaze head on. "Their hearse is sitting right there!"

And there it was. The reason why the journalist was suddenly knocking on his door out of the blue. And at such a late hour.

"Oh, no," Nick said, shaking his head. He turned back to Börne and Claudia, who were watching him quizzically, and smiled. Then he turned back to Nori where his smile died. "You're not coming in here. And you're sure as hell not talking to them. Not if I can help it."

Nori bit her bottom lip. Her expression softened. She began to tug on her right ear. "Come on, Nick. Maybe I can help."

Nick feigned a laugh, reminded himself to stay strong. Historically, intelligent and attractive women had been his kryptonite, and he already had one on the case.

"Oh," Nick said, conjuring some sarcasm, "I think you've helped enough, thank you."

"Think about it, Nick." The reporter in her was not easily deterred. A personality trait that Nick recalled from Opening Night. "Word's gonna get out they're here. It already has. How do you think I found out? So why not let me help publicize the fact? I can put a positive spin on it from the get go."

Nick thought about it. Then he thought better of it. "Thought that was the plan a couple months ago. And look how that turned out. You roasted me."

"I absolutely did not." Nori shook her head. "The story we ran was not the story I wrote. My editor made changes. Made it more salacious. In his mind, more interesting. You know what they say, Nick. 'If it bleeds, it leads.' He just made your story bleed more than you would have liked. This, though, this is different. This could be really good for you and the theater. Ergo, the town. I'm picturing an in-depth interview up front, get their insights on what's going on in the theater. Then I can chronicle the work they're doing here. And if all goes right, we put their stamp of approval on The Chamberlain, let everyone know it's okay to come back."

Nick could feel his defenses crumbling like a sandcastle at high tide. And Nori Park was a rogue wave. It wasn't even her intelligence or any perceived attraction on Nick's part. Problem was, the points she'd made were more than valid.

"And if all doesn't go right?" he asked.

"Aw come on, Nick." Nori smiled broadly. "Have some faith."

Nick chuckled, but it wasn't because he found what she'd said humorous. If there was one thing he lacked, besides customers, it was faith. He didn't have faith that F.A.U.S.T. could fix what was broken inside the theater. Didn't have faith that people would return simply because they said it was okay. And he sure as hell didn't have faith in Nori Park and The Standard doing a one-eighty where their views of him and The Chamberlain were concerned.

But Nick was finding it nearly impossible to poke holes in the iron-clad case Nori was making. The only thing for him to do was admit defeat.

Nick took a step back and opened the door wide.

"Awesome!" Nori wasted no time sliding through.

Nick had to hand it to her. Nori was nothing if not ambitious. She was already introducing herself to the Forresters by the time he had shut and locked the front door. As he rejoined them, a little voice told him he would come to regret letting the reporter in. He didn't know when or why, but it was the one thing in which Nick did have faith.

"So," Börne said, turning his attention from Nori back to Nick, "can we see this theater?"

FOURTEEN

Nick felt like the intro to a joke: Two paranormal investigators, a journalist and a failed businessman walk into a theater...

He just hoped the joke wasn't on him.

They left the equipment behind as they made their way to the pair of heavy, oak doors that separated the lobby from the auditorium. Traditionally, an auditorium's doors would be kept open right up to the time the previews started. At The Chamberlain, however, circumstances trumped traditional theater practices, and Nick kept the doors closed. At all times. Call it superstition, call it a former scout trying to be prepared. Confining the theater's phenomena to one area seemed like plain old good sense.

With his hand on the door handle, Nick hesitated. "Everyone ready?"

Everyone nodded except Nori, who suddenly didn't seem quite as sure about what she'd signed up to be part of. Understandable. As eager as she probably was to cover the story, she'd been there on opening night. No doubt she'd also heard the multitude of rumors since. In a small community like Angler Bay, rumors spread like the most aggressive of diseases. Sometimes with the same catastrophic results.

"Yeah," she assured, though the sullen look in her eyes said otherwise. Nori slowly took in a deep breath of air, held it for a second. Then, just as slowly, she let it out. "I'm ready."

Nick exchanged looks with both Börne and Claudia, then turned back to the doors and gave them a tug.

The doors didn't open.

Didn't even budge.

If anyone had been hoping for a grand reveal, they were understandably disappointed. Nick gave both handles another hard pull. Still, the doors remained closed. It was as if someone much stronger than Nick was on the other side holding them shut. He frowned.

"Locked?"

Nick considered Börne's question. They shouldn't be. He never locked the doors. Ever. Not since opening night. And not since simply keeping them closed had proven a sufficient sequester. He looked the doors up and down. Nothing seemed amiss. It made no sense. He let go of the handles and reached into his pockets for his keys.

Was it possible the doors had locked on their own? It didn't seem likely. It would be an entirely new wrinkle if they had.

Nick pulled out his keys and began sorting through.

"Shouldn't be locked," he said. "Haven't locked them since—"

The sound of creaking wood cut his thought short. When Nick looked up, he couldn't believe his eyes.

The doors stood ajar. Just as improbable as it was that they'd been unwilling to open, it was just as improbable that they had opened on their own.

"Interesting." Börne said, exchanging a look with Claudia. "This ever happen before, Nick?"

Nick shook his head, bit his lip. "Not at all."

Nori seemed to be finding the situation just as peculiar. Her eyes narrowed. A storm cloud of concern churned behind them.

Welcome to The Chamberlain, Nick thought.

"Now, before we enter," Claudia said, "I must ask. Nick, are you a religious man?" She turned to Nori. "You?"

Nick and Nori both shook their heads.

"In that case, please humor me as I ask for protection over us."

Nick's eyes widened.

"Protection?" He looked to Börne to see if he was being put on. The man's expression spoke of utmost seriousness.

"We find that it's better to be safe than sorry," Börne said. "And if you don't necessarily believe in prayer, that's okay. Sometimes people simply use this as an opportunity to put themselves in a positive frame of mind. Trust me, keeping an open and positive outlook can be highly beneficial to the process."

Nick briefly checked in with Nori. Her eyes studied the floor. He turned back to Claudia. Her eyes were closed, her hands stretched out toward them, patiently waiting.

Not without some hesitation, Nick reached out and took Claudia's hand. Nori eventually caught sight of what was happening and took the other. Finally, Börne took Nick and Nori's other hands, closing the circle.

"Saint Michael the Archangel," Claudia began, "defend us in battle. Be our protection against the wickedness and snares of the devil. May God rebuke him, we humbly pray…"

As the prayer continued to flow from Claudia, Nick lifted his head so he could see Nori. It appeared Claudia's insistence on prayer wasn't easing the journalist's anxiety any more than it was his. If anything, it was making it worse. *Protection?* Nori's face had lost all but a hint of color. Twice she turned and looked longingly toward the lobby. Nick thought she might bolt for the door, which, all things considered, might not be such a bad idea. When she remained rooted where she was, he offered her a tiny smile. She gave a half-hearted smile back before lowering her head.

"…all the evil spirits, who prowl about the world seeking the ruin of souls. Amen." Claudia's eyes opened. She nodded ever so subtly while releasing their hands. "We are safe to enter."

First protection, now mention of safety.

Before tonight, Nick had never considered that he needed either. The activity at The Chamberlain had simply been a nuisance. A hindrance to making a profit. But, now? Things felt suddenly different. It had taken bringing in the experts for him to feel threatened for the first time. A chill tickled his spine.

Silence played soundtrack to the moment until Nick realized all eyes were on him.

"Oh. By all means." Nick pulled the doors open fully and gestured for Claudia to enter. She did. Börne followed, hot on her heels. After one more top to bottom inspection of the doors, Nick joined the pair inside the auditorium. Only Nori lagged behind.

"I think I'll observe from here," she said, peering in from just outside the doorway.

In contrast, Claudia strolled down the center aisle like she owned the place, like fear was as foreign to her as intergalactic travel. Her eyes scanned the ceiling, repeating her behavior from the lobby. Halfway down the aisle, she stopped. A moment later, she turned to Börne.

"*Meine Liebe.*"

Their eyes met and held for several seconds. That was all it took to send him away. Börne returned a moment later, carrying two of his black cases. He set one of the cases down just inside the doorway. He carried the other with him around the back row of seats to the far rear corner of the auditorium.

Nick watched with interest, wondering what was in the cases. A question carried over from when he'd helped unload them from the hearse. At Mayor Blackwood's mentioning of it, he'd recently watched the movie Ghostbusters late one night when the stress of the job had rendered sleep obsolete. He doubted Börne would be pulling out a proton pack from either case, but one never—

"Floyd Cropper."

Nick jumped.

The introduction of Claudia's voice in the silence of the auditorium was startling. It echoed around the empty room before finally fading off into the void where all echoes go to die. Claudia and her flowing white gown had made their way down front where she'd stopped at the bottom of the aisle. Her head suddenly perked up. She tilted it to one side, then remained still for a moment, either concentrating or waiting. "Are you here, Floyd?"

Another chill rippled down Nick's spine as a thought occurred to him: what if the old man actually answered?

Approaching the screen, Claudia ran her hand along its shimmering surface. "Floyd? Are you with us?"

The floor started to tremble.

"What the…"

The vibration was subtle. It started in his feet and ran up Nick's legs. He shot his hand out to the seat beside him. He looked to Claudia. He looked to Börne. Neither appeared to notice the rumbling beneath their feet. If they did, they weren't fazed in the least.

The mild quaking coursed through the seats. They started to rumble. The overhead lights started to rattle, then sway back and forth. The creaking of metal filled the air. A faint humming sound joined in as overhead machines kicked on. An instant later, a fine spritz of water began to spit from the machines. A swift breeze began to circle through the auditorium.

Nick took in a deep breath and let it out. *Stay calm.* None of this was out of the ordinary. At least not by The Chamberlain's standards. Ironically, this was the very phenomenon some folks were coming to witness. The exact atmosphere Nick had paid a lot of money to establish. The difference now? No movie was showing to correspond with the effects. There was no trigger. No reason whatsoever for any of it to be happening other than the mere presence of the four individuals there to bear witness.

And the fact that Claudia Forrester was attempting to summon the ghost of an old man.

Nick checked in with Nori. She remained just inside the doorway, experiencing the phenomena for the first time. Both hands covered her mouth. Her wild eyes darted around the large room.

"Nick?" Börne asked. "Are you…"

Nick raised his hands in a show of innocence. "Nope. Not doing anything. And it's not part of the—"

A loud pop cut him off.

Everyone's attention hastened to the ceiling, where one by one, overhead light bulbs started to explode. Light bulbs flickered. Light bulbs burst. Tiny diamond-like shards of glass began to rain down upon the seats and concrete floor. The showers were sporadic at first, centralized. One sprang up down front by Claudia. Another in the back to Nick's left. As light bulbs all throughout the room violently snuffed themselves out, they quickly merged into one large storm of raining glass.

Covering her head with her hands, Claudia rushed up the aisle. Nick could hear glass crunching underfoot as she passed. At the doors, Nori greeted her. Nick soon joined them, and a moment later, so did Börne. Everyone breathed heavily. Everyone shook bits of glass from their hair.

"Now, that," Nick said, turning to watch the chaos unfold, "is new. Never on that…level…"

They all stood in the relative safety of the doorway, watching the light inside the auditorium gradually diminish as darkness slowly took over. Chaos reigned beneath its growing cloak. Mist continued to fall. Winds continued to gust. The popping of light bulbs sounded like an easily-entertained child with an endless supply of bubble wrap.

When the last bulb burst, an eerie calm settled over the nearly-pitch auditorium. The only remaining lights were the red glow of the exit sign down front, and the handful of ambient sconces mounted along the back and side walls. None of which dispensed with enough light to see much of anything. The mist had stopped. So too had the wind and violent trembling.

The faint scent of smoke wafted through the doorway. Barely noticeable at first, the odor grew stronger. Soon, there was no denying its existence.

Börne's voice floated over Nick's shoulder. "Smoke."

If Nick wasn't mistaken, a hint of excitement was present in the investigator's voice. Nick nodded, tried to steady his heavy breathing.

"From the light bulbs?" Börne asked.

"I don't think so," Nick said, wiping sweat from his forehead. "It's always been—"

Nori's brief coughing fit interrupted. The stench was growing stronger, becoming nearly unbearable. Like an invisible campfire had been set ablaze before them.

"Screw this," Nori said, and slammed the two heavy doors shut. She turned and faced the others with a sheepish gaze. "Sorry. But, you know, enough's enough."

Claudia raised a hand. "It's quite alright." Excitedly, she turned to Börne. "Tell me you got that."

Börne shook his head. His expression mimicked a sad puppy dog. "Happened too quick," he said. "I wasn't set up yet."

"Got what?" Nori asked. "I mean, what was that?"

A smile pulled at Claudia's lips, despite there being a hint of caution in her eyes. "I believe we just received a formal welcome from our Mr. Cropper."

FIFTEEN

"Well," Nick said, "that was more fun than my typical Tuesday night."

He didn't smoke, but he could have used a cigarette right then. His hands shook, which was why he slid them into his pockets. He thought of the tiny packet he used to keep there. The Xanax tabs that he no longer courted. For good reason, he reminded himself. He considered the unopened bottle of bourbon stashed in the desk drawer in his office. Considered it, then let go of the idea. Maybe later. For now, he'd have to calm himself organically. A tall order. Not since opening night had he seen The Chamberlain come so alive. Back then it had all been in his head. This time, however, he was pretty sure it had really happened.

"The shaking seats are one thing," he said. "A shattered light bulb here and there. Problems with the projector. But, that…"

Claudia reached up and put her hand on Nick's shoulder, ran it up and down his arm. "Well," she said, "we now have Mr. Cropper's undivided attention. Something you didn't have before. Things were bound to escalate once we connected."

Nick shook his head. He couldn't help but feel a little foolish. Like a child being comforted by his teacher. His beautiful teacher, which somehow made it worse.

Nori hugged herself, rubbed her shoulders. "That was a little scary. Not too proud to admit."

"It can be," Claudia continued. "Mostly, spirits just want something. That's why they hang around. Some want a wrong to be righted. Some just want us to recognize the fact they existed in the first place."

"That's a hell of a way to get recognition," Nick said, jabbing his thumb toward the auditorium. "I've seen toddlers throw lesser tantrums."

"Um, speaking of recognition," Börne said, "are we just going to gloss over the fact that it smelled like something was on fire in there."

Everyone took a collective step away from the set of doors. Everyone, that is, except Nick.

"It's alright," he said, giving the all clear with his hands. "It just smells that way sometimes. I don't know why. Sometimes the smell is so strong, so thick, it feels like you're about to be overcome by smoke. But, there never is any. Not actually. Not that I, or anyone else, has been able to find a source for. Somehow, it's just the smell."

Börne exchanged a look with Claudia. "So...where's the smell coming from then?"

"Damned if I know," Nick said. "Maybe you two could figure that out while you're here."

The group fell silent, everyone lost in thought. For Nick, the events of the past twenty minutes layered themselves atop those of Opening Night. There were similarities, and that bothered him. Was it just a hallucination he experienced that night? Or, could the rumors of a premonition actually hold some merit?

"So now what?" he asked, eyeing the auditorium doors warily, suddenly expecting them to fly open at any moment.

Börne bit his bottom lip and appeared to contemplate. "Contact doesn't usually occur so quickly," he said. "So, I suggest everyone just hang tight while I finish setting up the equipment. Then we'll try it again. In the meantime, use the restroom, grab a Coke and some popcorn. Get ready for the next show."

Nori snickered. "Well, if the second show is anything like the first," she said, "I'm gonna need something to mix with that Coke."

*　　*　　*

Nick pulled the bottle of bourbon from the bottom drawer of his desk. Drinking at work was a rarity, but keeping it on hand was one of two pieces of advice he retained from business school. You saw it all the time on television and the movies. Though, in all his years of doing business, Nick rarely had an occasion to get it out and offer a guest a drink. As for the other piece of advice, he never did learn to play golf.

"Hope this'll do," he said, twisting the bottle's lid. The seal broke free with a slight tearing sound in the otherwise quiet office.

"Works for me." Nori sat on the edge of Nick's desk, ankles crossed. She handed him her red and white paper cup, already three quarters full of Coke and ice. "And don't be shy."

Nick added a generous splash of Kentucky's finest.

"So," he said, handing the cup back to the reporter, "what do you think about all this? I mean, we've never really gotten the chance to talk about any of it. Not after...you know."

Nori stirred her drink with her middle finger, then slid the digit into her mouth and sucked the liquid off.

Nick struggled to keep his jaw from hitting the floor. The move had caught him off guard. It may have been the most sensual thing he had ever witnessed, and several seconds passed before he was able to erase the image from his mind.

"Well," Nori said before sipping from her cup, "this is definitely a first for me."

Nick laughed. "I assume you're not talking about the drink."

"Ha, ha." Nori smiled. It wasn't the schmoozing smile of a reporter chasing a story. This smile was genuine. Friendly. "I've seen some weird things in my line of work. Being an investigative reporter and all. But this…" She shook her head. "Never seen anything like this."

They both grew quiet.

Nori stared into her cup.

Nick cast his eyes to the floor. The dark grey carpet, while only a couple months old, was already showing signs of wear. A faint path split the room nearly in half. He would need to find somewhere else to do his nervous pacing before he ruined the carpet completely.

It was several minutes before either of them spoke again. When she did, Nori's soft voice floated between them, loud enough for only Nick to hear.

"Do you remember what you asked me on opening night? When you were showing me around?"

Nick didn't. He said so with a shake of his head.

"Before you left me alone in the theater," she continued, "you asked if I scared easily." Nori took another long sip of her drink, tucked a strand of hair behind her ear. "When I told you no, it wasn't a lie. But…I'm sorry to say that's all changed now. This has me completely unnerved, Nick. It feels… I don't know… personal somehow. Do you feel that way?"

Nick allowed the chill in his blood to run its course while continuing to gaze at the floor. When he looked up and met Nori's hollow eyes, he had to fight back his initial instinct: taking her by the hand, running away and leaving The Chamberlain for good. But life wasn't that simple. It probably never would be.

Nick screwed the cap onto the bottle of bourbon and slid it

back into the desk drawer.

"We should probably get back."

SIXTEEN

"That looks interesting."

By the time Nick and Nori returned to the auditorium, the double doors stood open. Claudia wandered the lobby, mumbling into what appeared to be a digital voice recorder. Nori headed toward the concession counter in search of something to go with her drink. Nick found Börne in the back of the auditorium, setting up equipment in the narrow strip of space behind the back row of seats.

Everywhere Nick looked, the floor sparkled with shards of broken glass. Only a few of the overhead lightbulbs remained intact. Nick shook his head while trying to estimate how much it was going to cost to replace the others. Thankfully, the ornate sconces mounted on the walls every twenty feet appeared to be working just fine. They provided only a modicum of light by which Börne worked, but at least they kept the investigator from having to work in the dark.

"This?" Börne wore a headset and swung the microphone away from his mouth. He held up a chunky green box that looked like a 90s-era cell phone on steroids. "It's an EMF meter."

"Oh." Nick considered playing along like he knew exactly to what Börne was referring. But he gave up on the idea just as quick. Can't learn anything if you act like you know everything. His father had taught him that when he was a child. And he had no clue what an EMF was, much less an EMF meter.

Börne detected as much.

"EMF. Stands for electro-magnetic field," he said. Börne crouched down and held the green box near an electrical outlet. Red and green bars zipped across the screen. White numbers blipped. Börne stood and offered Nick a better look at the box in his hand. "It's believed that the conscious mind contains an electromagnetic field that leaves residue behind, long after we're dead. This meter lets me know when a spirit is close. Before I can start taking readings of spirits, though, I have to take a baseline of all potentially elevated areas in the room—electrical outlets, light fixtures—so when I do get a spike, I can tell which are spirits and which are simply because I'm standing too close to a known power source."

Nick turned the box over in his hand, making great effort to appear as if he was checking out specific features. In reality, he only hoped to put on a convincing show. Nick was anything but tech savvy. He knew next to nothing about high-tech gadgetry. Even the blue shirts at Best Buy intimidated him. With a nod of feigned approval, Nick handed the meter back to Börne. "Cool," he said.

It wasn't a profound statement, but it was at least honest. Exploding lightbulbs aside, Nick was finding the whole experience with Börne and Claudia more interesting than he'd expected. He only wished he didn't have so much riding on it.

Börne made his way along the back wall, broken glass crunching beneath his heavy boots. He followed the wall as it curved sharply around the last seat in the row, then led down along the side toward the front of the theater. Each electrical outlet and wall sconce Börne came to got its EMF field detected and verbally recorded into the microphone on his headset. It was important to document everything, Börne had also explained. Time, location, every little aspect, no matter how minute and inconsequential it may seem at the time. The information would prove crucial in pinpointing any anomalies that may occur during the review of data and footage.

As the process of setting up and testing equipment grew more technical, Nick grew increasingly lost. Feeling lost soon led to disinterest. He was about to leave Börne to his work and go see what Nori and Claudia were up to when the sconce above Börne's head suddenly went batshit crazy.

The lamp grew brighter than normal. Brighter than the bulb should have been able to manage. Nick shielded his eyes, as looking at it became unbearable. Then, just as quickly, the light returned to normal before softening to the point of barely staying lit. Its bulb produced hardly any light at all. The sconce did this several times. Back and forth in rapid succession. Others joined in. All around the room, wall sconces went to animated extremes, high and low.

Nick scowled. *Not those, too.* It was as if the theater was excited about something. Or, trying to get their attention.

The wall sconce above Börne's head went out. Thankfully, it didn't blow or shatter like the overhead lights. It didn't burst with a loud pop. It merely went dark, and this time, stayed that way.

Nick stopped and stood just inside the doorway, his interest suddenly renewed. His heart rate started to rise. He scoured the room. In search of what, he had no idea.

Then, lest anyone think the first was merely a coincidence, one after another, individual wall sconces went dark. The lights were all controlled by two switches located just inside the door, but to Nick, it was as if someone was making their way around the auditorium's perimeter, systematically flipping switches. Within a minute of the first light snuffing out, the last of the sconces extinguished itself. The Chamberlain had slowly faded to black, as if a film were about to start. Only there were no films scheduled.

"Um, ladies?" Nick called into the lobby, though his focus remained on the action in the auditorium. "You might wanna see this."

The light filtering through the open doorway was the only reason there was still anything to see. That, and the subtle red glow from the exit sign down front. The room was otherwise perfectly pitch. Börne had made his way to the exit door. Standing beneath its sign, his upper body was awash in red. He appeared as though he'd been drenched in blood. A male version of Stephen King's *Carrie*.

Behind him, Nick felt a darkness closing in.

He turned.

The heavy wooden doors slammed in his face. He stood frozen in place as the concuss reverberated throughout the darkened room. It wasn't hard to read. The message was coming through loud and clear. Someone—or some*thing*—either didn't want them there, or didn't want them to leave.

Neither option fit into Nick's plans.

He looked to Börne beneath the exit sign. The red glow reached all the way to the floor. Börne was gone.

A chill ran the length of Nick's spine, and he shivered from the sudden cold.

"Börne?"

Nick got no response from the investigator. The EMF meter, however, had plenty to say. It was working overtime. It sounded to Nick as if the damn thing was about to pop a gasket. The high-pitched bleating echoed throughout the darkness. Tracing its location proved impossible.

The stench of burnt wood ignited around Nick.

He felt his heart rate spike.

"Börne!"

No answer. Making matters worse—or better, depending—the EMF meter fell silent. An unsettling hush joined its partner, darkness, in engulfing the room.

Where the hell was Börne? And why wasn't he responding?

A loud pop from somewhere down front reached out and grabbed Nick's attention. The darkness made it impossible to pinpoint exactly where the sound had come from. Then Nick noticed a change in the auditorium's atmosphere. There was no longer a red glow near the emergency exit. Something had happened to the exit sign as well. By the sound of the pop, the damn thing had exploded.

Nick felt a presence creeping toward him, encroaching upon his personal space. An energy gaining strength. A faint buzzing tickled his ears. His arm hair stood on end. The smoky odor grew more intense, more concentrated.

Remembering the set of doors behind him, Nick reached through the dark for a handle.

Something grabbed his forearm. A hand. Only it wasn't Börne's hand. Nor was it like any other. This hand was hot. Branding iron-hot. The grip seared his skin. The fetor of singed hair reached his nose. Sizzling flesh, his ears. Nick cried out in pain, ripping his arm free. From whom or what, he had no idea.

Frozen with shock, but not wanting to just stand there, Nick braved the consequences. He reached out into the darkness a second time. This time, nothing happened. This time, he found a door handle and pushed. *Déjà vu.* The door didn't open. Wouldn't budge. Nick found the other handle and came up with the same result. Flashes of opening night came flooding back.

Nick pounded the doors. Pounded until his hand hurt. The stench of smoke grew so strong, it was as if he, himself was on fire.

"Claudia! Nori! Somebody open the damn doors!"

He pounded even harder.

Smoke—but not real smoke?—continued to saturate the air. It left no room for anything else. Nick breathed it in, having no other choice. The last bit of calm drained from his body. He knew what he'd told Börne. *There's never any actual smoke. It's just the smell.* But he'd never experienced the smell this strong. He envisioned it literally engulfing him in a cloud. He'd eventually be reduced to a coughing fit, hands on knees, his chest heaving violently.

Miraculously, it never came to that. Strangely enough.

His throat never burned like he'd expected. It never constricted. In fact, he continued to breath just fine.

Still, Nick pulled his collar up over his nose as he pounded the door.

When the doors finally opened, Nori stood to one side. Claudia peered over her shoulder. The new flood of light swarmed Nick. Also caught in its spotlight was Börne, marching up the center aisle. With head lowered, he was halfway to the doors.

Nick didn't wait for him.

He rushed through the open doors and took up post across from Nori. As soon as Börne burst through, Nick and Nori slammed the doors home.

Only once the auditorium was sealed off, and the smoky stench contained on the other side, did Nick's thoughts turn to the agony inflicting his arm.

Four ugly red streaks curled around Nick's forearm. Burn marks that resembled tiny fingers, each imprinted on his skin. He turned his arm over. On the underside, a perfectly shaped thumb scorch to match the others.

"What the fuck?" There was no calm left in Nick. His chest heaved. He gasped for breath. He looked to Börne and Claudia, who were busy exchanging a look of their own. Concern etched their faces, like the lines on a roadmap to Hades. Börne, too, gasped for air.

"What?" Nick asked. Somehow, he doubted their concern was for his injured arm. "What are you guys thinking?"

The husband-and-wife investigative team exchanged another brief glance before Claudia met Nick's wide-eyed stare. She took a deep breath.

"I think we need to get some ice on that arm," she said. "And then, we need to talk."

SEVENTEEN

"Let's talk about spirits."

Nick sat on the concession counter balancing a bag of ice on his wounded arm. In his hand, he held a drink twice as potent as the one he'd made Nori. It was the most effective pain reliever he was allowing himself. Leaning against the counter beside him, Nori quietly chewed the end of her straw, eyes glued to the floor. The Forresters sat facing them in the two chairs Nick had retrieved from his office. Börne drank from a bottle he had run down and purchased from The Sand Dollar. He'd lamented the store's unimpressive selection of German imports, but didn't seem hindered by the choice he'd had to make. He was already on his second beer.

Claudia was the only one of them without alcohol. She'd declined, wanting to keep her mind clear and focused. Such was her state of being as she gave Nori and Nick an education on spirits of the non-alcoholic variety.

"Call them what you will – ghosts, phantoms, apparitions – these spirits were human at one time. For reasons no one is clear on, aspects of their humanity remain in this world. Lingering. Maybe they have unfinished business. Perhaps they're holding on to an unrequited love. These types of spirits are referred to as residual. Residuals may not even know they were supposed to have moved on. It's believed a residual's energy is the result of a traumatic experience, often attaching itself to an object or location having to do with that experience."

"Like a theater?" Nori asked.

Nick felt the brush of a cool draft. He glanced over to make sure the only door to the outside was closed and locked. It was, and he'd known it would be.

"Possibly." Claudia nodded. "Either way, these spirits generally pose no harm to the living. They simply go about their business, their actions repeating on a loop with no implications to us, short term or otherwise."

Nick lifted the bag of ice and surveyed the burn marks stretching across his forearm. *No harm, my ass.*

"So," he said, "can we go back to the unfinished business part? What do you mean by that, exactly? Like, they had things at the dry cleaners they never picked up, or what?"

"Revenge," Börne said. He gave Nick a mischievous smile and wink before taking a long pull from his bottle of quickly disappearing *Kolsch*.

To Nick's surprise, not to mention alarm, Claudia offered no contradiction to her husband's statement.

"Sometimes." She put her hand on Börne's knee as if to remind him to tread lightly. "And sometimes it's no more than the continued pull of an unrealized dream. Maybe they passed before closing an important business deal."

"Yeah," Börne chuckled. "The business of revenge."

Claudia tilted her head toward Börne and, this time, shot him a disapproving frown. Börne stopped laughing. He tipped his head back and filled his mouth.

Nick let out a chuckle himself. Albeit a sarcastic one. He knew what Börne was trying to do. The man was trying his best to scare him. Even if just a little. Unfortunately, though Nick hated to admit it, Börne's venture was a successful one. Hairs all over his body were on end. The idea that Floyd Cropper was still hanging around his beloved theater after torching himself on its very steps could no longer be denied. Claudia had even gone as far as calling Floyd out by name.

And he'd damn well responded.

Silence hung like a plague over the lobby.

Revenge.

The word resonated in Nick's mind. As far as motives went, revenge couldn't be ruled out. Especially considering how despondent Floyd had apparently been over losing The Chamberlain. Hell, it made perfect sense really. And who could blame him? After what Blackwood did to him? And in turn, what Nick had done. After all, he hadn't skipped a beat in swooping in to purchase the place, even before it had gone on the market. He had been just as eager to find a theater and get the ball rolling on his new idea as Blackwood had been to offer it up.

Nick swallowed hard against the hot ball of lead forming in his gut.

"What about demons?" Nori asked sheepishly.

Nick dropped his bag of ice. His jaw dropped with it.

Claudia gave Nori a studied look. "Why do you ask. Nori?"

The reporter shrugged and began tugging at her ear. "I don't know. It just… I guess I don't understand why the phenomena is happening inside the theater, when Floyd killed himself outside on the steps. Just wondering what else might be doing it."

"Whoa! Wait a second?" Nick dropped onto the floor and retrieved the squishy bag of somewhat frozen water. He placed it back on his arm. "Demons?"

"Non-human spirits," Claudia said, picking up the conversation. "Their energy is not of this world. Demons. Angels, as well."

"So, you're telling me these things are real. Demons? Really?"

Börne pointed to the auditorium. "As real as those lights that blew themselves up." This time there was no hint of merriment in his voice. His face was stone. His eyes cold.

"Shit." Nick's voice was soft and breathy. He felt his own face drain its color. "Holy shit." The hot ball of lead in his stomach sprang a leak. He suddenly didn't feel so well. He looked all around the lobby, from floor to ceiling, in every corner. "Suddenly the idea of a ghost doesn't sound so bad."

"Hell yeah," Nori quipped. "I say, bring on the effing ghosts."

Nick couldn't help but laugh. Nori's comment was the first spark of levity any of them had experienced in some time.

"Even if it's a vengeful ghost?" Börne asked.

Nick stopped laughing.

Börne's eyes were fixed solely on him as he spoke. "They can be pretty nasty." He nodded, gesturing toward Nick's arm.

Nick could no longer tell if Börne was pulling his leg. He looked to Claudia for help. Her hesitation before nodding, felt to Nick, like she was deciding whether or not to answer truthfully.

"For what it's worth, Nick," she said. "I believe that's what we're dealing with here. Not a demon, but a vengeful spirit. They do exist, even though they're not common."

"Shit," Nick said again.

Börne chuckled.

"So, vengeful, residual, non-human, whatever kind of spirit it is," Nori said, "my question, and I'm sure I speak for Nick here, is how do we get rid of it?"

Nick turned to Nori, who immediately returned to chewing on her straw. Her use of the word 'we' hadn't gone unnoticed. She'd said it like they were a team. Like he wasn't in this alone. Nick liked both the sound and the thought of it.

"Well," Claudia said, "generally, if this energy is connected to an object, you remove the object. Take it elsewhere and the spirit follows."

Nick's forearm was sufficiently frozen. The ice had completely melted at this point. He tossed the bag of water into a nearby trashcan. "And if it's connected to a location?" he asked.

Börne exchanged another look with Claudia before answering.

"You move."

*   *   *

The remainder of the evening proved as uneventful as the beginning wasn't. No more outbursts or busted lights, no more scent of smoke. Even Nori grew comfortable enough at one point to join the others in crunching up and down the auditorium's aisles in search of the paranormal. While Börne's equipment stood at the ready, eager to capture something either on film or audio, nothing of real importance made its way onto a recording.

It was as if the theater knew that cameras were rolling.

It was after four in the morning when Nori helped Nick toss the last of the broken glass-filled trash bags into the dumpster out behind The Chamberlain. The ground was damp. The alley was empty and still. And as Nori said good night and disappeared back into the theater, Nick realized how long of a day it had been. He was exhausted, too tired to think about anything except his warm bed. Not ghosts. Not the unexplained burn marks on his arm. Not even the burgeoning feelings he was beginning to have for Miss Nori Park. Sleep, and lots of it, was the only thing on Nick's agenda moving forward.

EIGHTEEN

The dream starts with Nick seated at the desk inside The Chamberlain's office. He's running the week's numbers. It doesn't take long. The numbers are few. Music flows from the tinny speaker on his cell phone. It could be day; it could be night. The atmosphere inside the windowless building is the same either way.

A sound from out in the hallway steals his focus away from his laptop.

It's not quite a laugh, but a raspy giggle.

As far as Nick knows, he is alone.

He slides his chair out and rises. He cautiously makes his way to the door. So far, the sound hasn't repeated. Nick questions whether or not he truly heard anything. He pokes his head through the doorway just to be sure.

The hallway is dark.

The hallway is empty.

Nick exhales. He isn't sure what he expected. A source of the giggling would have been ideal. What if he'd found an intruder roaming the darkened hallway? Would he have been prepared? Probably, not. He's not much of a fighter. Thankfully, the hallway is free of prowlers, so his lack of self-defense skills isn't an issue.

But, that's just the hallway, he reminds himself.

Responsibility urges Nick further. It propels him up the short hall toward the lobby, the need to be thorough. The lobby, too, is empty. Nick checks the front door. Locked, just as it should be. Still without explanation for the giggling, he shuffles back down the hall and returns to his office.

An old man sits at his desk.

Nick gasps.

The old man turns. As startling as his mere presence is, it is the old man's appearance that alarms Nick the most. Nearly all of the flesh on the man's face is gone. What remains is stringy and shriveled beyond any recognition of having once been skin. Singed black and crisp. The sinewy muscle underneath is a roiling, angry shade of red. A sound like bacon sizzling in a frying pan permeates the room. The smell isn't nearly as pleasant. The top half of the old man's button up shirt has been burnt away, exposing ruined shoulders that match the face. The lower half of the shirt hangs in midair. It covers the old man's torso, suspended, like a smaller version of a hula hoop. This seems impossible, yet somehow is not. The fabric's ragged edges are black. The fringe smolders with scarlet embers. Smoke emanates from them.

The old man sneers.

"This?" His voice is thick, full of charred gravel. A skeletal hand holds up the laptop in which Nick keeps track of his finances; and the lack thereof. "This is what you stole my theater for? This…pittance?" Spittle flies from the old man's blackened lips.

Nick's mouth fails to work. Words refuse to form in the face of judgment. The day has come. He now knows who the man is. He can finally put a face to the name, as horrifying as that face may be…

Floyd Cropper.

"I…I…" Words continue to abandon Nick. They scatter like cowardly friends facing a fight.

When the old man rises, Nick's feet succeed where his mouth fails. He takes a step back. When the old man steps toward him, Nick matches it, retreating a step further. He is back in the hallway. A quick glance in both directions reveals an unfortunate truth: he is all alone. A circumstance that proved reassuring earlier, but unnerving now.

Nick feels heat intruding on his personal space.

He turns back to the old man.

Floyd Cropper has taken great strides. He now stands directly before Nick. Heat radiates from the old man. He's a fire in a barrel.

Nick sucks in a sharp intake of air. The intense heat sears his throat. The closer the old man steps, the hotter the air grows. Standing face to—*face?*—the heat proves unbearable. It is as if the old man is still on fire. Yet, there are no flames.

Sweat breaks across Nick's body.

He coughs.

He turns to run.

The once short hallway is no longer. It can now only be described as a corridor. Its length has stretched to at least twice what Nick remembers. Twice what it used to be. He can barely make out the lobby's faint glow at the other end. Sanctuary feels impossibly far away.

A blaze of orange erupts along both sides of the corridor. Illumination radiates from the sconces that line the walls, chasing away the inky blackness. Only their light doesn't come from bulbs the way they were intended. The lamps don't glow softly with their normal 40 watts.

They rage with fire.

Within seconds, the flames begin to creep up the walls. A stifling heat overtakes the corridor. Nick coughs. His throat pays a price. Normal breathing becomes a memory.

Nick takes the first step toward the lobby. His second step shows more urgency. Soon, he is running up the corridor of burgeoning flame. Blaze after blaze licks at him, grabs for him as he passes. Sweat pours down his face. The distance between him and the lobby, however, never changes. The gap never shrinks, despite his best efforts. Sheer curtains of fire now drape the walls. Wallpaper sags, melts, and then drips onto the floor.

The mounting heat becomes all-consuming.

Nick is overcome with the inability to breathe. His arms start to sizzle. His face stings like the worst sunburn. The acrid stench of blistering skin infiltrates his nostrils. He gags. He shields his face the best he can as he sprints further up a hallway that feels longer with every step.

Nick stumbles.

His hands instinctively reach out.

He does not hit the floor. He doesn't catch his fall. Instead, his outstretched hands find the backs of two theater seats. The once-tight vinyl has become soft, molten. It gives way under his grip. Liquid vinyl oozes through his fingers, burning his hands. Nick cries out as he lets go of the seats.

He staggers back. The walls of flame are gone. The hallway, itself, has disappeared. Nick finds himself at the front of the auditorium, the silver screen to his back. He knows better than to feel safe. He doesn't relax. An energy resonates throughout the auditorium. The room is alive with electricity. The air crackles and spits. It feels like only a matter of time before—

The seat directly in front of Nick bursts into flame. It is the first of many. Within seconds, a dozen individual fires have ignited throughout the auditorium. Their numbers quickly double. Soon, full rows of the once plush seating are transformed into meandering bonfires. Their flames reach high into the air, their serpent tongues licking the ceiling.

The temperature in the room swelters.

Sweat soaks Nick's clothes. His skin starts to bubble. Smoke chokes back the air in his throat, burns his eyes. Terror becomes all-consuming, and Nick begins to panic.

Every seat in the house is now engulfed in flame.

The roar is deafening.

The inferno scales its way up the walls. The flames devour the drywall like famished piranha. Insatiable. When rain starts to fall from the ceiling, Nick is momentarily relieved. When drops begin hitting the back of his neck, relief turns to searing pain. The sprinkler system hasn't kicked on.

The situation is not getting better.

The aluminum light fixtures hanging from the ceiling have started to melt. Black rain falls throughout the auditorium. It soon covers the seats, the floor, any unfortunate thing in its path. The liquid metal scorches the top of Nick's head and burns holes in his clothing.

He cries out.

Flames, like hands, reach out from all directions, coaxing Nick into their embrace. He takes a step back. There is nowhere to go. Nowhere that isn't alight with soul-scalding fire and rain. Even the towering screen behind him is aglow with orange conflagration. Bent over, hands on knees, Nick chokes down what little oxygen he can find as everything around him burns.

A hand grabs his arm, bringing Nick upright.

Floyd stands before him, his naked body engulfed in an orange blaze. Head to toe. No part of the old man's body is free of dancing fire. He is a human torch.

Unfazed by his own burning flesh, the old man sneers as he thrusts something toward Nick.

The something strikes a blow to Nick's stomach, robbing him of precious air. His eyes are now swollen. Nick looks down through slits. He can barely make out the object in Floyd's fiery hands. The old man begins to laugh. His laughter overtakes the inferno's roar. It echoes throughout the room, swallowing what remains of the auditorium's available air.

Then the old man is gone.

Nick is left surrounded by a world on fire, holding an empty gas can.

He can only breathe smoke. There is no air left, no oxygen. There is only fire and smoke and unbearable heat. Nick drops the metal container and stumbles toward the emergency exit. His skin is melting, slithering off the bone. His vision is nearly gone. The door to the stairwell that leads to the alley is indiscernible. A phantom portal hidden among a giant fiery wall.

Nick staggers. He falls to his knees, engulfed in flame. He puts his hands to his cheeks, finds only a hot and mushy mess. His fingers sink knuckle-deep into his flesh before he can pull them away. Strands of skin, like stringy melted cheese, come away from his face. His vision has abandoned him. Nick's world is dark and loud and burning out of control.

He collapses.

He awakens.

Nick finds himself curled up on his bedroom floor. He's wrapped like a cocoon in his sheet, cloaked in sweat. He gasps for air. His mouth is hot and dry. It feels like he's been eating cotton swabs roasted like marshmallows over a campfire. The sunlight through his window warms his face. And as he realizes it's all been just a horrible nightmare, it is the lingering imprint of smoke in his nose that leaves Nick the most shaken.

NINETEEN

Nick dragged his feet getting to the theater that morning. No showings were scheduled at The Chamberlain until the afternoon, and despite the amount of work awaiting him, he was in no hurry. It had, after all, been a long night. Sleep had not come easy. And then there was the dream. It still had him rattled, if he was honest. A single cup of coffee usually got him through most mornings, but Nick was already halfway through his second by the time he gathered his wallet and keys. After chugging the last of the cup's offering, Nick set it in the sink and headed for the door.

The air was already thick with mid-summer heat and humidity. Perspiration immediately peppered Nick's forehead. He was still getting used to summer in the south. The heat and humidity never took a break, even during the small hours. He often felt the need for a shower, even when he'd already taken one that day. Nothing else, the intense sun would help wake him. If he was lucky, it might even burn off the remnants of that horrible dream.

Burn off?

Nick shuddered at the thought.

As he locked the door behind him, Nick urged his mind to change gears. He ran through the day's to-do list. He had replacement light bulbs in the storage room, though he couldn't recall how many. Surely it wasn't enough. Who could have predicted he'd be replacing them all at once? As for the exit sign, his initial hunch had been correct. It was a lost cause. For both items, he would have to swing by the hardware store on his way in. Nick wasn't entirely put out by the detour. The Chamberlain wasn't going anywhere. And apparently, neither was its uninvited houseguest.

*   *   *

With the thin white box tucked under his arm, Nick unlocked the theater's front door. He'd been lucky. He's scored the last exit sign the hardware store had in stock. He could probably get it installed before the four cases of light bulbs were delivered later that morning. Special delivery: one of the last vestiges of old school customer service still found in a small town. Nick was only surprised he hadn't gotten more of a reaction from Gene, the owner of the hardware store, when inquiring on the bulk supply of light bulbs. Not that he should be surprised. The people of Angler Bay rarely blinked anymore when it came to the strange goings on at The Chamberlain.

Nick gave the key a twist and pushed the door open.

A refreshing rush of frosty air greeted him as he stepped inside and pulled the door closed. The lobby was a welcome contrast to the tropical conditions outside. He carried the box over to the concession counter and laid it on the glass counter. He reached for a napkin to wipe the sweat from his face. And that was when he noticed it.

He scowled. "What the…"

Cool AC wasn't the only thing in the air.

Nick turned toward the double wooden doors of the auditorium. Closed, as usual. That wasn't enough to contain the muffled strains of a soundtrack from reaching the lobby.

Nick sighed. "Now what?"

Tossing his keys onto the counter, Nick strolled toward the double doors. The music grew louder. As did the sound of a man's voice. He recognized it immediately. It was the voice of the narrator of the kids' movie he showed during matinees. The hour-long film about the wonders of the planet Earth was the only kid-friendly movie he had for the 4-D experience. Plans for more had stalled due to budgetary constraints. Not to mention the fact that very few residents were bringing their kids around anyway. For this film, the cameras explored all corners of the planet with effects to match: a cool puff of air as the helicopter scaled the Himalayas; a fine mist as the audience trekked through the Amazon rainforest; slithering eels and graceful stingrays rippling through the vinyl seats as their submarine cruised along the Great Barrier Reef.

It was all great family fun.

Question was, why the hell was it playing?

Nick approached the doors, took a handle in each hand, and with a deep exhale, pulled them wide.

The best Nick could tell, row after row of seats sat empty. He was happy to see that they were solid, too, and not molten. He knew it had just been a dream, but having visual proof of the fact eased his mind further.

What did not set his mind at ease, however, was the glowing silver screen down front. A shaft of light beamed in from the tiny control room window, setting it aglow. On the screen, a helicopter's view as it flew above the Texas plains. Under any other circumstances, the setting would have appeared perfectly normal. Thunder rumbled through the overhead speakers. A bolt of lightning flashed across the boiling sky. The only reason the lights above weren't strobing in sync with the lightning on the screen was the lack of functioning bulbs.

Nick looked up at the control room window.

The other concerning aspect? He was the only one who knew how to operate the system.

And he'd just gotten there.

Backpedaling out of the auditorium, he made his way down the short hallway and up the steps to the control room. As far as he knew, Nick had never witnessed strange phenomena in the control room, so he typically left that door unlocked. A practice he might have to revisit given the circumstances.

Nick flung open the door and stepped inside.

He found the tiny room as empty as the auditorium. The control panel, however, was lit up and in full working order. Several icons were illuminated in red, indicating which particular functions were in use. A miniature version of the film played in a small window at the bottom right corner of the control panel screen.

The faint odor of smoke lingered in the air.

Waving the odor away, Nick approached the control pad. With his engineer gone, Nick had been forced to get out all of the manuals and learn the system. At least Manny had been right: it was easy. Nick wasn't sure a kindergartener could operate it, like Manny had said, but with kids' knowledge of technology these days, he probably wasn't far off. After a couple of strategically placed taps on the screen, the film stopped. The auditorium went dark. The speakers fell silent.

With a furrowed brow and a shake of his head, Nick looked through the small window, out over the vast sea of empty seats.

"Strange."

And it was. But then, strange pretty much summed up the daily existence of The Chamberlain Theater.

*   *   *

Nori climbed off her exercise bike, perspiration running down her neck and soaking into the collar of her Gwen Stefani concert tee. While she shook the circulation back into her wobbly legs, she grabbed her towel off the hook.

Thirteen miles.

Not her best, but certainly not her worst. Anything in double digits was acceptable. A full twenty miles would have been nice, but considering the little amount of sleep she was running on, she was happy with thirteen.

Tilting her head back and taking a long drink from her water bottle, Nori's thoughts turned to Nick. Something that was happening with relative frequency since she'd awoken. She wondered how he was faring this morning. She wondered how he was faring period. The stress of it all. The failing theater. The bizarre phenomena. Dealing with their asshole mayor.

And then there were the drugs. She knew he had a history of relying on them to get through. Nick had said he was done with them. She wanted to believe him, as much as anyone wanted to believe a former user when they said that drugs are no longer a problem. She also knew the stress he was under had to feel like a ten-ton brick. Especially when it all weighed on his shoulders and his shoulders alone.

Hang in there, buddy.

She had just stripped out of her damp workout clothes and turned on the shower when Nori heard her cell phone chime. Whatever the notification was, it would have to wait. The steaming hot water was playing tug-of-war with her sore and weary muscles, and her cell phone was on the losing end. She stepped into the shower and pulled the curtain closed.

*   *   *

The hardware store had sent just enough light bulbs. Which

was nothing more than sheer luck since Nick had had to guess how many he needed. Forty-eight brand new incandescent bulbs hung poised and ready to show patrons to and from their seats the next time The Chamberlain showed a film.

If there ever *was* a next time.

Nick was just replacing the plastic cover on the new exit sign when an abrupt beep filled the otherwise quiet auditorium. He clung to the ladder to maintain balance with one hand, while checking his pocket for his cell with the other. He didn't find it. Which was nothing new. Probably on the counter with my keys, he thought.

Then the beep rang out twice more.

What the hell?

From two-thirds the way up the ladder, Nick turned as much as possible and scanned the large room. Even with all of the lights on, the room was anything but bright. Shadows lingered anywhere light couldn't reach. As far as he could tell, he was completely alone. And as far as he knew, none of the 4D equipment made a beeping sound.

A tickle started at the base of Nick's neck.

I am alone…right?

When the beeping sound came again, it didn't stop. The shrill bleating now reverberated throughout the room.

Slowly, Nick made his way down the ladder. With the emergency exit at his back, he once again scanned the large room, this time from ground level. Row after row of red vinyl seats stared back at him. The rear double doors at the top of the center aisle stood open, patiently awaiting his exit. At least that's how he thought of it.

After folding the ladder and tucking it under his arm, Nick started making his way across the front of the auditorium. He observed the silver screen as he passed by. It offered no indication as to what might have been causing the beeping sound. It was after all, just a sheet of fabric. No electric ran to it.

What Nick soon discovered, however, was that the closer he drew to the center aisle, the more prevalent the smell of smoke. And the louder the beeping became.

At the center aisle, the beeping seemed to reach a crescendo. Nick looked all around the seats, stooped as much as he could and looked around the floor. And that's when he saw it. A small green box. *The size of a 90's era cell phone on steroids.*

It was Börne's little green box from the night before, presumably lost in the chaos as he retreated.

Nick reached under the seat and picked up the box. The beeping seemed hell bent on alerting someone of something. Green and red lights flashed across the top of the box's screen. The number 68.8 flashed in white just below. What the hell did it all mean? Was that good? Bad? Then Börne's words came back to him: *this meter lets me know when a spirit is close.*

The tickle that had started at the base of his neck shot down Nick's entire spine.

He dropped the green box. It bounced off of the arm of the seat in front of him and crashed to the floor.

The beeping didn't stop.

Nick took a step back and spun around. The aluminum ladder slammed the top of a nearby seat and wrenched itself from Nick's hand. It clattered to the concrete floor. He took another step up the aisle. Cold sweat broke out across his face.

The EMF meter didn't die with the fall. It continued to beep.

Nick took two more backward steps up the aisle before turning and running the rest of the way. A chill ran through him. Like he wasn't quite fast enough to outrun anything that might be behind him.

As he neared the back row of seats, the beeping stopped. Nick's blood froze in his veins. As much as he would have thought he'd be thankful for the EMF meter to go quiet, the fact that it did filled him with more fear than joy. Why had it stopped beeping? That was the question on his mind as he neared the doors. Why?

Nick wasted no more time wondering where the spirit may have gone. One after the other, he slammed the heavy wooden doors closed behind him. And as he stood there, back against the doors, breathing heavier than he had in a whole twenty-four hours, one thought came to Nick's mind.

"Knew I shoulda stayed in bed."

TWENTY

Hunched over the bathroom sink, Nick cupped his hands under the faucet. When the water reached capacity, he splashed it onto his face. He did this three times before reaching up and shutting off the water. A stack of neatly folded paper towels sat nearby on the counter, and Nick grabbed two off the top.

With his face patted dry and the crumpled paper towels deposited in the nearby trash can, Nick placed both hands on the countertop and leaned in. The man staring back at him in the mirror sported a grin. He shook his head.

"Crazy."

This whole experience with F.A.U.S.T. and—dare he say it—Floyd, was becoming a bigger deal than he ever could have imagined. And maybe more than he bargained for. More and more, Nick was finding himself needing a drink. More and more, he was fighting off the urge to call in a favor from his doctor for a bottle of pills.

"Stay strong," said the man in the mirror. "We'll get through this." Then he chuckled. "I mean, what else could possibly happen?"

Nick had just stood up straight and started to imagine the possibilities when the sound of adolescent chatter reached his ears. *Kids? Really? Is that really what I'm hearing now?* He couldn't be imagining it, though. The sounds of unabashed youth were only growing louder.

When Nick opened the restroom door and popped out, he was met with a parade of rambunctious school-age children marching their way through the lobby toward the auditorium. At the front of the line, leading the charge, was Mayor Blackwood.

At the double doors, the mayor swung them wide open and motioned for the children to enter.

"Mayor!" Nick shouted, rushing passed a second platoon of children invading the lobby.

One by one they marched through the open doorway and down the center aisle. Bringing up the rear of the first group was a harried young woman. When they reached the front of the auditorium, she ordered her little soldiers into the front row of seats. By the size of the group and the way the woman acted toward them, Nick could only assume they were a class of schoolchildren, and she was their stressed-out teacher.

That didn't, however, explain what they were doing there.

"Mayor, what the hell?"

"Nick!" The mayor's boisterous voice played well to the theater's professionally engineered acoustics. It may as well have been playing through the theater's high-tech speakers. "Been looking all over for ya."

"Wanna tell me what's going on?" Nick asked.

"It's called a field trip, Nick." The mayor's massive hand found Nick's shoulder, a gesture Nick had come to know and despise. "It's where students leave the classroom and get some real-world education. I'm sure you've heard of it."

A young man in a blazer, black rimmed glasses, and skinny jeans followed the next troop of school children into the auditorium. When they reached the front row, he motioned his class to take seats on the other side of the aisle from the first class. The young man didn't seem quite as stressed. But then, his line of students wasn't nearly as uniform, either.

With the events of the previous night still fresh in his mind, not to mention the EMF meter's terrifying reading, Nick's stomach turned over on itself.

"Not really sure what these kids are gonna learn here at The Chamberlain, Mayor."

Another, more disciplined, line of middle schoolers filed into the auditorium, followed by an older woman of about sixty. Her thick stockings disappeared up under her long skirt. Her set jaw would have rivaled the most hardened of drill sergeants.

Blackwood leaned in so that only Nick could hear.

"That The Chamberlain is not haunted, and is perfectly safe to patronize." The mayor nodded and winked at the older teacher. Her sour expression spoke to ill feelings about being at the theater. It also explained why her group of kids were much better behaved than the others. "Then they'll go home," the mayor continued, "and tell their parents how much fun they had at the movies. Safe fun, that is. Family-type fun. The kind of fun that makes it rain."

The mayor used two fingers from one hand to swipe at a stack of invisible money in the other.

Nick, meanwhile, cast a wary glance toward the ceiling and swallowed hard. Forty-eight new light bulbs stared back at him, a reminder of the stakes. "And you're thinking this will bring people back?"

"In droves." The mayor once again looked at the teacher like the old woman was in on the scheme. "Am I right?"

The teacher simply shrugged and took an open seat next to the last child in the row. Nick was fairly certain the woman had rolled her eyes as she turned away, but he couldn't be sure. If she did, the mayor didn't seem to notice.

But Nick couldn't concern himself with whether or not the old woman had offended Blackwood. He suddenly had his own problems. Alarms erupted in his head. The words *vengeful spirit* flashed off and on behind his eyes like a neon sign on the Vegas Strip. And then there was his forearm, wrapped in white cotton gauze. The scent of smoke, while no longer fresh in his nose, still hovered in his subconscious. It was enough to render him frozen with fear. His blood churned with slivers of ice.

Nick looked toward the entrance where children continued to filter into the theater. They were so young. So innocent. And there were so many. Blackwood must have brought the entire school with him. Nick imagined a small fleet of yellow school buses lining the street out front.

Damn it!

He turned back.

"Uh, Mayor?" Nick said. "This really isn't a good idea. Last night—"

"Aw, bullshit, Fallon."

Another teacher, who happened to be passing by, shot the mayor a disapproving look. Surprisingly, and most likely because this teacher resembled Halle Berry with the perkiness of a fully-caffeinated Starbuck's barista, the mayor actually offered a half-hearted apology for his language. When he spoke next, his voice was a little softer and didn't carry quite so far.

"Nonsense, Nick. This is exactly the kinda thing that'll turn business around at the Chamberlain." The mayor put his arm around Nick's shoulder. "Word'll spread. You'll see. These kids here? They're gonna have a great time. Little shits'll have so much fun they'll piss themselves. Now give 'em a few minutes to settle in, then start that movie." The mayor's grip on Nick's shoulder tightened as he spoke the last part. Interpretation: don't question me on this.

Nick's knees buckled slightly.

His stomach soured.

The wall sconces flanking the double doors flickered.

Nick noticed the action in the lights, but couldn't afford them much mental energy. Even though he interpreted the mayor's action as such, question he must. Blackwood's plan was a disaster in the making.

"Mayor, seriously," Nick said, speaking as sternly as he could muster. "This is a mistake. Last night—"

Mayor Blackwood spun around, eyes squinting, lips pursed. He leaned down, placing his forehead within inches of Nick's. He spoke with as much purpose as Nick had ever heard.

"I don't give a flying fuck what happened last night." Blackwood's eyes searched Nick's for recognition of the threat he was mounting. "What I do give a fuck about is showing these damn kids a fucking movie. Do you understand me, Mr. Fallon? Nod once for yes, and fuck off for no."

And with that, Blackwood exited the auditorium.

Mic drop.

This time the wall sconces beside the door glared a bright white before eventually settling back

Never in a hundred years could Nick match the mayor's intensity or ferocity. The battle was lost. The battlefield lay in smoldering ruin, his defenses crushed. With an impenetrable sense of dread souring his gut, Nick started down the aisle toward the ladder and Börne's little green box, wondering what else he stood to lose that morning.

TWENTY-ONE

The burden of responsibility for the students' safety weighed heavily on Nick's shoulders. He could practically feel an angel on one side, urging action. Her horned nemesis perched on the other shoulder, recommending Nick grab a tub of popcorn, find a seat in the auditorium, and watch what was about to unfold. Thankfully, Nick found it easy to ignore the latter.

If the mayor insisted on giving these kids the 4D experience, then they would get one, alright. Just not to the full extent. Luckily, the technology was configured in a manner that allowed him to shut down certain mechanical features if he so chose. And today he was.

Both his heart and mind clamored at high speed.

His entire being teemed with dread. His laundry list grew more extensive with each child he passed; things Nick would need to take care of before he could even think about starting the movie. If he was going to keep these kids safe—if that was even possible—precautions would need to be taken.

Nick crested the aisle, holding the ladder high so as not to decapitate any kids with the it along the way. Sweat broke out under his collar, made his hands slippery. He didn't bother returning the ladder to the storage room. He simply dropped it in the hallway with a clatter. Wiping his hands on his khakis, he started toward the control room.

A thought hit him. A memory from the opening night fiasco. Nick spun on his heels and returned to the ladder. A moment later, it sat propped against the back wall *inside* the auditorium.

Just in case.

"Hey, Nick!" The voice's normally soft, quiet tone was gone. A sharpness replaced it. Like razor wire. "What the heck's going on?"

Nick bit his bottom lip as he waited to greet the voice's owner.

Nori's face wore a mask of concern as she made her way through the lobby. Following impatiently close behind, she played caboose to the train of students barreling toward the auditorium. Once the last pre-teen disappeared through the double doors, Nori joined Nick in his rush to the control room.

"Blackwood had one of his bright ideas." Sweat now streamed down the side of Nick's neck. It was as if the devil on his shoulder had just relieved himself in disgust at Nick's decision to side with the angel. Nick ran his gauze-swathed forearm across his brow. "Feel warm in here to you?"

Nori didn't answer, as if it mattered. Nick wouldn't have heard. His mind was taxed at the moment. It could only do so much thinking at one time.

At the door to the control room, he hesitated and turned to Nori with a frown. "What are you doing here, anyway?"

Nori's gaze lingered on the auditorium doors, the previous night's events no doubt on her mind as well.

"The mayor sent me a text," she said. "Told me something was going on here that I'd want to report on." Nori shook her head, eyes wide and cavernous. Apparently, her journalism classes hadn't covered how to report on innocent children intentionally put in harm's way by a town's sworn leader. "I had no idea he'd do something like this."

Nick opened the door and scaled the two steps to the control room.

"The children," she continued, right on his heels. "How could he…why would he…" They were not questions in the usual sense, nor were they statements of fact. It was simply a reporter processing the situation laid before her. Nick had no answers to offer, though he doubted she was seeking any. At least, not from him.

For the second time that day, Nick brought up the touch screen control panel. He immediately started swiping and tapping, turning the effects on and off, making judgment calls on each one. Given the circumstances, misting machines that would spray anything at all onto the kids seemed like a bad idea. He shut them off. Armrests that sent a brief and buzzing shock? Nope. Shut those off, too. About the only thing he couldn't control ahead of time were the light bulbs if they decided to blow themselves up again. If and when they did, he would simply have to get everyone out as quickly as possible.

"Do me a favor," Nick said, fingers swiping through a catalogue of options.

Nori didn't hesitate. "Anything."

Nick handed over his set of keys, holding out one shiny silver key in particular. "Down the hallway, past my office, is the storage room. There are metal cases containing old movie reels stacked in the corner. Grab the biggest, heaviest one you can carry, and meet me back at the auditorium."

Nori disappeared without further instruction.

Nick turned back to the control panel. What to do about the seats themselves? They rocked a little. Jostled up and down. Had mechanical sensors hidden in the cushions that, when triggered, made it feel like you had accidentally sat on a small animal. All in all, the seats seemed the least likely to pose a threat. Besides, he had to leave the kids something to experience, right? How else were they supposed to—in the mayor's words—piss themselves with laughter?

They could always piss themselves with fear, instead.

Nick shook the thought free from his head.

Satisfied he'd done everything in his power to keep the kids safe, Nick cued the movie. Of course, keeping the kids safe was not entirely within his control. He could shut off all the effects he wanted. If The Chamberlain (or, more specifically, the spirit of its previous owner) got a hair up its ass to lash out...

The movie took a moment to upload. Once it had, it still wouldn't start until he pressed play. Good thing. Nick wasn't ready for it to start just yet. Grabbing two spare electrical cables from a cardboard box on the floor, he exited the control room.

They met again at the auditorium's double doors. Nori had done just as Nick had asked. She held a large grey metal case, both hands through the handle. The films had been left behind by the previous owner. Not knowing what to do with the oversized paperweights, Nick had allowed them to continue collecting dust in the storage room until he could find a use for them.

Finally, an opportunity had presented itself.

"Perfect." Nick took the case. In exchange, he handed Nori the cables. "Be right back."

While the town's children were discovering the stereoscopic effects of their 3D glasses, Nick made his way down the aisle toward the front of the theater. Turning right brought him to the emergency exit. He pushed open the door and wedged the reel case between it and the doorjamb. By propping open an emergency exit door, Nick may or may not have been violating a fire code. He didn't know, and he didn't care. Nor did he have time to research it even if he did. Legal or not, it was necessary. If the kids suddenly needed a way out, they would damn sure have options. Key word: unrestricted. A door that couldn't close, sure as shit couldn't lock.

Nori remained in the doorway where Nick had left her, cables in hand.

"Thanks," he said, taking one of the thick, black cables from Nori. Fashioning a loop with one of the ends, Nick slid it around one of the door handles. Pulling it tight, he wrapped the other end of the cable numerous times around a nearby wall sconce. Keeping the double doors open would allow an annoying amount of light in. There was sure to be grumbling. But at least it would keep the exit free and clear. It was, after all, for their own protection. The kids would just have to deal with it.

Protection.

Nick shuddered at the very thought of them needing it.

"Good idea."

"Huh?" In his haste, Nick had forgotten Nori was still hanging around. He was reminded of how difficult it had been to lose her on opening night. This time, her persistence worked in his favor. Despite their rocky start, the reporter was quickly proving a valuable ally. Whether or not this showing would result in a positive story, Nick wouldn't have wanted to guess. Nor could he predict how long this budding kinship would last. For now, he was just glad she was on his side. Having a mutual enemy in the mayor certainly didn't hurt. "Oh, thanks."

He took a deep breath, tried to calm his racing heart. He ran through his mental list. The conclusion Nick came to was this: the kids were as safe as he could hope to make them. Short of standing up to the mayor and refusing to show the movie altogether, there was not much more Nick could do.

"If you could secure the other door the same way," he said, handing the remaining cable to Nori, "I'll go start the movie."

TWENTY-TWO

Nick took a deep breath.

Beyond the control room's tiny window, the auditorium was nearly full to capacity. Under normal circumstances, it was a situation for he would have happily given an appendage. However, these weren't normal circumstances. These circumstances had the potential to become dire really quick. After his conversation with Börne and Claudia, Nick couldn't believe he was actually going through with this.

If there's a repeat performance of last night...

Nick closed his eyes, forced the thought into the dark recesses of his mind. The kids would be scarred for life if that happened. He also didn't see where he had a choice. There was no getting out from under the mayor's thumb on this one. Not if he wanted to keep The Chamberlain long enough to turn it around. He'd seen how easily the mayor had pulled the theater out from under...

Cropper.

Nick breathed in deep.

With a single tap to the control screen, the theater lights slowly dimmed. All the chatter from the room devolved into a hush, save for a smattering of giggles that required a hard "shh" to quell. Another deep breath, another pensive exhale. Nick tapped the screen once more and exited the control room.

The mayor stood outside the double doors talking to Nori. From all appearances, the conversation wasn't going well. The mayor kept adjusting his tie. Nori looked even more perturbed than she had a moment ago.

Nick braced himself as he approached.

"What's up?" he asked.

Nori jabbed a thumb at Blackwood. "Mayor here's skipping out on the movie."

Nick looked at Blackwood who appeared as sheepish as a man with a four-hour erection walking into an emergency room.

"Sorry, Nick." The mayor tapped his watch. "Got a meeting at noon. Only came along to make sure you understood the plan here." Blackwood shot a quick glance into the darkened theater. Opening credits were already rolling. His façade cracked and his anxiety showed through. The mayor tapped his watch again. "Gotta get back to the office."

"But Mayor—"

"Sorry, Nick." The mayor turned, gesturing with half a wave. "Places and people."

And then he was gone, the heels of his loafers click-clacking all the way through the lobby.

When Nick turned back to Nori, the brief time away had done little to dampen the inferno behind her eyes.

"You believe that guy?" Nori looked as angry as the mayor had looked anxious. "He's got balls enough to fill the theater with innocent children, but not enough to sit in there with them?" Nori raised a middle finger toward the front door. "Meeting my ass. I was his kid, I'd run away, too."

If Nick had to pinpoint the moment that he first detected honest to goodness feelings for Ms. Nori Park, that would have to be it. The break from her usual poised and mild-mannered way of carrying herself was refreshing. There was a realness to it.

Her furrowed brow rivaled the most melodramatic of toddlers. The flared nostrils and pursed lips. All genuine. All cute as hell. Nick had heard people say, "you're adorable when you're angry," but it wasn't until that moment that he saw what they meant. He stifled a grin.

Nori must have noticed. "What?"

Nick did his best to play it straight. "Sorry?"

"You had a look." Nori's eyes narrowed briefly, then relaxed. "Like you had something to say."

Nick shook his head. "No, not really."

Nori exhaled. "Never mind. Sorry. And sorry for that back there." Nori gestured toward the door. Nick took the reference to mean her outburst over Blackwood. "But, sometimes that man…"

The sound of calliope music wafted through the open doorway.

Nick reached up and gently touched Nori's elbow. "It's fine. Trust me." Second guessing himself, Nick dropped his hand. "I'm right there with you."

Inside the auditorium, a man's voice started talking over the music.

Nick raised his eyebrows. "Here we go."

Nori nodded and mustered a slight grin. "It's gonna be okay."

Nick returned the gesture, knowing full well she didn't wholly believe it.

That was okay.

Neither did he.

And from the doorway of the auditorium, Nick and Nori held their breath and watched the opening scenes of the movie, one eye on the overhead lights, the other on over two hundred and fifty of Angler Bay's youngest and brightest.

*   *   *

The film was only four minutes old when the first scream erupted.

From the open doorway, Nick and Nori exchanged a look. Their expressions mirrored each other's emotions: fear, dread, horror.

Nick bolted into the auditorium, Nori within his shadow.

The scream had come from down front and somewhere to the left. A young girl, by the sound of it. A cluster of students and a few teachers rose to their feet in the front row. Murmurs filled the air. A commotion poised to spread like a California wildfire.

Alarming scenarios ran through Nick's mind, each contributing to his growing queue of questions. What had caused the scream? Was it something he'd seen before? A phenomena familiar to The Chamberlain? Or, was it some new horror to add to its catalogue?

He filed them all away. The what's and how's weren't important. He was focused first and foremost on reaching the girl. After all, her scream had turned his stomach inside out.

The film continued to play on the screen.

Nick's pace slowed as he neared the bottom. Over the music and narration, he could hear Nori's footsteps behind him. At the front of the auditorium, he turned left. It wasn't until he did so that he realized the oddest of truths: the scream and now the giggling had both come from the same area.

Turned out, it was the same girl.

"Sorry," she said, as Nick and Nori approached, hair on fire. The girl with long brown curls and a Harry Potter t-shirt had returned to her seat, hands folded over her lap. In the glow from the nearby screen, an embarrassed grin graced her face. "The ripples in the seat," she continued. "They scared me is all."

The mob of whispering gawkers dispersed, and everyone returned to their seats.

Nick rubbed his forehead. He let go of the breath he'd been holding. Within seconds, relief allowed his rigid shoulders to deflate. His heart rate, however, would take longer to normalize. *Guess I should've turned off the damn seats, too.*

On the screen behind him, a killer whale rose entirely out of the sea before twisting and splashing back down.

Nick looked skyward. The overhead misters would have kicked on at that very moment, spraying something—who knew what—over the crowd. Thank God, he'd shut them down.

Nick looked to Nori. Nori looked to Nick, her face showing more relief than annoyance. "False alarm?"

He nodded.

Nori ducked down and started back toward the center aisle.

Nick looked to the cowering girl once more. She mouthed the word 'sorry.' Nick replied by mouthing, 'it's okay,' and gave her a thumbs up. When he turned to leave, the teacher sitting at the end of the row offered an apologetic smile. Nick simply nodded and hurried up the aisle.

The following fifty minutes of film played on without disturbance. Without a hitch, as the mayor would have said, had he the nerve to stick around. For nearly an hour, Nori and Nick stood in the doorway, tense as sentries, poised to attack if the need arose. Several times their eyes met. Several times they exchanged a raised eyebrow. The fact that everything was going so smoothly surprised them both. Especially Nick. It seemed anytime he set foot in the auditorium anymore something bizarre, or at least out of the ordinary, happened.

But, as two hundred and fifty raucous students and a dozen relieved teachers filed out into the lobby, then on to their awaiting buses, The Chamberlain felt like any other movie theater in any other town. A cool place to while away the hours on a hot summer day. Relaxing. Fun. Safe.

And that caused a knot of worry to tie up Nick's stomach.

Whatever spirit was calling The Chamberlain home had just shown its ability to pick and choose when to go bat shit crazy and when not to. That meant the spirit wasn't only vengeful, but it had the ability to scheme.

And Nick couldn't imagine a more frightening scenario.

TWENTY-THREE

"Whatcha lookin' at, *meine Liebe*?"

Sipping the hotel's finest dark roast from a paper cup, a robed Claudia sat on the edge of the bed, wet hair wrapped in a towel. Her transformation was just beginning, from the everyday Claudia Forrester who cherished yoga pants, oversized t-shirts, and DIY landscaping shows on Saturday mornings, to the elegant and mysterious Claudia Forrester, goth-themed paranormal investigator and one half of F.A.U.S.T. The entire process—hair, makeup, wardrobe—took most of two hours.

Börne, whose transformation took considerably less time, sat quietly at the narrow desk, laptop open in front of him, while an episode of *Big Bang Theory* played on the television in the background.

"Floorplans." Börne sipped Matcha tea and checked his watch. "8:40, by the way."

Claudia ignored her husband's gentle prod. She was in a playful mood, and wasn't about to be rushed tonight. "Floorplans, huh? Finally building me my dream home?"

Börne tilted his head and eyed Claudia over the rims of his glasses. The way the hotel's standard issue white robe draped her slender form gave new meaning to the word "complimentary." She hadn't tied the robe together. She never did. Börne sometimes questioned why she bothered wearing a robe in the first place. Other times, he just sat back and enjoyed the view. Like now. Her damp cleavage and baby soft naval taunted him to no end. The sheer black panties that peeked out when she uncrossed, then re-crossed her legs made matters worse. In Börne's mind, he saw himself rise from the chair and go to her, slide his hands inside the folds of terry cloth and send the robe to the floor.

But, only in his mind. They had someplace to be. They had things to do.

If only they hadn't already made plans with Nick.

Börne shook the fantasy from his mind and turned back to the laptop. "The Chamberlain, my dearest Claudia. Been comparing these original floor plans from 1912 to what the theater looks like now. At least from what I can remember."

"And?" Claudia unwound the towel and shook her head. Damp, red ringlets cascaded down over her shoulders. "Find anything interesting?"

Börne leaned in and squinted at the laptop's small screen. If only he had access to his much larger desktop computer at home. "Not yet."

Claudia slapped at the mattress. "Well, keep at it. I'm sure you'll find something."

She swung her legs off the bed and got to her feet. While doing so, she allowed the robe to slip off her shoulders. The garment gathered in a heap on the floor. Failing miserably in concealing a wicked grin, Claudia sashayed around the end of the bed, exaggerating certain anatomical aspects as she did. Halfway to the bathroom, she cast a glance over her shoulder to see if Börne was looking.

He was.

Then he was on his feet and headed her way.

It was almost an hour before Claudia made it to the

bathroom to continue her transformation.

*   *   *

The last showing ended at 9:50 pm.

For the entirety of the show, The Chamberlain held not a single soul. Floyd Cropper's notwithstanding. So far, the mayor's plan had yet to produce results. In all fairness, his plan would require time for word to get around. If it was to work at all. Bad news travelled quickly in small communities like Angler Bay. Good news? Not so much. It wasn't as interesting, didn't demand the same urgency.

Unfortunately, Nick didn't know how much time The Chamberlain Theater had. Bills were piling up, and his dwindling rainy-day fund wouldn't get him through a mild sprinkle. With that in mind, Nick had to give Blackwood at least a little credit. Begrudgingly. And only because things had gone so well. It wasn't necessarily a bad plan, just ill-advised. They had gotten lucky.

Had things not gone so well…

While he waited for Claudia and Börne to show, Nick went about shutting things down in the control room. With three quick taps, the screen went dark. The system's soft humming came to a rest. The theater fell as quiet as an underground cave. The only exception being the occasional rumble of thunder somewhere out in the night.

Nick looked through the small window and out over the still auditorium. For the hundredth time that day, he tried wrapping his head around the events of that morning. Or, to be more exact, the *lack of* events. He couldn't even remember smelling smoke while the students were there. It all left him with so many questions. Why had Floyd's spirit not shown itself? Why not rear its ugly head? It had been daytime. Did that matter? Did the time of day really have any bearing on when a vengeful spirit chose to act out? Nick didn't think so. Especially when it was virtual nighttime twenty-four seven in the auditorium due to the lack of windows.

Nick flipped off the light in the control room and closed the door behind him. He was anxious to get F.A.U.S.T.'s thoughts on what had and had not transpired that morning. They were, after all, the experts.

Nick started down the hallway, but soon stopped in his tracks. He trained his ear, heard the opening and closing of the front door. He glanced at his watch. They were also prompt, it seemed.

Nick continued down the hallway toward the lobby, making a mental note to grab the broom and dustpan. He may not have had any paying customers that day, but in hosting an auditorium full of pre-teens, there was no shortage of cleaning to be done. Nearly twelve hours later and Nick was still finding stray candy and gum wrappers laying around. And he hadn't even sold the students any concessions. Kids were just resourceful like that.

Nick chuckled to himself. Perhaps that was the reason the morning's showing had gone off without a hitch. Maybe ol' Floyd was too scared, too held in check by the prospect of a theater full of unpredictable kids.

Nick couldn't blame him.

He was still finding the idea amusing when he rounded the corner and came face to face with an empty lobby. Nick's grin slowly dissolved. He could have sworn he'd heard the front door open briefly, then close. Outside, rain was coming down at a good clip. The transient throng of wind and rain while the door had been open had been unmistakable.

Right on cue, a clap of thunder rattled the roof above.

"Hello?"

Nick looked all around the deserted lobby. There were very

few places for someone to hide. He looked behind the concessions counter. Nothing. And that was pretty much it. There really was nowhere else. Despite what he thought he'd heard, Nick was undeniably alone.

A shiver tiptoed down his spine.

He shook it off.

Maybe he hadn't been hearing things. Maybe he'd simply been too slow to appear. Börne and Claudia had arrived after all, he told himself. They'd poked their heads in, and having not found him in the lobby, retreated to their car to grab their equipment. *Of course.* That was it. That was the most likely scenario.

At the front door, Nick placed his forehead against the glass and cupped his hands around his eyes. The outside world was saturated, shrouded in darkness. The street glistened as it slept beneath a blanket of rain. Buildings shimmered with the light of nearby streetlamps. Rainwater ran down the theater's steps, converging into a swiftly flowing current that swept the gutter clean.

What Nick didn't see was a hearse.

Or any other vehicles, for that matter. Not a single soul was out and about, leaving the town ghost-like. The brewing storm was keeping everyone huddled at home. Everyone except—

"Nick."

His feet left the ground. A spider having tip-toed over an arachnophobe's bare foot. Nick spun around.

Mayor Blackwood stood in the doorway of the men's room. *Leaned* was maybe a more accurate description. Propped. Only one foot supported the man's heft. Only his shoulder lodged against the doorjamb afforded him the ability to remain upright. His nose was red, his hair damp, and the way his necktie was loose and pulled to the side spun a tale as old as time. His light blue button-up poking through his fly backed up the story.

There was apparently one person in town whose good time wasn't being hampered by the weather. And by all appearances, Mrs. Blackwood hadn't been in on the fun. Which was a shame, because Valarie Blackwood was by far the best and most palatable aspect of the mayor. Nick didn't envy her having to deal with the mayor when sober. He couldn't imagine having to deal with the man after an evening spent in the bottle.

Blackwood let a world-class belch escape, then smacked his lips like he was savoring his bourbon a second time.

Nick pursed his lips. Forget the man's wife. Currently, Nick didn't envy his own damn self. "Mayor. What can I do for you?"

"You got shit to eat around here, Nick? And for fuck's sake, call me John."

Nice try, but no thanks.

Nick wasn't falling for it. Not again. The night Nick had signed the paperwork acquiring The Chamberlain, the mayor had taken him out for a celebratory dinner and drinks. That's when the mayor had given Nick a lesson on how to punish a liver. What the mayor's liver had ever done to deserve it, Nick had no idea. But damned if the man hadn't given it a sound beating. It was at some point during the assault that he'd instructed Nick to stop calling him Mr. Mayor. Or even Mayor. Said it was too formal for the two of them at this stage in the game. Two days later, though, when they'd met up to do a walk through and discuss prospective plans, Nick made the mistake of calling the mayor by his first name. As he'd been instructed. For being such an obedient pupil, Nick had received a head spin and a stern, third-degree scowl for his efforts. Blackwood didn't actually say anything. Didn't have to. Nick could tell by the man's reaction that addressing him informally would be hereby frowned upon.

Literally.

"The usual," Nick said. "Twizzlers, Sno Caps, Raisinets. Didn't make popcorn tonight. Didn't have the demand for it."

Nick spread his arms wide, further making his point. "But I could whip some up if you'd like."

Nick held his breathe. He just knew the mayor was going to make him fire up the popcorn popper. He'd be here all night cleaning out the damn thing. Nick was pleasantly surprised when the mayor declined the offer.

"No, no." Blackwood shook his head and mumbled. "Won't be here long. Jus' wanted to stop on my way home, hear how well the showing for the kids went."

How well?

Nick sighed.

Assumptions were a heavily-wielded weapon in the mayor's arsenal, always on his hip, always at the ready. They immediately informed you that, not only was he right, but that any attempt at disagreement would be futile. In Angler Bay, Blackwood was akin to the chef of a mob-run restaurant, always proclaiming his meatballs were the best, most authentic in the city. Who's going to argue with the chef of a restaurant backed by the mob? No one, that's who. The same no one who was going to tell the mayor his assumptions were wrong.

"Surprisingly, it went well," Nick said. "No casualties."

The mayor righted himself and shuffled toward the concession counter.

"Jesus H, Nick." A chuckle and sour breath exited the mayor's mouth. "Certainly, you weren't actually expecting… casualties."

Nick moved behind the counter so as to serve the man if he changed his mind, and not simply turn him loose on his inventory.

"It's not like we haven't had our share of chaos around here." The burn on Nick's arm started to itch. As if he needed reminding. Nick thought about sharing his injury with the mayor, but quickly dismissed the notion. "Very real chaos the last couple days. Claudia calls them manifestations. Whatever you call it, something's definitely not right here. Or, not happy, if you believe those two."

"And do you?"

"What?"

"Believe those two?"

Nick shrugged. "Well…"

The mayor practically vomited laughter.

It wasn't the response Nick had expected. He also couldn't claim to be surprised. He was, after all, dealing with the man who, on opening night, while Nick sat shaken and bleeding, asked how soon he could be up and running again. Nick shook his head at the memory. He was truly blessed to be graced with the mayor's inebriated presence on this glorious evening.

He started to speak, to defend either F.A.U.S.T., himself, or both, but immediately saw the uselessness of it. *Fuck it.*

Nick was about to reach for his broom and act like he was too busy to chat when an honest to goodness blessing walked through the door. A blessing in the form of Börne and Claudia Forrester.

"Thank, God," Nick muttered.

TWENTY-FOUR

Turned out, Nick wasn't the only one anxious to get Börne and Claudia's thoughts on the morning with the students. Hot on the Forresters' heels was Ms. Nori Park. When the door closed shut behind the trio, Nori and Claudia were already in mid-conversation.

"It was a false alarm," Nori said. "Something about the seat startled her."

"And that's it?" Claudia walked further into the lobby, her head cocked toward Nori. The investigator was quite literally lending her an ear. "Nothing else?"

Claudia's flowing white evening gown, along with Börne's 'Goth butler about town' attire, must have struck the mayor's funny bone. He snickered. His exaggerated attempt at concealing it proved just as embarrassing. His ability to censure himself proved just as futile.

"Ho-ly shit," the mayor said. "Would you look at that. Halloween come early this year?" The mayor seemed insistent on *not* putting his best foot forward. Attempting to flirt with Claudia showed him in no better light. "And what, may I ask, is your name? Or, shall I just call you, Beautiful?"

Nick's stomach turned. He felt bad for Claudia. Not to mention, more than a little embarrassed for himself. He felt even worse for Börne. If there was one thing Nick had learned about Claudia, it was that she was capable of standing up for herself. But here was the mayor, hitting on Börne's wife right in front of him. Nick didn't have a wife, but if he did, he doubted very much he would enjoy watching some drunken ass-hat hit on her.

Nick unbuttoned his collar, responding to the room's sudden rise in temperature.

As expected, Claudia handled the situation, and the mayor, with her usual aplomb.

"My name is Claudia Forrester," she said. "And this is my husband and partner, Börne." She offered no smile of greeting. It would have assuredly been fake if she had. "And you can only be Mayor Blackwood."

The mayor beamed, oblivious to the slight.

"Why, yes," he said. The most arrogant grin Nick had ever seen graced the mayor's flushed face. The besmirching of his reputation had sailed right over his head. Even as Blackwood asked Claudia how she knew his name, it was obvious to everyone in the room that he was more than pleased that she did.

Claudia answered, "I've heard enough about you, Sir."

Nick smirked. *Classic.* Not 'I've heard *a lot* about you,' but 'I've heard *enough* about you.' Enough to form an opinion, apparently.

A second shot across his bow failed to put a dent in Blackwood's sloppy smile. His red-rimmed and bloodshot eyes didn't so much as blink.

If Nick wasn't still reeling from the mayor's earlier repugnance, he might have cracked a full-on smile. As it were, smiling floated near the bottom of his list of current emotional expressions. He looked to the others. Not surprisingly, Börne's scornful eyes were fixed on the mayor. Nori was rolling hers, and Claudia's were on anything and everything except the mayor. Awkward was the name of the game. Nick loved The

Chamberlain. It was his home away from home. But, at the moment, he would have rather been anywhere but standing in its lobby.

And to think, he had actually been looking forward to the evening.

"So," Nick said, turning to the Forresters and doing his best to ignore the mayor's very presence, "sounds like Nori's been filling you in on our morning."

"She has." Even as he answered, Börne's stare remained on the mayor, who leered hungrily at Claudia. "Sounds like our friend has a soft spot for children."

"I'm sorry," the mayor said, his leering eyes finally taking a break from Claudia. "Our friend?"

"The spirit haunting The Chamberlain," Claudia said. "Floyd Cropper's spirit to be exact."

"Someone," Börne chimed, "with whom I'm sure you're well-acquainted."

Another gut-busting bellow exploded from Blackwood.

Nick shook his head, looked to Claudia, and mouthed the words 'I'm sorry.' To the mayor, and no one else, everything coming out of either Claudia or Börne's mouth was apparently the funniest damn thing. He shouldn't be surprised. Adding alcohol to an asshole generally makes for a bigger, more tactless asshole. Nick was embarrassed. Slightly ashamed. But, not surprised.

"Ridiculous," the mayor said, once the last of his chuckles died off. "First of all, yes, old Floyd loved kids. Shame he and Helen never had any of his own. But you think the old guy's haunting this place? Never heard something so absurd. I mean, don't get me wrong. Floyd Cropper loved this damn theater more than most men love their wives. Even more than they love their mistresses. But I don't think he had ambition enough to spend his afterlife running around causing problems for ol' Nick here. Ambition to that degree would have kept The Chamberlain from going under while he was alive."

One after another, Nick's eyes met everyone else's. Were they all thinking the same thing? *Was this guy for real?* If they weren't yet, they soon would be. Nick rarely went a week without questioning the mayor's authenticity. Whether he tried to or not, the man simply couldn't keep his size eleven foot out of his mouth.

It didn't take long for him to prove Nick's point.

"Look," Blackwood said. He walked around the group, taking measure of each of them. "You two come in here dressed like you just walked off the set of a seventies B-movie, filling Nick's head with stories of spirits and grandeur. No wonder he can't make any money. He's too busy looking over his shoulder for the ghost of owners past to concentrate on running this damn place, let alone come up with a new business strategy."

Nick's eyes widened.

Blackwood had sobered at an astonishing rate. He no longer resembled the town lush, stumbling and fumbling. He spoke clearly and with purpose. He was now the captain of his ship, and everyone else in the room, his vassal.

It was the Blackwood that Nick had grown accustomed to seeing these last few months.

"And you," the mayor said, stopping behind Nori. He leaned in as if to whisper in her ear, but the words came just as loud and biting as those previous. "You're perpetuating this nonsense? Clouding Nick's head even more? Arming him with even more lame-ass excuses?"

"But, Mayor—"

The mayor silenced Nori with a raised finger. He was on a roll, stonewalling to maximum effect, hardly a waver in his gate.

"I would expect more professionalism from you, Ms. Park. Perhaps I should give my pal, Preston, a call. Ask him why he doesn't have better control over his journalists."

Everyone stood in silence, like schoolchildren being chastised after being caught smoking behind the bleachers.

Nick looked at Nori. Her head shook with irritation. Her teeth held her bottom lip hostage. She wanted to say something; wanted to rage against the Blackwood machine. Nick wished she would. But, Blackwood's threat of calling her editor had real teeth. She had already written one story about The Chamberlain, her shred-piece about the opening night fiasco. There was no upside to a second story about the failing theater. So far, she was working the follow-up on her own time, out of her own curiosity. One call from the mayor's office had the potential to kill a new story before she could determine whether or not there even was one. Much less pitch it. A journalist's worst nightmare.

The storm churning behind Börne's eyes told Nick all he needed to know about the man's first introduction to Angler Bay's beloved mayor. Börne was pissed. Like he was ready to pack up his shit and go home pissed. A death blow, for sure. The final nail in The Chamberlain's coffin. There was nothing else. Nick was out of ideas. Bringing in F.A.U.S.T. had been a final Hail Mary.

Nick was about to say something, to try and stop the bleeding, to turn the tide back in his favor, when Claudia opened her mouth and proceeded to poke the bear.

"Well, then, Mr. Mayor," she said, "I don't suppose you'd like to meet this spirit for yourself?"

A guffaw. That is what they call a spontaneous eruption of laughter. And that is what came out of the mayor. If it had been anything but hot air, it would have ended up all over his shoes.

"Darling, I think I've got better things to do with my evening than to hang around here playing ghosts and robbers." The mayor straightened his tie, the universal gesture of someone important, with somewhere important to be, and something important to do. He may have been okay, if only he'd stopped there. "Nick, if this is how you want to spend your time and money, well, I can't stop you. But there are two things I know about my bank: it closes every day at five; and if they don't get the lease payment from you, they'll gladly get it from someone else."

The mayor turned on his heels, shirt still sticking out of his fly like a blue tongue, and headed toward the door.

Nick fumed. He didn't know exactly where his line lay, but somewhere during his speech, Blackwood had crossed it. Nick needed to speak up. Stand up not just for himself, but all of them. Someone had to put the son of a bitch in his place.

Since it turned out not to be him, Nick couldn't have been happier that it was Nori.

"What's wrong Mayor?" she called out before the man could reach the front door. "Afraid to face Floyd after what you did to him?"

The soles of Blackwood's loafers sent out a sharp squeak as he stopped. He didn't turn around at first, just stood there with his back to them. When he finally did turn to face them, his face was the color of a Mexican chili, his temper just as hot. His lips were pursed, but it didn't stop him from speaking through them.

"Let's get on with it."

TWENTY-FIVE

"Black tourmaline." Claudia reached out her hand. "Its protection against negative energy and spirits have always served me well." Two strands of black leather cord, identical to the ones hanging around her and Börne's necks, hung from her fingers. A stone, about an inch and a half long, swung at the bottom of the cord. It was rough-edged, resembling a piece of jagged black chalk. Claudia looked around the group, concluding her survey with Blackwood. "Though I'm afraid I only brought four necklaces, Mr. Mayor. I didn't know you would be joining us."

The mayor chuckled.

"That's quite alright, Miss." The smirk on his face affirmed that not receiving a gemstone was indeed alright. He didn't need the protection any more than he needed alcohol counseling, apparently. "I'm good."

Nori took a necklace from Claudia.

Nick followed suit. He had never given a moment's thought to things like crystals, oils, or anything else of the spiritual persuasion. As far as he was concerned, only people who liked to dance naked in the forest under a full moon believed in their powers. And while the image of Claudia dancing naked among the trees tried to enter his mind, Nick successfully blocked its entrance. He didn't feel the least bit foolish slipping the necklace over his head. That is, not until he noticed the mayor's derisive expression now aimed in his direction.

Nick quickly turned away.

"The black tourmaline," Börne said, "is considered one of the most effective gemstones for protection. At least it's the one we feel most confident using. Stones and crystals generally work differently for different people, but these have always served us well."

Nick ran his fingers up and down the length of the course stone. "And how many times have you dealt with a spirit this...vengeful?" he asked.

"A time or two," Claudia answered, but only after exchanging a look with Börne.

"What?" It was Nori who noticed. "What is it?"

Claudia reacted like a teenager caught kicking an accessory under the table. "What do you mean?" she asked, feigning indifference.

Nori looked to Börne with her reporter's eye, then turned it back on Claudia. "Feels like there's something you're not telling us."

Claudia checked in with Börne again. After a moment's hesitation, he gave her a slight nod. She cleared her throat while everyone, including Blackwood, looked on. "It's just...well...to be honest, we've never really experienced manifestations this...pronounced. This tangible."

Nick's jaw squared. "This pissed off, you mean."

Börne answered with a nod. "Which is why we're forgoing the EMF meter and much of the other detection equipment tonight," he explained. "There's really nothing to try and detect at this point. We already know it's here. We've seen its handywork. This spirit is being anything but subtle."

"Floyd's spirit," the mayor mocked.

"As far as we've seen," Börne continued, "nobody has ever

caught evidence of the afterlife like what we've seen here at The Chamberlain on video. Not like this. Most images captured on film have to be interpreted. And I mean interpreted just to determine whether the image is actually something, or just an anomalous trick of light everyone hopes is something. So, basically, the next time the shit hits the fan in there," Börne pointed toward the auditorium, "we're catching said shit on video." Börne bent and pulled two hand held camcorders from a black duffle bag. He handed one to Nick.

Nick turned the device over in his hands and started familiarizing himself with its controls.

"What about sage?" Nori asked. "I've heard of people burning sage to cleanse a house."

Nick looked to Nori with eyebrows raised. "Is that an option?"

"Two problems," Claudia said. "In order for sage to work, there must be windows in the space. Somewhere to flush the spirits, allowing them somewhere to escape. As the theater has no windows, I don't think burning sage would do anything but fill the room with a pleasant fragrance."

Nick stopped fiddling with his camera. "And the second problem?"

Claudia sucked in her bottom lip, wedged it between her teeth. She cast pensive eyes in Börne's direction. "*Meine Liebe?*"

"The thing is," Börne said, having a difficult time hiding the mischief that crept into his grin, "we don't actually want to get rid of the spirit. Not yet."

Nick's eyebrows drew up in high arches.

Nori's eyes narrowed.

The mayor belched, otherwise remaining uncharacteristically quiet and indifferent.

"Wait a second," Nick started.

Börne raised the camera for all to see. "Not until we get

some footage." He met everyone's gaze one by one, reading their reactions, before settling on one in particular. "Nick," he continued, "I'm not exaggerating when I say this could be huge."

Nori, ever the probing reporter, was quick to interject. "For your website, you mean."

"For all of us," Claudia said.

"I don't know." Nick dropped the camera to his side. "Riling up this spirit just to get some video of it? Sounds a little risky to me. Not to mention irresponsible. Kinda like pouring gasoline on a fire just so you can see it better. Honestly, I'd just as soon get rid of this damn thing, whatever it is, and move on with our lives."

"We will," Börne assured. "But—"

"Aw, come on, Nick," the mayor busted in. "Where's your sense of adventure?" He looked Claudia and Börne up and down. "These two are obviously professionals. If they think we're sitting on something big here, then by God, why are we standing around with our dicks in our hands debating it?"

Börne's grin stretched to a full-on smile. Not because of the mayor's sophomoric humor, but because he had convinced at least one person in the group to see the value of his plan. Keyword being *value*. In Nick's experience, if the mayor saw dollar signs in a particular plan, that was usually all of the dangling carrot he needed.

"Let's get on with it!" The mayor clapped his meaty hands and lead the way toward the auditorium doors. The rest of the circle broke rank. Börne followed hot on the mayor's heels, a puppy shadowing a toddler with a cookie. Nori didn't seem as anxious. She trailed a few steps behind, her investigative mind no doubt processing the change in F.A.U.S.T.'s plans.

Only Claudia and Nick hung back, watching the others walk away. Nick had his reasons for not immediately following. He assumed Claudia had hers. With that in mind, he decided to make the most of the one-on-one time.

"You don't seem as excited as your husband." Nick searched Claudia's face for a tell-tale sign. Something that would foreshadow an explanation. His investigation came up empty.

"Let's just say I take the paranormal a little more seriously than my beloved." Claudia continued to watch the group retreat as she spoke. "Specifically, the dangers it can present."

Nick swallowed hard. His hand went to the pendant hanging around his neck. If she was trying to put him at ease, she was off to a piss poor start.

"Um…dangers?"

Claudia nodded, but remained silent. Nick sensed there was a story behind that silence. A story he decided he'd very much like to hear before he stepped foot in the auditorium again.

"So," he said. "You've only felt the need to use the crystals for protection, what, a time or two? Have they ever failed you?"

"Once," Claudia said, finally meeting Nick's gaze. "They've failed me once."

Nick eyed her warily. The sudden softness of her voice. The lack of confidence in her green eyes. It was all out of place. A side of the paranormal governess he had yet to see. It filled Nick with unease. Enough so, that it caused the contents of his stomach to whirlpool with nausea. "I'm almost afraid to ask, but what happened?"

Claudia's expression was that of a time traveler's journeying back to a memory as she looked away. "It didn't go well."

Nick expected a loud clap of thunder to erupt outside, the lobby lights to flicker, or a phantom orchestra to play an ominous dun, dun, dun. Something to portend a dramatic revelation. Neither happened. This wasn't a movie, after all. He checked in on the group standing before the closed auditorium doors. Closed doors was the new protocol. Nick saw no benefit in leaving them open anymore. Only the mayor seemed to be growing impatient. He cast Nick a questioning glare, not used to people keeping him waiting. Nick ignored the look and turned back to Claudia. "Wanna tell me about it?"

Claudia shook her head, let out a sigh. "Not exactly."

The nausea in Nick's stomach solidified into a greasy mass of dread. "Okay, then," he said, running a hand through his hair. "Maybe we should just—"

"Her name was Shelby Ann Creek." Claudia's voice was meek, her words a virtual whisper. "She was my mentor. My teacher. Most of all, she was my friend."

The repeated use of the word 'was' didn't slip by Nick unnoticed.

"She taught me everything I know," she continued. "Investigation after investigation, I soaked up every bit of knowledge I could. Under her guidance, I honed my own skills and sensibilities. She was an encyclopedia of information. Of strategy." Claudia paused briefly, casting her eyes down. "Then Dieburg happened."

Another pause, eyes now closed.

Nick found himself wondering what healthy alternatives former addicts turn to when anxieties mounted. What did herbal tea taste like anyway? He waited as long as he felt reasonable before prying. "What's a Dieburg?"

Claudia raised her eyes. "It's not a *what*," she said, "but a *where*." She placed a trembling hand to her temple, visibly uncomfortable with having to relive the experience. "She should have seen it coming, should've known. But she was overconfident. We thought we were ready. We had no idea. The spirit was too powerful. More powerful than Shelby Ann had ever encountered."

"And the spirit here at the Chamberlain…"

"Let's call him by his name, shall we?"

Nick nodded. "Floyd. Is it, or, is *he* as powerful as others you've encountered?"

Her downturned look told him everything.

Nick's heart sank. His pulse quickened. His neck sprouted baby beads of sweat. All while his mind broke in ten different directions, reeling with this new information. Truth, they were all in potential danger. He knew that now.

He wanted to warn Nori. He wanted to excuse himself and hide in his office, letting Börne, who was braver than he, videotape to his heart's content. For a brief moment, Nick even thought about calling off the whole damn thing. No videotaping. No summoning of spirits. No prayers for protection required, because nobody was going in. *No way in hell.*

Nick took a deep breath.

The only thing that stopped him from cancelling the investigation were the consequences of doing so. If this thing didn't work out, if Claudia and Börne couldn't rid The Chamberlain of Floyd's pissed off spirit, then he was toast. Finished. Through. The doors would close on the theater, possibly forever, and Nick Fallon would be adding one more busted business venture to his ever-growing resume of failures.

"So," he pressed, but cautiously, "what happened in Dieburg?"

A visible shudder made its way through Claudia's shoulders. Her eyes remained closed.

Nick wondered how far back in time her mind was having to travel. He glanced over at Nori. She remained at the auditorium doors, talking to the other half of F.A.U.S.T. He wished he could hear their conversation. Was Börne expounding on his wife's fears? Was he sharing with them the potential dangers they faced? Nick doubted it. Why risk shitting on a plan that barely had support to begin with? Especially when the only one showing said support was Mayor Blackwood. Not exactly an immoveable object. As eager as the man was to make a buck, he didn't come across as an adventurer-type, and would probably turn tail if he was privy to what Nick was learning.

Scratch the herbal tea. Healthy alternative or not, Nick considered the bottle of bourbon sitting in his desk just down the hall.

Claudia took in a deep breath and exhaled, pulling Nick's attention back around.

"The details don't matter," she said. Sucking in her stomach, she smoothed out the lace of her white gown, straightened her posture. "What is inherently important is that I made it out of that house before it crumbled in on itself. Shelby, God rest her soul, did not."

And there it was. The danger of which she had earlier spoken. *The house crumbled in on itself.* Nick shivered from a phantom breeze. *What the...* Who knew that was a thing? Who knew that a spirit could do more than flicker a few lights and slam a door or two? Who knew they actually had the means to cause you harm?

Me, Nick thought, eyeing his bandaged arm.

You know damn well.

"Okay," he said. "So, I'm thinking—"

"Hey, Nick!" The mayor's voice split the quiet of the lobby, causing Nick to jump. "Stop hitting on this man's wife, would ya? I need to get home before mine locks me out."

TWENTY-SIX

Asshole.

For the first time ever, Nick hoped something happened inside the theater. Nothing too big. Nothing too dangerous. Nothing like Claudia's story. But something. New light bulbs be damned. As he and Claudia walked toward the auditorium, Nick felt the need to apologize for the mayor's overall lack of human decency. He just wasn't sure he could open his mouth right then without causing further damage to his pride.

They joined the rest of the group outside the auditorium doors.

Somewhere in the night, thunder rumbled on its way out of town.

"First things first," Claudia said, reaching out her hands. "We didn't offer a prayer of protection the last time, and Nick's arm suffered the consequences. It was irresponsible of me. I insist we return to that practice considering the spirit's temperament."

A chuckle of derision escaped the mayor's lips. No one appeared surprised. Nick had long grown wary of Blackwood thinking everything was funny tonight. He could only assume everyone else had, too. He wasn't about to indulge the man, though. He wouldn't acknowledge the mayor's behavior and risk giving him an opening.

In an uncharacteristic moment of weakness, Claudia didn't, or maybe couldn't, let it go.

"Something amusing you, Mr. Mayor?"

Nick took her in, brows raised. It wasn't weakness after all. Just the opposite. Her moxie had returned. Her confidence. Claudia was prepared to defend what they did and squash the mayor like a cockroach in the process.

Blackwood's palms went up in front of him, the international sign of apology.

"Sorry," he said through droopy eyes. "But, temperament? You talk as if these things exhibit differing behaviors. I wasn't aware that ghosts had good and bad days."

Nick watched and waited, eyeing the mayor closely. He considered the man's remark. It actually sounded legitimate, but was that his strategy? Was Blackwood wanting to have a serious discussion on the subject of spirits? Or, was this yet another attempt at mocking the situation. Veiled as it might be.

"Mr. Mayor," Claudia said, dropping her outstretched hands to her sides. She bit her lower lip, mining for just the right amount of tact. "There are different types of spirits. And just as they did while alive, all possess different personalities. Behaviors. Temperaments. Whatever you want to call it. They are no different than any other creature in nature."

"No different?" The mayor looked all around the group. "So, you're telling me that these so-called spirits are as natural as you and I? As Ms. Park? As…I'm sorry. Your name again?"

"Börne."

"As natural as good old Börne here?"

Nick remained a fly on the wall, watching the tennis match play out between Claudia and the mayor. It was both fascinating and, as best Nick could tell, far from over.

"We refer to the supernatural," Claudia continued, "as

simply that which is beyond our scientific understanding of the laws of nature. At least, as we know them thus far. However, just because we can't wrap it up in a nice little package with these laws, does not mean they are any less a natural force. There are many forces of nature that we don't have a complete grasp on. The supernatural is just one such force."

"A force to be reckoned with," Börne chimed in. Then he added, "at times."

Everyone took a beat, processing Claudia's explanation. Even the mayor seemed momentarily lost in thought. Or, simply too drunk to process all the information he'd just been given.

Nick wondered if it made him a bad person because he hoped the mayor's head was hurting from all of the thinking he was being asked to do.

After several quiet moments, Claudia silently reached her hands back out to the others. Without hesitation, Nori took one. Nick took Nori's, and so on. Eventually, a circle had formed by all members of the group except one.

"That's quite alright," the mayor said. To emphasize his point, Blackwood shoved his hands deep into the pockets of his slacks. "Think I'll pass on the talking to God portion of the show. Never been much of a believer."

"In what?" Claudia inquired. "God or the supernatural?"

Blackwood nodded. "Yes."

"Interesting." Claudia took a moment, appearing to turn something over in her mind. "Normally, I'd say that your lack of belief in our vengeful spirit might be enough to protect you. It's a popular theory that how much credence we give spirits determines their strength."

The mayor cocked his head. "Normally?"

"I'm sorry?"

"You said *normally* my lack of belief might protect me." An uncomfortable grin broke across the mayor's face. "What did you mean by *normally*?"

It was Nick who answered for Claudia. Answered for all of them. "Like I keep telling you, the situation here is anything but normal."

"Now," Claudia continued, "I usually say the prayer, covering the group." Claudia glanced around, taking a moment to make eye contact with everyone. "This time, however, I would prefer if everyone said it with me. Everyone who believes, that is."

Everyone but the mayor nodded in agreement.

"Please, repeat after me." With eyes closed and face tipped to the ceiling like she was sunning herself, Claudia took a deep breath and let it out. "Saint Michael, the Archangel, defend us in battle…"

Everyone did as asked. In unison, they repeated Claudia's prayer line for line, word for word. Despite being a product of a devout family, Nick teetered on the fence. He was still unsure as to whether or not he believed in God. He'd always found the arguments both for and against His existence compelling. Each swayed the needle in their direction at different times in his life. Each had felt right. Tonight, however, he took no chances. Nick said the prayer and said it well. Said it like a sinner in church the morning after a particularly unholy Saturday night.

To the mayor's credit, he did nothing to disrespect their invocation. No awkward coughs, no clearing of his throat meant to distract. No guffaws. For all anyone knew, the man was silently repeating the words right alongside them. Perhaps all of the talk about spirits had changed his mind after all.

Or, as was more plausible, maybe the drunk was sobering up.

"Alright," Börne said once they were finished, "video recorders out, set to record." His smile, if the group wasn't careful, had the potential to be contagious. "Let's make history!"

TWENTY-SEVEN

Nick flipped the switch. The one that turned on the camcorder Börne had given him without first asking if he wanted it. A good move on Börne's part. Had he been asked, Nick wasn't sure he would have consented. If Börne was looking for someone to hang around and film the shit as it hit the fan, Nick probably wasn't the guy. In fact, he would have bet money on it. But, Börne had explained himself. He didn't want to risk missing something by having only a stationary camera setup somewhere in the theater. The idea was to split up mobile cameras so that the room was covered from both sides, fluidly covering all possible angles and corners. It all seemed very plausible as far as game plans went. Börne's only regret was that he did not have a third camera for Nori.

For her part, Nori didn't seem too put off by not having one. Otherwise, Nick would have gladly relinquished his.

The camcorder clicked and buzzed its way to life. The shutter snapped open. A roving white light came on. Nick swung the camera around, taking turns bringing everyone in the group within its grainy viewfinder.

"Mr. Mayor, since you are without black tourmaline," Claudia said, genuinely trying to be helpful, "I would suggest sticking close to someone in possession of one."

Blackwood showed his appreciation as only he could: with a wave of his hand and a show of his backside as he sauntered down the center aisle toward the front of the auditorium.

In the doorway, Nori and Nick exchanged a look. Both shrugged, then went their separate ways. Nori and Börne went to the left, while Nick took a hard right and cautiously made his way behind the back row of seats.

He couldn't see any smoke, but as soon as he entered the auditorium, Nick could smell it. No trace of it caught in the ray of light coming from the hallway. Only his nose told him it was there. He wondered if he was alone in that fact. Was it possible he smelled it only because he expected to? Because he anticipated it at this point? He had no idea. For all he knew, the musky stench of char had seeped deep into the theater's pores, promising to linger there until the day The Chamberlain was torn down.

"Floyd Cropper? Are you here?" Claudia's voice cut through the quiet like a katana blade.

It was the second time she'd caught Nick off guard like that. He nearly gave himself whiplash spinning in her direction. That made him realize he was entirely too jumpy for this kind of work. *Damn it, man! Calm yourself.* Ten seconds in, his heart rate was already off and running. He forced himself to take a deep breath. It was too early in the evening's festivities to start freaking out. There was no telling what they might encounter in the next few hours.

Nick's hand went to his chest where he found the gemstone beneath his shirt. He should have asked Claudia if she and her mentor had been in possession of black tourmaline that day. Seemed like an important detail now.

"Floyd?" Claudia's voice sounded a tad different than it had a moment earlier. It held something that wasn't previously there. It wasn't fear. It wasn't anxiety.

It was caution.

Nick slowly swept the camera around the room twice, then brought it back around to Claudia.

"If you are here, Floyd, please make your presence known."

A long, drawn out silence followed. It stretched for thirty seconds. Sixty. The auditorium remained at rest.

Nick brimmed with unease. It was that feeling of knowing something was coming, but not knowing what or when. His spine literally tingled. He could feel an energy growing in the air. Be prepared for anything, he told himself. He was counting on the others to do the same. Except for Blackwood, of course. Nick knew better than to count on that man for the simplest of things, much less preparedness.

Proving the point, the mayor plopped into a seat in the front row. He kicked back, legs out, ankles crossed. He clasped his hands behind his head. Just like anyone else who might sit in that seat, he was simply settling in for a good show.

Nick expected nothing less.

All it took was a flickering of the lights to change the mayor's posture.

The brief strobe brought the mayor upright in his seat. He turned around with an exaggerated chuckle.

"Nice try, you assholes." Blackwood's deep voice broke through a tension that had suddenly befallen the room. "Gonna take more than jacking with the lights to scare me."

Nick spoke up. "Nobody's jackin' with anything, Mayor."

"It's becoming quite a common occurrence here at the Chamberlain," Nori chimed in. "Welcome to the show."

Once, then twice more, the sconce lights on the walls blinked off for several seconds. The overhead track lighting followed suit. The new bulbs extinguished themselves. Extinguished, but not blown as far as Nick could tell. He held his breath that they remained that way. The darkened auditorium proved unsettling, despite the commonality of the occurrence. For Nick, it somehow didn't get easier with each passing manifestation.

What Nick *was* growing accustomed to was the pace at which his heart now thumped. What was normal anyway? And would his heart remember what that rate was once this was all said and done?

A moment later, all of the lights came back on.

"Floyd," Claudia continued, looking toward the ceiling. "Is that you making—"

The luxury of visibility was short-lived. This time, all of the lights went out simultaneously. The sconce lights. The overheads, too. Went out and stayed out. The auditorium had once again plunged itself into sheer darkness. Only two scant sources of light saved the room from going pitch: the soft red glow of the new exit sign in the front corner; and a narrow shaft of light coming through the doors to the lobby.

Neither reached into the back corner where Nick stood. He slowly lowered the camera to his side, his heart throbbing in his ears.

For several seconds, no one said a word. The room was like a morgue at midnight, still and quiet. Eventually, it was Börne's voice that broke the silence.

"Hey, Nick?" His words travelled through the dark from the other side of the room, somewhere near the front of the auditorium. "There's a tiny button just south of the on/off switch. It'll turn on the night vision. Probably shoulda mentioned that beforehand."

Night vision, huh? That would be handy.

Nick fumbled blindly in the inky blackness, jostling the camera in search of the night vision button. He felt sorry for Börne. Or, Claudia. Or, anyone else who might have to watch his footage later. He envisioned the viewer growing seasick from all of the jarring.

It took a few seconds for Nick to find the button, click it, and right the camera. On the screen, objects in the room lit up in washed-out shades of eerie green. It looked as if a glowing, toxic liquid had washed through the auditorium, staining everything in its wake. The lighter colored the object, the more the green clung to it. Claudia's flowing white gown looked as though the contaminant itself cascaded over her shoulders and down the entirety of her body. Across the sea of seats, Nori and Börne's faces took on a soft green pallor. Their eyes, however, gleamed a stark white. Almost alien-like.

The auditorium itself remained a shadowy black.

As Claudia once again attempted conversation with The Chamberlain's resident spirit, Nick panned the camera down the sloping rows of seats, toward the front of the auditorium. Was this what Börne wanted him to do? Just randomly work the camera over the room in the hopes of capturing something on film? He had no idea. He'd been given no instruction, after all. Simply handed the camera and turned loose.

Despite the change in atmosphere, the mayor remained in his front row seat. The way he sat slumped with his head back against the headrest, Nick couldn't tell if he had settled in for a show or a quick nap.

It suddenly didn't matter. The theater came alive before either could commence.

The rows of overhead lights began to swing. Like fingernails on a chalkboard, the sound of metal wrenching against metal twisted the muscles in Nick's neck. The riggings swayed. They pitched forward first then back. Their momentum grew with each arc.

Nick took a deep breath. His pulse doubled.

Here we go.

The smell of smoke grew stronger in his nose, lest he try to forget. Nick checked the camera's viewfinder, hoping the infra-red technology was picking up what his eyes couldn't. That wasn't the case. There was no sign of smoke on the screen, white, green or any other color. Yet, the growing stench was undeniable.

"Anyone else smell that?" Nick asked the darkness.

Nori's voice emerged from beneath the veil, sounding a million miles away. "How could we not? Smells like a campfire."

A sizzling joined the sound of metal coursing throughout the auditorium. Static-like. The air around them buzzed with energy. Light emanating from the rows of lightbulbs slowly brightened.

Nick pulled the camcorder away from his face. The increasing light wasn't exactly friendly to the infra-red. Soon, even without the infra-red, he was squinting against the auditorium's brilliance. The brightening of the room caused the temperature to increase. Sweat soon peppered Nick's forehead. He wiped his mouth on his shoulder. The illumination was pushing the bulbs beyond their capacity. He held his breath.

Then, together in one joint maneuver, all of the overhead light bulbs fizzled and went dark.

The auditorium plunged once again into pitch black.

For several seconds, no one said a word. The tinkling of tiny glass particles hitting concrete never came. Not like the evening before. When it became obvious that the lights weren't coming back on, it was Claudia who spoke first.

"Everyone alright?" When the investigator's voice reached through the dark, Nick detected a shakiness within. A fracture in the normally confident façade. He didn't like it. His mind replayed Claudia's story about her friend.

We thought we were ready. We had no idea.

A collection of murmurs answered Claudia's question. Everyone was alright, but too on edge to verbally form words. If they were anything like Nick, they were too preoccupied with corralling their fear.

Nick's hand trembled as he raised the camera. Trying his damnedest to keep it steady, he slowly scanned the auditorium for whatever might come next.

Instantly, the room flooded with light.

Nick ripped his eyes from the camera's viewfinder.

"Damn it!" Just that quick, the blinding light had burned white circles in his vision. He blinked, squeezed his eyes shut. Blinked some more. "Make up your mind already! We gonna have light or not?"

"Nick?" Nori inquired.

"Nothing," he replied. "Just talking to myself."

Once his eyes started to regain focus, Nick looked to the ceiling with renewed hope. The illumination wasn't coming from the overhead lights. The new bulbs he'd replaced that morning remained dark. So where—

He blinked again.

The movie screen.

The large, sixty by twenty-foot rectangle at the front of the auditorium glowed a ghostly white.

At the back of the room, Nick frowned. He turned to the control room window. In order for the screen to be illuminated, a shaft of light had to come from the control room window. There was no shaft. There was no light. The control room supplied no more light than the busted out light bulbs above.

The lines across Nick's forehead deepened. *How the hell?*

He turned back to the screen. It still glowed as brightly as if a film was about to begin. How could that be? The screen had no power source of its own. No electricity ran to it. It was a simple vinyl sheet with a silver, paint-like coating.

Yet, somehow…

"Um, Nick? Buddy?"

Nick ran his free hand down over his chin He sometimes wished he had a beard to stroke when thinking things through. "Yeah, Börne?"

"Wasn't aware there was a showing scheduled."

"There's not."

"Then…"

"I have no idea."

TWENTY-EIGHT

Nori had either read his mind, or she'd done her own quick investigation and had come to the same conclusion. "It's not coming from the control room, Nick. How is that?"

Unseen in the dark, Nick shrugged.

A rumble of thunder came and went somewhere beyond The Chamberlain's walls.

"Floyd?" Claudia's voice was a bit shaky, but controlled. "Floyd, are you manipulating the screen in some way?"

All remained quiet.

With the night vision switched off, Nick swept the camera to the rear of the auditorium. He found Claudia standing in the back, fingering the stone round her neck. He allowed the lens to linger, capturing her unease. It wasn't until a moment later, when she looked his way, that Nick turned and drew the camera down to the front. Here, he zoomed in on the front of the room and settled. If anything else was going to happen, the chances of it happening near the well-lit screen, that had no business being so, were as good as any.

Call it a hunch.

"Floyd?" Claudia continued. "Floyd, are you wanting to show us something?"

Nick's chest pounded as he tried to anticipate the spirit's

next move. Ridding the auditorium of all possible lighting, only to somehow illuminate the room with a large piece of fabric? What was the ultimate plan? Where was all of this leading?

The mayor, however, didn't appear the least bit concerned. His posture hadn't changed. Even after the events of the last few minutes, Blackwood remained slumped in his seat, unstirred. Was he asleep? Couldn't be. Who could sleep with everything that was going on?

There was only one logical explanation: the mayor's evening had caught up with him. He had succumbed to liquor's sweet embrace and was now passed out in the front row. It was unbelievable, really. The man was nearer the screen than anyone, yet completely unaware it had somehow come alive.

Crazy.

It was Börne who saw it first. His voice coming slow and breathy. "Holy shit."

Instinctively, Nick brought the camera around to the investigator. He kept it momentarily trained on Börne before turning it in the direction of Börne's open-mouthed gape.

He didn't see it at first. In fact, it took several seconds before...

Nick's jaw dropped. His eyes came off the camera's viewfinder. He voiced an expletive or two.

Claudia must have seen it, too. When she spoke, Nick wasn't sure who she was encouraging. The three of them, or herself. "Everyone stay calm."

It was the screen down front.

A series of shadowy impressions had appeared. Not so much on the screen, but within it. Finger-like protrusions pushed against the material, as if stretching it outward from behind. They weren't normal sized fingers. They were much larger, nearly the size of baseball bats. A simple flick from any one of them would do substantial damage to life and limb. As the fingers stretched further outward, the hands they belonged to soon followed, literally growing out of the screen. The aluminized piece of vinyl gave no more resistance than a large bed sheet.

"Nick? Are you getting this?"

There was genuine excitement in Börne's voice. Nick couldn't match it. The feeling in his stomach was anything but enthusiastic. He simply nodded in response to Börne's question.

More shadows emerged on the screen. A second pair of hands. Together, all four stretched out, reaching for something beyond Nick's imagination. It wasn't until the hands turned to the left that their intent became clear.

Their apparent target slumped in his seat a mere fifteen feet away.

"Mayor!" Nick shouted. If Blackwood heard, he didn't acknowledge. He didn't stir. He didn't so much as flinch. Nick tried again. "Blackwood!"

Still no response.

"What the hell?" Nori's voice came from somewhere nearby. She was no longer down toward the front with Börne. She was making her way toward the doors. And wasting no time in doing so. "Why isn't he moving?"

Nick didn't hazard an answer. He was busy wondering the same thing.

It took a minute, and startled looks from both Claudia and Nori, for Nick to realize the sound he was suddenly hearing wasn't that of his own heart beating in his ears. Apparently, the screen wasn't the only thing that had animated. From somewhere deep inside the theater, a heart was beating.

The whole damn auditorium was alive.

"Börne?" Claudia sounded strange. The concern in her voice had risen to a level Nick hadn't heard before. Borderline fearful. "*Börne, meine Liebe! Komm schon!*"

Twenty steps were all that separated Nick from the doors.

Might as well have been a hundred. He couldn't move. He was transfixed. His eyes darted back and forth between the hands reaching out of the screen and the man they reached for.

"Blackwood!"

Though higher-pitched and shrill, Nori's shout proved no more effective than Nick's. Four of the largest hands the world had ever seen crept toward the mayor like a pair of stealth hunters. Still, he remained oblivious. God only knew what their intentions were once they reached their prey.

From the dark, something grabbed Nick's arm.

"Nick!" Nori shouted, shaking him. "Come on! Let's get out of here!"

Nick looked first to Nori, then to Claudia, his lead. The one running the show. But she was too busy to set any examples for anyone. From just inside the open doorway, she implored her husband to join her with words Nick didn't understand. Their meaning, however, was universal.

Turning away, Nick locked eyes with Nori. He saw fear. He also saw confidence. She was stepping up. Nori had taken charge.

Nick nodded. "Okay."

Nori turned toward the doorway.

Nick took a step to follow, then stopped. "Wait! Nori!"

Nori stopped and turned, but made no move to return to his side.

"What about the mayor?" he shouted.

"What about him?"

"We can't just leave him!"

Nori threw out her arms, looked to the man still slumped in the front row. Seconds later, when she turned back to Nick, she had made her decision. "Screw him!"

Nick's chest deflated as he watched Nori turn and continue toward the doors. Her reaction wasn't what he had expected, but he wasn't exactly surprised. There was no love lost between Nori and the mayor. Blackwood threatening to call Nori's editor had set fire to that already crumbling bridge. Still…

"We can't just leave him," he repeated. Despite his protest, Nick's feet were moving forward, increasing the distance between himself and the mayor. He followed the aisle along the back row of seats, using the vinyl seatbacks as a guide. At the open doorway, he stopped and took a quick head count. They were still shy two people. Nick had thought it might be only one at that point. "Where's Börne?"

Claudia nodded down the center aisle, her eyes fretful, pendent clutched in a white-knuckled fist.

Nick turned in the direction of Claudia's fearful gaze. Börne's silhouette crept across the brilliantly-lit screen down front. The investigator was heading right for the large hands growing from it. As far as Nick could tell, Börne still had his camera running. He was capturing everything. And at such close range, the footage would indeed be extraordinary.

The mayor, for his part, remained motionless, painfully unaware of the circumstances surrounding him. Nick supposed there was a silver lining in being able to account for his whereabouts. Now, if Börne could just get Blackwood to move his ass.

"Shit." Nick bit his bottom lip. Decisions, decisions. On one hand, he felt the pull of the lobby and its relative safety. He also knew that Börne could probably use a hand extracting the mayor from his seat. Nick hated good Samaritans, always feeling the need to do the right thing. It was annoying.

Damn it.

"Here." Nick handed the camcorder to Nori with a half-hearted smile. "If I die epically, make sure you get it on film."

Nori's face was stone. She wasn't sharing Nick's levity as she took the camera. "Be careful!"

As Nick drew closer to the screen, three things began to

happen: his pace quickened, adrenaline fueled his heart rate, and the stench of smoke grew stronger. The air also seemed to thicken by a degree. It was suddenly harder to breathe. His throat burned. He brought a fist up to his mouth and coughed into it.

By the time Nick met up with Börne, the phantom fingertips were only inches from reaching Blackwood, all but ignoring Börne as he ran the camera with one hand and shook the sleeping mayor with the other.

"Asshole!" Börne yelled. "Wake the fuck up!"

The guy was pulling out all the stops. Which was good, because Nick didn't think he had it in him to speak to the mayor that way. Even though, speaking to the mayor that way was apparently what the situation was going to require.

The mayor finally showed signs of life just as one of the ghostly hands snaked in between him and Börne. The mayor's eyes burst open. Confusion overtook his face.

He screamed as the hand latched onto his leg.

Thin streams of white smoke billowed up from the mayor's pant leg. A sound like sizzling bacon accompanied the smoke. His grey slacks turned black and disintegrated.

"Son of a bitch!" Only then did Börne drop the camera to his side. Handing it to Nick, Börne took a deep breath. He grabbed hold of the glowing white arm, alarm registering on his face as soon as he came in contact. Börne powered through his obvious discomfort and wrenched the hand free of the mayor.

Eyes wide and clutching his injured leg, the mayor looked helplessly up at Börne and Nick.

"Come on, damn it!" Nick urged. "Don't just sit there!"

The mayor's attention turned back to the four hands about to engulf him. For a split second, Nick thought the old fool might be too frozen with fear to move. Thankfully, that proved not to be the case.

Already slumped deep in the seat, Blackwood slithered the rest of the way out, underneath the grasping hands, and onto the floor. Crawling on his hands and knees got him to the aisle. Börne grabbed the mayor under one arm. Nick grabbed him under the other. Together, they lifted the mayor to his feet and held him until his legs stabilized. Once the man's legs seemed up to the task of supporting his own bulk, they cautiously let go.

"Come on!" Nick shouted.

Neither he nor Börne looked back as they scaled the center aisle. Neither one of them thought to check on the mayor, not until they were at the doorway. If they had, they would have realized the mayor had only managed to reach the aisle's midway point before the silvery hands halted his progress.

One arm wrapped itself around the mayor's substantial belly, crumpling and burning his suit jacket, while another had ahold of his face. It covered his mouth and nose. Even in the relative darkness, Nick could see the mayor's eyes bulging nearly out of their sockets as smoke formed a cloud above him. Anywhere on the man's body where the screen hands touched generated the same sizzle and smoke.

Blackwood cried out in agony.

"Oh, my God!" Claudia gave voice to everyone's thoughts as they sucked in a collective breath.

"What do we do?" Nick immediately looked to Börne for the answer. It was reactionary. The man had proven himself a natural leader, and Nick was comfortable in his role as devoted follower.

Nick wasn't surprised when that leader once again stepped up.

Without a word to any of them, Börne turned back down the aisle, digging into his vest pocket as he picked up the pace. He didn't fumble. He didn't break stride.

"Here!" Nori handed Nick the camera, then followed in Börne's footsteps.

Nick raised the camcorder on a scene his eyes dared him to believe. All four hands clutched some part of the mayor now. Resembling half of an octopus, each tentacle-like arm worked independently. The mayor's attempts at screaming were stifled. His movement, bound. Smoke continued to waft from his body as the hands dragged him back toward the screen. One after another, his attempts at grasping the seat backs for leverage proved futile.

A haze of honest to goodness white smoke had developed and enveloped the auditorium.

It wasn't until Börne raised his hand over his head that Nick realized what he'd pulled from his pocket. Specifically, when the light from the screen glinted off the metal. Börne brought the knife down. The blade sliced through the arm that held its hand over the mayor's mouth. The arm disintegrated, vanishing into a puff of grey smoke and taking the hand with it.

The mayor gulped air like a tarpon in a cooler.

Nori grabbed the mayor by his arm and started pulling. He didn't come free, but she was at least able to slow the screen's progress.

The screen's progress.

A bizarre thought, to say the least. But that was the only way Nick could think of it. It was the *screen* that wanted the mayor. Not a spirit. Not Floyd.

The. Fucking. Screen.

Börne took a swipe at the arm that held the mayor's shoulder. Like the first, this arm and hand both disintegrated. Particle evidence of their demise plumed into the air, caught in the light of the screen's glow like dust in a ray of sun coming through a window.

Nick continued to run the camcorder, capturing all of Börne and Nori's heroics. Four animated barriers had kept Blackwood from making his exit. Börne had literally cut that number in half.

Nori slowly stepped her way up the aisle, pulling the mayor with her. Each severed limb made her task that much easier. Though none of what they were doing looked particularly easy, and Nick looked on in awe of their determination. Blackwood continued to sob and periodically cry out in either pain or fear. Nick could only hope that the mayor stayed on his feet long enough to make it out of the auditorium. Once in the lobby, with the doors shut behind him, he was free to collapse if he so chose.

Ten seconds and two arcs of Börne's blade later, the mayor was set free from the screen's grip altogether. The ordeal had left him injured and weak. Nori and Börne had to practically carry the man up the incline toward the waiting doors. His feet went through the motions of taking steps, but it was clear his wobbly legs alone weren't capable of supporting his weight.

Watching them struggle, Nick felt foolish just standing there running the camera. He also knew Börne wouldn't have it any other way. To the investigator, the footage of the mayor's rescue was more than likely more valuable than the mayor himself. To some degree, Nick had the most important job among them.

"Come on!" he urged. Nick tore his eyes from the trio long enough to check the status of the movie screen down front. He half expected to see more hands—or who knew what—reaching out from flat surface. *Reinforcements?* There were none. It was a plain old movie screen. As it should be. It was as if they had never been there to begin with.

But they had.

The burns on the mayor's suit and face were proof enough, regardless of what the cameras did or did not capture. Scorch marks darkened the suit's otherwise grey fabric in several spots. A hand print stretched from one cheek to the other like a pink sunburn across his face. As he passed by Nick on his way through the double doors, the fetor of burnt flesh competed with that of smoke and soot.

Nick tried to ignore the movie screen, but found it impossible to do so. His eyes kept returning, needing verification. It was all too surreal. All too unfathomable.

Claudia and Nori slammed the doors shut. And as the clamor echoed throughout the otherwise silent lobby, one thought registered in Nick's mind. Much like the mayor's once-pristine suit, none of them would be the same after that night. They now shared a scar, so deep, it would never truly fade.

TWENTY-NINE

"Mr. Mayor?"

Claudia was the first to speak. Everyone else stood wide-eyed and shell-shocked. By paranormal standards, they had just witnessed the equivalent of a car wreck resulting in white sheets littering the ground. Even the lobby remained silent, as if holding its breath, anxious to see what would happen next.

"Mayor Blackwood. Are you alright?"

The mayor slowly exchanged sheepish glances with everyone huddled around him. The skin on his face was already turning ten shades of pink and red. Either he also suffered from the group's collective loss for words, or the burns on his face made it too painful to speak. Tears filled the man's eyes. They rolled down his scorched cheeks as he leaned against the wall for support. And to top it all off, the front of his grey slacks, all down one leg, was darker than the rest. Not from the burns, but from fear.

"Nick?" Nori asked. "Do you have a first-aid kit around here?"

Nick nodded. "Yeah, I think so." Stepping toward the mayor, he asked, "John? Are you okay?"

Even when addressed by his first name, the mayor didn't react. He only stared hollowly at the others, his mind seemingly in a different dimension, in another time. He didn't so much as blink. Gone was the arrogance he traditionally wore like a fraternity pin. Gone was the aura of brute strength. The man was broken.

"Can't be," the mayor muttered to no one but himself. "Not possible."

Nick turned away, embarrassed to be witnessing someone's rock bottom.

Beside him, Börne subtly reached for the camcorder, which Nick was only too happy to surrender.

It was when Nori reached out her hand and touched his elbow, that the mayor pushed himself off the wall and turned away from the group. Without another word, without any indication as to where he was going, he stumbled his way through the lobby and out the front door. Like a shadow after sunset, Blackwood disappeared into the night. He'd given them no opportunity to say, "we told you so." Not that anyone would have. Cruelty at that level resided in none of them. Even as despicable as the mayor had been only a half hour before.

For several minutes, no one said a word. The calm of the lobby was a sharp contrast to the mayhem of the auditorium. And very much welcomed. Nick was still trying to process everything he'd just seen. He assumed their silence meant everyone else was as well, all of them dumbfounded in the light of everything.

Everyone, that was, except Börne, who was already eagerly fiddling with the camcorder.

When Claudia finally broke the silence, her uncharacteristic use of profanity provided some much-needed levity. "These fucking doors. Do we have to stand so close?"

*   *   *

"Way to be prepared," Nick said, as he and Börne followed

the ladies further into the lobby. "The knife, I mean. Must have seen some scary things in your line of work, huh?"

Börne shook his head. "Not really. I've carried a pocketknife since I was eight. Grandfather gave me my first. A small Solingen Bulldog with a bone handle. Never know when you'll need one."

Nick glanced over his shoulder at the auditorium doors. "Guess so."

Börne drew in a deep breath, then released it. He shook his head. "Never seen anything like that, actually." A hint of adrenaline still permeated his voice. "Surprised I didn't piss *my* pants."

When they reached the concession stand, Claudia embraced Börne, burying her face in his chest. He wrapped his arms around her shoulders and planted his chin atop her head. Soothing words passed by his lips.

A few feet away, Nori took Nick by the arm. Her slim fingers gently stroked the soft skin of its underside. "You okay?"

Nick nodded, offering a wan smile. "I'm alright. How about you, Wonder Woman?"

Nori's smile was just as weak as Nick's. "Never better."

Nobody said anything for several minutes. The storms, both outside and inside the auditorium, had passed, taking their theatrics with them. The night was calm. Peaceful.

When Nick finally did speak, it broke a seal that had bound them all. "Anyone want—"

"Screw it, I'm just gonna ask," Nori interrupted. "What in holy hell was that?"

"And did you see how it went right for the mayor?" Claudia asked. "In all the years—"

"It reached right past me!" Börne chimed.

"It went after the mayor like it knew him!"

"Like it had a score to settle."

"Kinda makes sense," Claudia said. Everyone stopped

talking and looked her way. "I mean, I would imagine Floyd might feel some blame toward the mayor for losing the theater."

Nods were offered from everyone involved as imaginations ran with that theory. Nick thought briefly of the piece of black tourmaline hanging around his neck. Thought also of the fact that the mayor—the only one of them who was attacked—was also the only one of them without a piece of the so-called protective gemstone. Coincidence or cause and effect? Nick would need more time to decide.

"And why did it burn when it touched him?" Nori asked.

"Right?" Börne, chimed. "The heat coming off the arms. My God, it felt like a coal furnace. Just glad my leather jacket…"

It went on like that for several more minutes. Questions came so fast that no one could stop asking them long enough to offer any real answers. It took more than a minute, but once their cache of questions was spent, the group once again fell silent. They searched each other's faces for explanations. They came up empty.

"So," Nick said eventually, "guess the only question left is, what does it all mean?"

The blank stares continued. It seemed Nick's latest was just another question in a long line without answers.

"I think we need to take a break." Claudia reached up and tucked a loose strand of hair behind her ear. "Floyd, the spirit, however we want to refer to him, is pretty riled up." Her statement came as a revelation to no one. She was greeted with knowing nods.

"This was the biggest…what do you call it…manifestation yet," Nori said. "And so aggressive."

"Right." Börne lifted one of his black cases onto the counter, started packing up his camcorders. "Something was definitely different this time around."

The mayor? Nick knew he couldn't be the only one thinking it.

"But, yes," Claudia continued, "I think we need to shut the investigation down. Just for a day or two. It's not safe. That'll give us time to do some more research and think this thing through. I may even make a phone call or two. Get some colleague's opinions on the matter. I mean, seriously, this is…" From that point, Claudia could only shake her head.

Börne snapped the clasp on the black case. He slid it off the counter and stood there as patient as a kid waiting for the okay to dive into their beggar's night haul. He turned to Nick. "Are you good with keeping the theater closed for a day or so?"

"Yeah, Nick," Nori chimed in. For the first time that night, a genuine smile cracked her stoic face. "Can you afford to lose that $22.50?"

Nick chuckled. He could afford to lose the little money he'd make over the next couple days a lot more than he could afford to lose his sanity.

Or worse.

THIRTY

"Two pair of hands."

Börne was talking to himself again, working his way through the Chamberlain case. It was his way; how he did things. With his laptop open on the desk in front of him, he reclined in the hotel's sad excuse for an office chair. "What does that mean, four hands? Pretty sure ol' Floyd only had the two."

The fact that they had witnessed such a salient manifestation of phenomena firsthand was unbelievable in its own right. To capture it on film was remarkable. Beyond remarkable. Astonishing. Yet, here he was, sitting in a darkened hotel room watching that very footage. He needed pinched. Despite the fear he'd felt at the time, Börne was all smiles now.

The paranormal community—hell, the entire world—would collectively shit themselves once it caught a glimpse of what F.A.U.S.T. had captured on film.

He couldn't get enough. While Claudia snored softly in the bed beside him, Börne ran the footage back once more, this time slower than before. He sat up straighter in the chair. He leaned in. With elbows on the desk and chin in hand, he watched the evening's events play out for the eighth time since returning to the room…

First, the lights in the theater flicker, brighten and then went out. A moment later, the night vision kicked in and everything turned varying shades of green. Then nothing—everything was calm—until the moment the movie screen illuminated the auditorium.

And all the while, the mayor sat slumped in his seat down in the lower right corner of the monitor.

Börne shook his head. The mayor was something else. Ignorant and arrogant, a bad combination. Not to mention rude. Still, it was hard for Börne not to feel some empathy for the poor bastard. The situation had progressed well beyond anything they'd prepared for. Much less anything they'd prepared *him* for. Börne shouldered his share of guilt. Whether or not that guilt was deserved was debatable. In the end, the mayor was simply in the wrong place at the wrong time. It was out of everyone's—

In the video, the movie screen gave birth to hands.

The emergence of the first two was gradual. Börne leaned in until his face could feel the heat coming off the screen. He slowed the footage even further. The hands, first one and then the other, pressed against the screen as if from behind. The screen gave and stretched outward. It was pushed well beyond what its construction should have allowed. And as he watched the second pair of hands sprout forth a moment later, Börne's focus turned to the Chamberlain's previous owner.

"So, what's the story, Floyd? It appears you have a friend we weren't aware of."

*   *   *

On the nightstand beside his bed, Nick's cell phone erupted.

He pried his eyes open, one and then the other. His shrieking ringtone had interrupted a very good dream, the interruption made more irritating by the fact that dreams had been few and far between as of late. Especially good ones. His hand blindly searched the nightstand, finding the lamp, the empty bottle of bourbon he'd swiped from his work desk, and a nearly-empty glass of watered-down sleep aid before finally landing on his phone.

Despite the stupor that held him in its clutches, Nick managed to find the talk button. He pushed it while clearing his throat. "Yeah?"

"Nick, you up? It's Börne."

Nick sighed. The man didn't have to introduce himself. Even while half asleep and with his mind desperately clinging to a fading dream, Nick recognized the accent.

"Did I wake you?"

Nick lifted his head and took a look around. His bedroom, not to mention the sky outside his window, was pitch black. *Did I wake you?* His eyes slowly adjusted to the red numbers on his bedside clock.

"Börne. It's three o'clock in the morning. What do you think?"

The silence on the other end was answer enough, and Nick considered letting it continue. Just maybe, given the opportunity, Börne would hang up. It wasn't likely, assuming Börne had a good enough reason for calling at that hour. Nick thought again of the dream that had now nearly vanished from memory. He ultimately decided that he wanted to know, had to know. So, he asked what was so damn important that it warranted the middle of the night phone call.

"I need you to come down to the theater." Börne's voice was edged with excitement. "There's something you need to see."

* * *

When Nick arrived at The Chamberlain, still groggy and bleary-eyed, Börne was waiting in the lobby. A camcorder and a paper cup with a hotel logo on it rested on the concession stand counter. Perfectly dressed for a Victorian funeral, Börne wore his usual black boots, black slacks, white button up, black and red vest, and a long black frock with large silver buckles running down the right side. It was the same outfit he'd worn the night before. Nick concluded the man probably hadn't been to bed yet. Maybe giving the investigator a key and after-hours access to the theater hadn't been such a good idea. When Börne had initially asked about investigating on his own, Nick hadn't seen an issue with it. Summoning him in the wee hours of the night might changed matters.

"This could be huge!" Börne wrung his hands, shuffled his weight from one foot to the other, then back. His eyes were lively despite the early hour. Nick couldn't tell if the man was really excited, nervous, or if that cup of coffee on the counter was just one in a line of many. Börne stripped off his frock, folded it over his arm, and then laid it on the counter. He swiped the camcorder, and before Nick could ask what the hell Börne thought was so huge, the investigator turned and started toward the auditorium. "Come on."

Nick watched him go, slow to follow. Unlike Börne, he hadn't had coffee yet. Not that he hadn't considered grabbing some on the way over. He'd refrained in the hopes of returning to bed at some point in the near future. The lack of caffeine was also a convenient excuse. Nick was lagging behind because, quite simply, he wasn't mentally ready to deal with The Chamberlain's auditorium just yet.

Especially if Börne really had found something 'huge.'

Nick covered his mouth with a fist and let out a massive yawn. Through squinted eyes, he briefly considered the cup of coffee Börne had left unattended on the counter. Ultimately, and through a ridiculous amount of effort and will power, he decided against grabbing it.

"Ah hell."

Nick dragged his feet along the linoleum floor, following the path Börne had set.

"I couldn't sleep." Börne stood waiting outside the auditorium doors.

"Really?" Nick said. "I was doing just fine." It was only a partial lie, but a lie nonetheless. He had, in fact, been sleeping well. Very well. It had just taken an unhealthy amount of bourbon to get him there. Which quite possibly had something to do with why he was dragging ass, too.

Börne turned away from Nick and his remark. Instead of entering the auditorium, though, he started down the long hallway where Nick's office and storage room were located. "So, I thought I'd come over," he continued, "and do a walk through with my EMF meter."

"You're a fun guy, Börne. I can tell."

Börne stopped, turned, and eyed Nick quizzically. "What do you mean?"

Nick chuckled, waved him off. "Never mind."

Börne shrugged and continued down the sloping hallway. "So, I'm walking around the auditorium, finding nothing of interest. Then I started thinking back to last night's events. You know, with the screen. Its behavior, I guess you'd say. So, I walked up to it—"

Nick stopped. "Wait a second. The screen? Why the hell would you wanna do that? Just how short is your memory?"

Börne stopped, looked back at Nick.

"Uh, because that's how you investigate?" Börne smiled. "Don't worry. I propped the doors open and would have high-tailed it out had anything happened."

Nick stared at the investigator with his jaw slightly slack.

Börne continued. "Anyway, I go up to the screen and the meter suddenly goes apeshit—"

Nick raised his hand. "Hold on. Germans use the word, 'apeshit?'"

"They do when they've lived in the States for over ten years." Börne smiled like a schoolboy who'd just found out the girl on the monkey bars liked him. "And…when we come across something like this."

They continued down the narrow hallway, their footsteps echoing through the dimly lit corridor. They passed the door to Nick's office first, then the one to the small storage room. The occasional wall sconce lit most of the way, but as they neared the end, darkness awaited.

"Another stupid question for ya," Nick said. "If the screen made your EMF meter go apeshit, then why are we out here in the hallway? Why aren't we checking out the screen?"

"Ah," Börne said, raising both his eyebrows and index finger. "Because, I don't believe the energy was coming from the screen last night."

"Oh? Did you not see—"

"It was coming from *behind* the screen."

Nick's brow pulled off a classic furrow. "Behind it?" He shook his head. "Not possible. There's nothing behind the screen except a wall. Behind that, an alley. And I've been in that alley. Trust me, there's nothing out there except cigarette butts, broken beer bottles, and a trash dumpster that smells like something crawled inside and died."

"Well, my friend, I hate to contradict you. But I think you're wrong."

Nick guffawed. "Seriously. If you smelled it—"

"Not the dumpster," Börne said, resting his hand on the wall that ended the hallway. "I think you're wrong about there not being anything behind the screen."

THIRTY-ONE

"I think there's a room on the other side of this wall."

Nick stepped up beside Börne and looked the wall at the end of the hallway up and down. It was difficult to see much of anything in the dim light. He could, at most, take stock of its location in relation to the auditorium. Where they stood coincided with the front of the auditorium, down near the screen. Börne was right about that much. Nick turned to him.

"So…"

Börne nodded. "Behind the screen."

"Like some kind of—"

"Secret room." Even in the shadows, Börne's smile shone brightly. "In fact, I'd bet money on it."

Nick placed a hand on the wall, ran it back and forth over the red and gold striped wallpaper, now only a few months old. There had been no mention of The Chamberlain having a secret room; not that he had ever heard of. As far as he knew, the theater consisted of the lobby, auditorium, control room, office, and storage room. Any other rooms would have been detected during renovation, wouldn't they?

Not if it was a secret one.

Nick tried to find the seams in the wallpaper, but there were no raised edges where the strips met. No subtle humps or divots.

No evidence of anything impermanent about the wall. He even rapped his knuckles against it. Solid. Like any other.

Börne raised the camcorder, flipped on the LED light mounted on top, and handed it to Nick. From his vest pocket, he pulled out a cell phone and swiftly brought the screen to life.

Together, they directed their lights at the narrow wall. Up and down, side to side. They left no corner or wallpaper seam undetected. Still, they found nothing. If there was a secret door or panel present, it was hidden pretty damn well.

"Guess that's why they call them *secret* rooms." Nick lowered the camcorder. "And not 'come on in and make yourself at home' rooms."

Börne turned to the right, slapped his hand on the adjacent wall that ran the length of the hallway. "What's on the other side of *this* wall?"

That was an easier question to answer. "Storage room," Nick said.

Börne raised his eyebrows. "Then let's have a look at this storage room."

Nick led Börne back to the last doorway they'd passed. Camcorder tucked under his arm, Nick held his collection of keys up to its light and began sorting through. Growing up, his father had been the maintenance manager for several area apartment complexes. His enormous key ring was perpetually packed full of jangly keys. All combined, they represented a massive jumble of authority and pride in Nick's eyes. Now that he had amassed a respectable set of keys himself, Nick saw them for what they truly were: a time-sucking pain in the ass.

After finally finding the silver key marked in black Sharpie with a large "S," Nick unlocked the door and swung it inward.

Darkness welcomed them.

Nick ran his hand along the wall just inside the doorway. Finding the light switch, he gave it a flip. A long, fluorescent bulb illuminated the room, painting the otherwise blank walls with charcoal-colored shadows. All in all, the space wasn't much larger than a walk-in closet. It felt even smaller due to everything one would expect to find in a theater's storage room. Cardboard boxes filled with everything from paper cups to boxes of candy to toilet paper and hand soap lined the walls. A tall garbage can full of rolled up movie posters sat in one corner. Towering stacks of metal movie reel containers sat in another. The posters, Nick had acquired to hand out at special events. The old film reels had been unceremoniously gifted, left behind by the previous owner, and had been collecting dust for as long as Nick had been there. Nobody had touched the storage room or office during renovations. Nick had concentrated his money on the areas of the theater that mattered most: the lobby, control room, and auditorium. After all, the 4D movie experience didn't come cheap.

Börne went immediately to the stacks of film reels. One by one, he began sliding the metal cases away from the wall. The scraping of metal against the concrete floor pierced the room's placidity and sent a shiver coursing through Nick's shoulders. He wasn't sure what the investigator was looking for. He wasn't sure Börne even knew. Still, he wasn't raised to be the guy who stands around watching others do all of the work.

Nick tossed his keys onto a nearby carton, slid the trashcan of movie posters away from the wall, and set about inspecting Börne's wall from the opposite corner.

Within minutes, a determination had been made: the wall was as common as any other. They'd found no loose panels, no areas that sounded hollow when tapped on. If there was a secret room, it was certainly living up to its name. Nick's doubt grew with each passing minute, with each square foot of wall they inspected and subsequently ruled out. It wasn't like experts were incapable of being wrong. Especially experts on something as unsubstantiated as the paranormal.

Nick checked his watch.

His heart sank.

One would never know from inside the windowless room, or anywhere in the theater except the lobby, but dawn was approaching. His chances of catching a few more hours of shut-eye were quickly slipping away. There was almost no going back to bed at this point. Which made caffeine all the more necessary.

Nick was about to suggest a java run when Börne interrupted his thoughts.

"Wait a second." Börne studied the far wall, where an electrical panel peeked out from behind cardboard boxes.

"Okay?"

Börne pointed to the room next door. "When we were in your office last night," he said, "didn't I see an electrical panel?"

He did. Nick had needed to access it a couple of times in the waning days of the renovation. The new popcorn popper kept overloading and tripping the circuit breaker. An upgrade was performed and the problem was solved. Nick relayed this information to Börne.

The investigator's shoulders did a quick up and down. "We're a long way from most of your mechanicals. Not sure why the theater would need two electrical panels in this area."

Nick considered it. "There are two in the control room."

Börne considered that, then nodded. "Makes sense in there. But, back here?" His attention returned to the metal panel that now seemed not only out of place, but highly unnecessary.

A mountain of cardboard sat in front of the suspect panel. Börne approached and began removing boxes from the top of the summit. When the mountain had been reduced to a small hill, he nudged it aside with his boot and studied the metal door.

"Let's see what we have here." Börne reached up and grabbed the panel's latch.

A low rumble reverberated throughout the room. The stack of film reels rattled and chattered against one another. Movie posters danced like popcorn inside the trash can. Börne pulled his hand back from the panel.

The rumbling ceased.

Nick and Börne exchanged a look.

"What the...?" Nick let the question run out of steam. Eyes wide, he nodded toward the panel. "Again."

Börne placed his hand on the metal door.

This time, nothing happened. No vibration. No rumble.

Were their minds playing tricks? Were their imaginations getting the better of them? Neither was likely, Nick thought. They couldn't both be imagining the same phenomenon.

After a full half-minute of inactivity, Börne shrugged. He reached up, engaged the latch and opened the panel door.

The tiny hinges creaked, protesting the notion of being put to work.

What lay on the other side of the thin metal door were the insides of an ordinary electrical panel, only much older. Corrosion, dust, and more than one spider's handywork covered the tubular fuses. The handwritten notations along the side, indicating which fuse was for which mechanical, had long since faded.

"Looks old as hell," Nick said, interrupting a well-developed silence. "Original?"

Börne frowned, seemingly unconvinced. "Maybe."

"Probably explains it," Nick offered. "More than likely, it was just easier to install a new panel than to go through the hassle of bringing this one up to code."

"Ordinarily, I would agree with you." Börne looked at Nick with a sparkle in his eye. "If this were an actual working panel."

Nick didn't understand the inference and said as much.

"This," Börne said, tapping on the panel's façade, "this panel is a dummy. A fake."

Nick wasn't sure he followed. It certainly looked real to him. "And how do you know this?"

"Simple. Before Claudia and I decided to take this paranormal hobby full-time, I spent my twenties as an electrician's apprentice." Börne ran his fingers along both edges of the panel, apparently in search of something. What that something was, Nick had no idea. He did, however, recognize the 'a-ha' moment on Börne's face when the investigator found it.

"Bingo."

There were two soft clicks and the squeal of metal sliding free. The electrical panel swung away from the wall. What was left in its place was a large cavity of mostly nothingness. No holes in the wall, no wiring passing through. Just a black rectangular box with a long iron lever, its thick, grey paint chipped and peeling.

Börne looked back at Nick, his grin now a broad-based smile. "Tell me you're not dying to pull that."

*   *   *

Nick was familiar with secret doors, secret rooms. He was, after all, a product of the Scooby Doo age, where the use of such plot devices ran rampant. But he had never seen a secret room in person, much less been inside one. Haunted fun houses had never been his thing. He didn't grow up in a Victorian-era home. When it came to secret rooms and passageways, Nick was an unabashed virgin.

One that was about to lose that designation.

He took in a deep breath, held it, and pulled the lever.

A series of three loud, heavy metal thunks echoed in the tiny storage room.

With a whoosh of air several decades in the making, a section of the back wall separated itself from the rest. Two vertical seams ran from floor to ceiling. The section of wall, roughly the width of a door, sat inset from the main wall by a couple of inches.

Nick released his own long-held breath, then looked to Börne. If the investigator's chest was pounding as hard as Nick's, it didn't show through his getup. His eyes were on fire, though. A child's eagerness played across his face.

Börne nodded to the camcorder sitting on a box beside Nick.

Nick picked up the camera and proceeded to press the power button, despite feeling wholly unprepared for what its lens might capture.

Börne walked over and placed both hands on the moveable section of wall. "Are we ready?"

Nick was not. To be fair, he doubted he ever would be. Börne, on the other hand, showed no signs of fear or anxiety. Only adrenalized excitement registered in his character. The look on his face told the story: there was no turning back now. It was obvious the man was in the right business. It was just as obvious that Nick had made the right choice in bringing in F.A.U.S.T. Nick only hoped his trembling hands wouldn't broadcast his own level of fear when Börne reviewed the footage later on.

Nick verified the flashing red dot on the viewfinder and nodded.

Börne took in and let out a deep breath, then started pushing.

A sorrowful creaking sound hit their ears.

Years of immobility giving way to progress.

Once the section of wall had slid back a few inches, the left side caught and locked into place. The right side, however, continued to move. Specifically, it swung inward. A moment later, Börne stopped pushing and took a step back. The resulting doorway opened large enough for an adult man to slip through.

Or two.

Which was Nick's fear, him running the camera and all. His empty stomach knotted up. Not for the first time he fantasized about being back in his bed, lonely as it sometimes was.

"So, uh, should we say that prayer or anything?"

Still mesmerized by the open doorway, Börne shook his head. "That's kinda Claudia's thing."

Nick thought back to the night before and the mayor. "Tourmaline?" he asked. "'Cause I left mine—"

Börne shook his head. "Claudia."

Nick offered a scowl. "So, what are you saying? You don't believe in that stuff?"

"Oh, I do," Börne said. "Just not as much as she does." Dropping his eyes to the floor, Börne nodded his head. "I know, it's become a topic of discussion around our house from time to time. She says that if I knew what she knew, I'd take it more seriously. And it's not like I don't, it's just, well, I doubt we'll be needing it. If that makes you feel any better. I mean, here at The Chamberlain, all manifestations have occurred inside the auditorium. Am I right?"

Nick nodded despite the fact Börne wasn't looking his way.

When Börne finally did turn and look back at Nick, adrenaline blazed in his eyes. "So? Rock, paper, scissors?"

Nick shook his head. "Oh, hell no." He extended an inviting hand. "Lead the way."

And that's exactly what Börne did. Turning his cell's screen on, he slipped through the opening and was instantly swallowed up by a blackness that now awaited Nick.

THIRTY-TWO

The smell was the first thing to greet him. Even before the pitch-black. There was must. There was dust. The usual suspects one would expect from a room that's been closed up for who knew how long. But it was the overwhelming scents of residual smoke and charred paper that reached out like an overeager salesman, grabbing Nick by the gut before he was fully through the doorway. The brute force of it caused him to recoil.

"Son of a…"

Nick pulled the collar of his shirt up over his nose while searching the darkness for Börne. The room was windowless, void of any and all light, save for the ones they brought in.

"Hey, man, where'd you go?" Nick swung the camera to the right, finding nothing but a shadowy wall. The room extended to the left, so he swung the camcorder in that direction. When he briefly caught Börne in his light, Nick started. Börne's visage appeared ghostly in the ray of light. The sight of someone standing there caught Nick off guard, even though he'd expected to come across him.

"Chill out, dude," Nick whispered to himself.

He took a deep breath, exhaled, and brought the camcorder back around, training the bright LED light on Börne.

Börne raised his hand, shielding his eyes. "Nick. Seriously."

Nick lowered the light until it no longer shown on Börne's face. "Sorry."

Their words bounced back and forth in a hollow echo. The room felt tight. Small, like a cave. A chill filled its air.

"Gotta be a light switch somewhere," Börne said, scanning his cell light around the doorway.

Nick turned his light on the rest of the room.

An array of charred and smoke-damaged wooden crates lined a wall on one side of the room. Of traces of their packing straw remained. The tops of two round and very old wooden tables leaned against one wall, their legs removed and stacked on the dingy concrete floor beside them. A heap of wooden chairs held the tables in place. Everything was covered in fine layers of black soot and what looked to be ash. Including the structure standing against the far wall, which itself seemed to cut the room off at an awkward angle.

"Behold!" Börne said, and Nick jumped. The impersonation was a near perfect Vincent Price. "The proverbial writing on the wall." Then, Börne dropped the Vincent Price voice, and in his normal voice asked, "any idea what this means?"

Nick preferred the normal voice. This expedition was creepy enough without either of them making it moreso. Shaking off the chill that Börne had sent through him, Nick stepped up beside the investigator. He raised the camcorder and married its light with Börne's.

The stone wall beside the doorframe had once served double duty as a chalkboard. An entire section was smeared with old chalk marks, still visible beneath a transparent layer of black soot and ash. Nick leaned in and blew on the wall. The ashy black powder came away from the wall and disappeared into the dark. Words had clearly been written on the wall. They had also been erased and rewritten many times over. Only four chalk-scribbled words remained…

Corn…brown…foot juice…butts…

"What the hell is foot juice?" Börne shined his light all around the large doorway. If he was searching for more words, his search came up empty.

Nick smiled on the inside. Not because he was thrilled about the scent of smoke currently permeating his clothes, but because he knew what the words meant. Add them to other items he'd seen in the room, and Nick basked in the opportunity to teach Börne something for a change. He had learned of these things in college. Specifically, in his course on Early 20th Century America. It was a 7:30 am class, which meant he slept through more than his share of lectures. There were a few subject matters, however, that he found interesting enough to keep his eyes propped open. And in those days, the only topic that captured his attention more than pretty coeds had been alcohol.

"It's a shopping list," Nick said, turning and shining the camera's light around the room. "This was a speakeasy." Nick turned back to Börne, whose face looked ghostly pale and shadowy in the camera's downturned light. "That's what this room was used for at one time. That's why it was hidden and kept secret."

A furrowed brow spoke to Börne's question before he voiced it. "What the hell's a speakeasy?"

Nick chuckled. "Like a private club. A secret drinking establishment back in the 1920s and 30s. Back when alcohol was illegal."

Börne's jaw dropped. His eyes grew in size. "Wait a second. There was a time in this country when alcohol was illegal?"

Nick nodded. "We called it Prohibition."

"Wow," Börne said, nudging a nearby crate with his boot. The sound of clinking glass came from inside. "You Americans are way too uptight."

Nick snickered. "Says the guy dressed like Queen Victoria's

butler.""

Börne laughed. "Touché, my friend. Touché."

"Anyway," Nick said, returning the camera's light to the words scribbled just inside the doorway. "Corn means bourbon. Brown is Scotch. Foot juice is another term for cheap wine, I think. Butts would mean cigarettes."

"Scotch, bourbon, cheap wine," Börne said. "Now that's my kind of shopping list."

Nick turned and shined the camcorder's light onto the far wall. "Might not have to go far."

Covering the entire stone wall was a stout system of wooden shelving. From one end to the other, a good fifteen feet across, the shelves stretched from floor to ceiling. On those shelves, an array of black, wooden crates took up nearly every square inch of space. And resting in those crates were, by Nick's estimation, several hundred glass bottles of Prohibition-era contraband. All of which was coated with black soot. Though, not a fine layer like that which covered everything else in the room. The soot and ash on the crates and shelves had been disturbed. Smeared. Smudged. Even wiped clean in some places.

Börne's whistle brushed past Nick's ear. "Any chance they're still full?"

"Only one way to find out."

As Börne made his way over to the wall, Nick felt his shoulders sag. Not in a bad way. Discovering that The Chamberlain did, indeed, possess a secret room had initially filled him with unbridled anxiety. His vivid imagination had devised all sorts of macabre and deviant reasons for its existence. Finding out it was used for drinking and gambling, and not a serial killer's torture chamber, was allowing some of that tension to ease.

"Empty," Börne said, dropping a bottle into one of the wooden crates. A hollow clank cut through the dark as the bottle returned to its original resting place.

Nick wondered what other treasures the secret room might hold. The tables and chairs, crates full of liquor bottles, and the writing on the wall told the story of a run of the mill speakeasy. None of it, however, explained the soot and ash that seemed to cover everything in the room. Everything except the floor, that is. It had been cleaned to an extent. Possibly mopped. Hints of dark swirls remained where the mop water had become too soiled to be efficient. Turning away, Nick left Börne to investigate the vast inventory of bottles alone.

The table and chairs showed the same thin layer of black as everything else. Nick ran his finger along the leg of an upturned chair. He smelled the residue on his finger. It smelled of paper or wood. All signs pointed to a small fire having taken place in the room. It would have made sense if some of the patrons in the speakeasy had been smoking in the room and caught something on fire. What didn't make sense was that the soot and ash coated the tables and chairs where it sat against the wall. Like the fire had happened after the speakeasy had already been shut down.

But who…?

Nick let it go. It was too early in the morning to think too hard. In fact, now that they'd discovered the room behind the movie screen, Nick was ready to leave. They could return later with better lighting. Better lighting and a shop vac. He was about to suggest as much when his thoughts were interrupted.

"Now we're talking!" Börne's voice cut through the quiet like a thrown axe. He held out an unopened bottle toward Nick. "You a gin man, Nick?"

Nick took the cloudy bottle. Tilting it toward the camera's light, he read the yellowed label. "Booth's? Never heard of it. Not sure I've ever tried gin."

At the very edge of Nick's light, Börne smiled like a kid separated from his parents and locked inside a candy store.

"Your life's about to change, my friend."

Nick set the eighty-year-old bottle of liquor on one of the chairs. "Ya know," he said, "I think you were on to something, Börne. Pretty sure we're directly behind the scree—"

Something brushed Nick's ear.

He ducked, picturing a spider swinging by its ass string, He cringed. He despised spiders. No creature on Earth should have that many legs. He could practically hear the tip-tip-tip of those hairy legs crawling across the floor and over his head.

Nick immediately swatted the unknown object with the back of his hand. It swung away. A second later, it swung back and hit him again. Without thinking, Nick reached up and grasped the object, intent on yanking it down and quickly casting it aside. As soon as it was in hand, however, he realized what it was. It wasn't a spider. It wasn't a creepy crawly at all.

It was a pull string for a light bulb.

Relief washed through Nick.

He was set to give the string a tug when the darkness exploded. Not with light, but with sound.

THIRTY-THREE

Börne's shout was brief, cut short by a deafening crash.

The shattering and splintering of glass and wood.

Nick recoiled as shrapnel pelted his legs. A bottle pinwheeled off his ankle bone. He yelped and bit his lip. He retreated from the chaos a couple of steps, losing the pull string in the process.

It sounded as if the room was collapsing in on itself.

When the mayhem finally settled, only two sounds could be heard: liquid dripping onto the concrete floor.

And Nick's heavy breathing.

"Börne!" Nick swung the camcorder back to where he'd left Börne standing. The investigator was gone. To Nick's horror, so was a large section of the shelving. Only a bare brick wall remained behind.

"What the…"

A brief clinking of bottles. A creak of old wood. A thick gurgling sound, like someone gargling with motor oil.

Nick turned the camcorder toward the floor. A cold inhale caught in his throat. He couldn't see Börne buried beneath the mountain of shelving, crates, and broken bottles. He could only hear him. And the sounds turned Nick's stomach.

"My God!" Nick raised the camera, used its light to search for the pull string. He didn't even know if the lights inside the room still worked. He had to try. He would need both hands free if he had any hope of lifting the massive section of shelving. The structure itself had to weigh several hundred pounds, at least. That wasn't even counting the crates, some of which still held their contents. He also feared what condition he would find Börne in underneath it all. If there was ever a situation that called for light and being able to see what you were doing, this was it.

The gurgling continued to drift up from beneath the pile.

Nick reached for the string above his head. In his rush to do so, his fingertips grazed it and sent it swinging.

"Shit!"

His heart pounded. Panic gripped him by the back of the neck. Nick continued to search the air, his hand trembling. His fingers grazed the string, lost it, then found it again. This time, he held on. Held on like Börne's life depended on it, well, because...

Nick wasted no time in giving the string a yank.

The darkness was instantly reduced to a collection of scattered shadows. A row of three yellow light bulbs hung from the ceiling. Together, they illuminated the narrow room.

One bulb burst immediately, extinguishing itself. The light inside the room dimmed by a good measure. Within seconds, one of the two remaining bulbs followed suit, cutting Nick's ability to see in half.

"Come on!" Nick shouted. The third light bulb had to cooperate. It had to stay lit. *Had to!*

He realized he couldn't waste time waiting to find out.

Setting the camcorder on a nearby box, Nick rushed to where the section of shelving teetered atop splintered crates, broken bottles, and Börne. The task seemed insurmountable. The structure, so stout. His mind flashed to stories of frantic mothers lifting cars off of toddlers. Nick hoped his own white-hot adrenaline would help him perform what felt like an equally daunting feat.

"Hold on, man!" Nick wasn't sure Börne could hear him. It didn't stop him from extending the line of communication. Until he knew differently, he would hold out hope. "Gonna get you out! Just hold on!"

For a moment, Nick feared he might be lying. The wooden structure was slow to cooperate. It was even heavier than he'd anticipated. Even with his back strained, the shelving raised only slightly. Two, three inches at most. It released a groan of defiance. Unable to maintain his grip, the structure fell back onto the pile of debris.

"Shit!"

Sweat broke across Nick's forehead, trickled down the back of his neck. He wiped his head with his bandaged arm. Was the room getting warmer? He wasn't sure. The stench, however, was certainly growing stronger. Nick coughed. He put the room's changing atmosphere out of his mind and refocused. It was the sudden onset of silence that worried him most.

The gurgling had stopped.

"Börne?" Nick's pulse raced. Blood pumped through his ears. His heart threatened to beat its way out of his chest. "Hang in there, buddy!"

Nick wiped his damp hands on his jeans before attempting to lift the unit again. This time, he knew what he was up against and bettered his grip. This time, there was progress. Glass tinkled to the floor as the structure rose into the air. He managed to raise it only a few inches, but it was enough. With his arms and back protesting the load, Nick shuffled a few steps to his left, dragging the top of the shelving unit with him. One foot slipped, then the other. A growing pool of blood and liquor made the trek a slippery one.

When his grip was about to give out, Nick lowered the shelving onto a wooden crate. It teetered precariously, but remained in place. He raised and relieved the ache in his back.

Then he gasped.

Börne's face.

It was unrecognizable. Crimson painted it, leaving no trace of skin unmasked. Blood bubbled from a gash across the bridge of Börne's nose. Slivers of glass protruded from both face and body. It was the jagged top half of an amber-colored bottle sticking out of his throat that had done the most severe damage. It had sliced through skin and muscle without impediment and had driven itself deep.

Nick had to remind himself to breathe.

He stood frozen over Börne's ruined body. The investigator lay motionless, eyes wide, mouth agape. He made no sound. The only movement, a subtle twitch of his right hand. As Nick stood watching, it too came to a stop.

The conclusion Nick came to was a difficult one. Börne was gone. There was nothing he could do, and Nick's focus started to shift. Even though he was sure it was too late, he needed to get help. He needed to alert someone.

He needed to exit this fuckin' room.

When he turned to go, Nick's heart stopped.

The room apparently had other plans. The door leading out was closed.

Fear unleashed a frozen river. Ice crystals flowed through his veins, chilling his insides. Nick placed his hands on the slab of wood. He was certain they'd left the door open. He was the last one through, and he hadn't closed it. He was pretty sure Börne hadn't, either. Why would he? They had no reason to close it, and every reason in the world not to.

Nick ran his hands over the door. Just like on the outside, there wasn't a handle on the inside, either. *How do you open a door without a handle?* He pushed the edge of the door abruptly, hoping to pop it open somehow. He slid his fingers over the seams in search of a latch or trigger. That's where his hopes died. The door to the secret room offered no indication of how to open it. Much like the room itself, the trick to opening the door from the inside was meant to remain a secret.

Sweat now streamed down Nick's face. The walls were definitely closing in, the sparse amount of air in the room less willing to give itself up. He pounded the door with his fists. He kicked it, not once, but twice. Nick screamed for help. It was a fool's errand. There was no one in the theater to hear.

Nick fell silent.

Or was there?

Nick glanced around the shadowy room before closing his eyes. He took in a deep breath, then released it slowly. It was a crazy thought. A terrifying notion. He tried to force it from his mind, tried to reject it. The last thing he needed was another...manifestation.

He shook his head, unable to let it go.

Was there someone, something, in the room with him?

Opening his eyes, Nick placed his back against the door, and once again surveyed the room. There was no denying it. Perfectly sturdy shelving units don't just topple on their own. Doors don't just close. And it wasn't as if The Chamberlain hadn't already set the precedent. Absurd as it might seem, the idea that he wasn't alone in the room was the only explanation that actually made sense.

Nick used his already saturated bandage to wipe sweat from his eyes. He sucked in another deep breath. He couldn't believe what he was about to do, what he once would have considered unthinkable.

He had no choice.

"Floyd?"

Nick's voice echoed off the stone walls. The sound of it within the quiet room caused the hair to stand on the back of his neck. He thought of Claudia and the first time she'd tried to summon The Chamberlain's previous owner.

Claudia.

His heart wanted to break at the thought of her. His eyes wanted to tear up. Nick shook himself free of the emotion. He shoved the pain down into a cavern somewhere deep. There would be time enough for heartache later.

"F-Floyd," he repeated. "Are you here?"

A bottle slid from its crate near Börne's lifeless body. It clanked onto the concrete floor and rolled out from under the heap, the label counting off each revolution. The green bottle didn't stop until it had made its way across the room to Nick's feet.

His blood ran cold.

His spine tingled.

His question had been answered.

THIRTY-FOUR

Claudia opened her eyes.

A shallow sense that something was wrong greeted her.

She sat up in bed, pulling the comforter up to her chest. Reaching for Börne, she found only a cool sheet. Her husband's side of the bed was empty. She looked over at the desk where Börne had been working before she drifted off to sleep. A streetlight outside the window spotlighted the chair. It, too, was empty.

"Börne?"

A large mirror flanked the wall at the foot of the bed. In it, she could faintly see the bathroom door. It stood partially open, revealing nothing but pitch inside.

"*Liebling?*"

A feeling of dread woke the butterflies in her stomach. A long time had passed since she'd last experienced that feeling. Not so long, however, that she would have forgotten. The last time she'd felt it, like something was seriously wrong, her intuition had been dead on.

Which didn't soothe her soul one bit.

Casting off the comforter, Claudia swung her legs over the side of the bed. Her slippers awaited her at the foot, as did her robe. She sidestepped them both on her way to the bathroom.

"Börne?"

She didn't wait for an answer. Wasn't sure she expected one. Claudia pushed the door open and reached for the light. The sudden brightness made her squint. She looked behind the door, pulled back the shower curtain. The bathroom, like the rest of the hotel room, was empty. Claudia returned the bathroom to darkness and walked out.

She was at a loss. Where the hell could he be? Had he gone downstairs to the lobby? Outside? Börne was certainly no stranger to late-night walks. They helped clear his head, helped him to think. Especially when they were engrossed in a difficult case. But he always left a—

Claudia went to the desk and turned on the tiny lamp. She found Börne's laptop, a half-empty bag of pretzels from the vending machine, and two pens and a small notepad, all three emblazoned with the hotel's name and logo. What she didn't find were any scraps of paper or scribbled-on napkins. No note whatsoever. She lifted Börne's laptop and felt the underneath. It was cool to the touch. He had, more than likely, been gone awhile. Setting the laptop down, she noticed the cord to his cell phone charger. One end was plugged into the nearby wall. The other hung limp off the side of the desk.

Hope seeped into Claudia's heart. Börne had taken his cell phone, something he didn't always remember to do when his mind was consumed with work. She'd chided him about it on occasion, and he'd promised to try harder moving forward.

Grabbing her own cell off the nightstand, she checked it for messages. The screen was blank. No texts. No calls. Biting her lip, she brought up Börne's contact info and hit the call button. As she waited for the call to go through, Claudia used her thumbnail to pry at the small gap between her two front teeth. She stared out the second story window, where night was just giving way to morning. Except for a white and black squad car slowly making its rounds, the street below was empty. The buildings across the way showed very few lights in their windows. Angler Bay was still asleep.

A single ring came through the phone, then a voice.

But it wasn't the voice she'd hoped to hear.

"I'm sorry. The person you are trying to reach is unavailable."

*   *   *

"Shit."

Nick stared at the green bottle at his feet. He ran his hand through his increasingly dampening hair. "Shit. Shit. Shit."

When he'd first considered calling out to the Chamberlain's previous owner, he'd failed to consider what he would do if he got an answer. And if a bottle mysteriously rolling across the floor wasn't an answer, he'd hate to see what an answer might look like.

"Floyd," Nick started, making it up as he went. "I need out. I need to get help for my friend."

It was a lie. He was no doctor, but even Nick knew that Börne was dead. He was gambling on the hope the spirit wouldn't be as observant. The *vengeful* spirit, he reminded himself, who may or may not be responsible for Börne being in that state in the first place.

Nick also wondered what the repercussions were for trying to deceive a vengeful spirit.

Tread softly, ol' buddy.

Silence controlled the room. Nothing stirred. The only hint of movement came from the flashing red light on the camcorder, signaling that it was still recording. Everything remained as still as when he and Börne had first discovered the secret room. How long had it been? Minutes? An hour? Nick had no idea. He only knew he didn't care to stay any longer.

After getting no response to his plea, Nick returned his efforts to finding his own way out.

He ran his hands along the walls beside the door. There had to be a panel, a switch, something. There had to be a way out. In the days of the speakeasy, the door would have been kept closed. Even if there were patrons inside. *Especially* if there were patrons inside. There had to be a way of opening the door from inside the room, purely for safety reasons. Nick ran his hands along the edges.

"Come on, dammit!"

Coming up empty yet again, Nick's panic began to feel more like anger. He punched the door. The hollow thud resonated in the room's thick air, but that was it. He'd achieved nothing, receiving only bruised knuckles for his effort. A wooden chair sat nearby. He kicked at it, then grabbed it and swung it through the air, smashing the chair against the door. A barrage of splintered wood ricocheted and flew in his direction as the chair disintegrated in his hands.

He heard a giggle.

Nick spun around, dropping the chair's legs, the only parts that remained. "What the—?"

His heart was in his throat. Was he seriously hearing things now? Had he really just heard…laughter? He couldn't be sure. It had been faint, brief, making little sense. He snorted. *Tell me, Nick. What about this whole fucked up situation* does *make sense?*

Sweat now soaked his hair and shirt. He was dehydrated, could feel it. Light-headed. Dry-mouthed. Perhaps he was hallucinating. Perhaps…

Nick tried to forget the phantom laughter. At the very least, he needed to stow it in the back of his mind for processing later when his mind was more reliable. He chuckled at the thought. *A reliable mind.* When would he ever possess one of those again?

The whole ordeal was reminiscent of opening night and his drug-fueled hallucinations. The only difference this time was that it was real. Every horrifying detail. No matter how much he wished them not to be.

For the first time since that night, Nick actually wished he had a stomach full of too much Xanax. It would be better than the alternative.

Nick leaned his back against the wall and slid down to the floor. Scared, angry, and growing increasingly exhausted, he lowered his head. He cradled it in his hands, the weight of his circumstances nearly too heavy for him to bear. The voice of reality was determined to make things worse. It crept up to his ear and whispered: *Nobody will be coming to look for you.* And it wasn't lying. There was no one at home to miss him. No one to notice he was gone. Even when Claudia grew concerned over how long Börne had been gone, a secret room in the bowels of the theater would be the last place anyone would know—or even think—to look.

Bowels.

Nick chuckled at how appropriate his word choice was. Not only was it how most people would describe the location of this room in relation to the building, but he was also in some seriously deep shit.

THIRTY-FIVE

Nori Park's alarm clock went off at 5:45.

It was the same time as every other day, only this morning its bleating irritated her more than usual. She'd gotten little to no sleep the night before. She hadn't been able to get the mayor and the events at The Chamberlain out of her mind long enough to allow more than a few minutes of restless slumber here or there. She'd tried pulling the covers up over her head. Even barricaded her head beneath her pillow in an attempt at stifling the mayor's screams. Nothing blocked them out. It was only once she turned on her police scanner and lost herself in the chatter that her mind became distracted enough for sleep to take over.

Then the damn alarm had gone off.

Giving up on the idea of sleep at this point, Nori pushed herself up in bed, resting her back against the headboard. The sun wasn't quite up. The first of its rays were just starting to infiltrate the darkness outside her bedroom windows. She reached for the water bottle she kept on her nightstand, took a long drink, then returned the bottle and retrieved her cell phone.

Static cackled through the tinny speaker of the archaic police scanner.

Nori spent the next several minutes scrolling through unread emails. She thumbed passed one after another until a day-old email from her mother halted her progress. Nori tapped the screen. Her parents were confirming the flight itinerary for their visit next month. Nori sighed. It wasn't that she wasn't excited to see them. She was. It had, after all, been six months since their last visit. What she wasn't excited about were all of the questions they would undoubtedly pack in their luggage to bring with them. Why doesn't she ever visit? Why wasn't she married yet? Why does she hate them so much as to deny them becoming grandparents?

Nori rolled her eyes and sniggered. Her parents had never quite phrased it that way. That's just how she took it.

Nori closed the email. Her thoughts turned to the new box of green acai tea sitting in her kitchen. Callie had recommended it, and she'd been excited to finally give it a try. Her stomach rumbled, as well. She could eat. With nothing on the news wires catching her attention, Nori swung her legs over the side of her bed. Only a quick trip to the bathroom stood between her and the day's first cup of tea. She tossed her cell onto the bed and was off to greet the morning.

*   *   *

The video camera beeped.

Nick raised his head. The recording device still sat on the box where he'd set it when the shelving had first collapsed. He'd forgotten it was still recording. From where he sat, Nick could see the battery symbol flashing on the screen. It was dying. Nick leaned over and retrieved the camera. After clicking the button to stop recording, he set it on the floor beside him. Better to save the battery. For lighting purposes, if nothing else. For all he knew, it just might come to that.

Looking up at the last remaining light bulb, he hoped like hell it wouldn't.

What he really needed was his cell phone. He doubted very seriously he'd get much of a signal down there, though he could have used the flashlight app, if nothing else. But he could see it resting in the console of his car where he generally left it, more often than not. He'd never been one to take it everywhere he went, especially since he'd been dodging his accountant. Nick shoved his hands into his pockets just to be sure. He found nothing more than his set of keys and his wallet. Neither of which did him any good at the moment. Nick felt like cursing himself, but didn't have the energy.

Börne.

He'd had his cell phone. He'd used it for the same reason Nick was saving the camcorder battery: to light the way.

Nick visually surveyed the mountain of rubble and the body caught halfway underneath. Hidden somewhere beneath the mass of wood, glass and Börne was the man's cell phone.

Nick's stomach turned over on itself.

What he was thinking would have ordinarily been unthinkable.

"Have to," he told himself. If there was any possibility of getting service in that underground room made of old stone and concrete, any possibility at all, he had to try. Nick just hoped the payoff would prove worth the gruesome endeavor. And that the accident that had killed Börne hadn't also killed his cell phone.

The rancid odor of death grew more stringent as Nick approached the mass of debris.

Footing proved treacherous the closer he got, too. By now, any bottles that hadn't survived the crash had emptied their contents. The floor was awash in varying shades of rust, brown, and red. Swirled in with the liquor was more blood than Nick had ever seen. There was also enough broken glass scattered about to cut him from stem to stern if he wasn't careful.

After turning his head and taking a deep breath of the freshest air he could find, Nick knelt down in the blood slick. The fluids immediately soaked through his jeans. The warm sensation on his knee wrenched his stomach, and he willed its contents to remain where they were.

Börne's dead eyes looked on as Nick began sorting through the muck.

Börne's hand was the first place he looked. Börne had been using light from his cell to check the contents of bottles, so Nick hoped that would be as far as he needed to venture. A splintered wooden crate pinned Börne's right arm to the floor. Giving the man's shirt sleeve a tug did nothing to free it. Nick took a second to breath and run through his options. Crawling back out and trying to move the heavy structure again held no appeal.

He was already knee deep in it.

"Ah, man." Nick kicked the crate. Then again. Soon, he was giving the crate hell with the toe of his shoe. Each blow splintered the wooden box further and sent Börne's arm splashing in the pooling sludge. Each splash made a sickening, slurping sound. Nick cringed, while forcing bile back down his throat. He was probably causing further damage to the man's arm. He considered stopping.

Why? Did it really matter at this point?

The next kick sent the crate collapsing in on itself. The shelving that had rested on top of it shifted slightly, but immediately settled. Thankfully, other crates continued to support its weight. Nick wrenched the ruined crate out and tossed it aside. Börne's arm, caught on the splintered wood, slid out with the crate.

Nick's rising hope plunged.

Börne's hand was empty.

"Shit." With his head turned so as to breathe in as little death as possible, Nick reached back under the shelving. One by one, he began clearing out broken bottle after broken bottle. He'd already pulled out several when he grabbed one that was larger than most, squishy, and not a bottle at all. Nick drew back his blood-covered hand in disgust. He immediately felt another retch building. This one, he wasn't so confident he'd keep down.

He'd inadvertently grabbed ahold of Börne's ruined thigh.

The only thing that kept his stomach from releasing its contents was the distraction of seeing Börne's cell phone lying face down only inches away.

The glow from the cell's screen was turning the nearby muck into a makeshift lava lamp.

Nick's eyes widened.

Yes! It still worked!

It took vomiting once, and more than a few scrapes to his arm before Nick was able to retrieve the phone. It was soaked. Bourbon, gin, and a fair amount of blood dripped from the cell's black case. The sum of it ran down the inside of Nick's arm. The screen was shattered, but the damage wasn't so extensive as to render the phone completely useless. The bright light shooting from the back was enough to keep hope alive.

Nick couldn't help but cackle. He raised the phone to the ceiling in a triumphant fist.

"Fuck you, Floyd! I don't need your help after all."

It took only a few seconds for the pride of independence to start fading. There were no bars at the top of the phone's screen, no battery meter. In fact, there was nothing on the screen at all. Nothing except a thousand hairline fractures.

"Come on…"

Nick started tapping the screen—here, there, everywhere—trying desperately to bring the phone to life. It didn't react like he wanted. It didn't react at all. Despite the fact the light from the screen still worked, the screen remained blank. No matter where he tapped or what buttons he pushed, the phone had made up its mind not to respond.

"Fuck!"

His frayed nerves got the better of him. He reacted before thinking.

Nick turned and sent the cell phone sailing through the air. It met with a nearby wall and exploded into several pieces. Nick regretted his actions even before those pieces hit the floor. Swear words made their way from his mind to his mouth. This time, he directed them at himself.

Nick leaned both hands on the grimy wall and hung his head between them.

How could he be so stupid?

He kicked the wall.

Because the damn thing wasn't working, that's why!

He reared his foot back, cocked and ready to deal the wall another blow.

A most welcome sound saved him the pain. Somewhere in the theater, a phone rang.

Nick popped his head up, tuned his ear and waited.

Seconds later, the phone rang again.

He stood straight, alert. The only landline phone in the theater was the one in his office down the hall. But it was too far away, and he was too sequestered. There was no way he could hear it with the door—

Nick's breath caught in his throat.

The door, once closed, now stood open.

Tiny fingers tickled the back of Nick's neck. Light from the storage room cut a rectangle of yellow across the secret room's concrete floor. How? When? Why hadn't he heard the moaning of the hinges like when the door had opened the first time? A thought struck him. He hadn't heard the hinges when the door closed, either. What if…

He didn't want to finish the question.

It was too late. The thought had already overtaken all others in his mind. He had to indulge it. What if the door never did close? What if it had actually been open this entire time? The implications froze Nick to his very soul.

Maybe it really was opening night all over again.

The phone in his office rang out, snapping him back to the present.

Nick didn't waste any more time before darting through the open doorway. He stumbled his way across the storage room—plowing over cardboard boxes and metal film canisters—and out into the hallway. The ever-present scent of buttered popcorn had never smelled so good.

The phone rang.

Thankfully, he didn't have to go far. Fifteen feet away stood his office and its open door. Nick's chest pounded. His nerves tingled as he ran up the sloping hallway. His breaths came rapid and shallow.

At the doorway, Nick tried to stop and failed. The hallway's flat carpet may as well have been a sheet of ice. His bloody shoes slipped and slid right over it. He grabbed the doorframe, righted himself, and swung into the office he'd briefly wondered if he'd ever see again. He collapsed into his big black office chair, sending it crashing into the wall. He spun the chair around. And with his chest heaving and lungs fighting for air, Nick snatched up the phone receiver.

"Hello!"

Silence. Nothing on the other end. Had the caller hung up?

"Hello!"

He was about to replace the receiver and start dialing 9-1-1 when a soft and fearful voice came from the other end.

"Nick?"

The sound of Claudia's voice split his heart in two. Nick's eyes flooded with tears. He couldn't speak. He had only one thing on his mind and couldn't bring himself to say it out loud.

I'm so sorry.

THIRTY-SIX

He'd never seen someone die. Had never seen a dead body, save the one belonging to a grandmother he'd hardly known. Nick could still see Nana Irene laying in her champagne-colored coffin, lips curled scandalously to the point of a grin, arms crossed over her abdomen like she was simply asleep. So calm, so tranquil, so at peace with her circumstances.

It was nothing like the corpse being rolled out of The Chamberlain on a stretcher.

A white sheet draped the body from head to toe. Blooms of red blossomed in areas where blood caused the sheet to cling. The thick, black sole of a leather boot peeked out from under one side as a man and a woman went about their day's work. The backs of their dark blue windbreakers read 'CORONER' in large white letters.

As the stretcher rolled through the lobby, Nick watched it over the shoulder of a detective intent on getting his statement 'while it was still fresh.' Like it would expire at some point. Like the sights and sounds of what happened in that secret room would somehow, someday fade from his memory. Nick scoffed at the notion. There was no chance of that happening. Just like there was no chance of him waking up and it all being a dream. A horrible, messed up dream.

Börne was dead.

That was as real as it got.

Question after question was lobbed his way, only a few of which Nick had an answer for.

Did you see what happened?

No.

Was anyone else around at the time of the accident?

No.

What were you two doing in the theater so early in the morning, anyway?

What does that matter?

When the stretcher reached The Chamberlain's front door, Nori Park was there to greet it. She stepped out of the early morning sunshine and into the lobby, hair damp, face drained of color. She held the door open as the coroners steered the stretcher through. With mouth agape, she watched as they carried it down the concrete steps to the awaiting white van. It wasn't until they lifted the stretcher up and into the back that Nori finally turned away.

Seeing Nick sitting in a folding chair beside the concession stand, she rushed to him.

"Nick!" Nori knelt beside him. "My God!" She laid a hand on his knee. "What happened? Who…"?

Nick looked at her with blank and distant eyes. The rims were red. Until very recently, tears had been present.

"What are you doing here?"

The commotion in the room proved hard to ignore. Detectives, paramedics, and police officers all shuffled about, communicating through shouts. To a passerby, The Chamberlain might have appeared the site of a major crime scene.

"Police scanner," Nori said, turning back to Nick. She wore concern on her face like a mask. "When I heard there was an accident at the theater, well, I just…"

"Why's your hair wet?"

Nori scowled. "What? Nick—"

"Your hair. It's wet."

Nori added a shoulder hitch to her scowl. "I'd just stepped out of the shower when I heard." She looked briefly to the detective, then back. "Nick…"

His focus drifted. His mind couldn't help but wander. Through the glass of the front door, Nick watched as one door on the van closed, then the other. A moment later, it pulled away. Only an empty space remained. That, and a melee of emergency vehicles and gawkers being held at bay by police barricade.

"Nick." Nori patted his knee, trying to bring him back around. "Nick, who was that? Who was on the stretcher?"

Nick's gaze turned back to Nori, but his focus lagged behind.

"I'm sorry." He searched her expression. He was fairly certain he'd been asked a question, but was unable to recall what that question was. "What did you ask me?"

"Excuse me, Mr. Fallon."

A second detective approached. This one was tall, dark and imposing, his head shaved clean. A badge hung from a chain around his neck, and his sleeves were rolled up on his light blue button-down. A faint stain marred the breast pocket, looking to Nick like the result of dribbled coffee. Nick stared at the stain. He couldn't take his eyes off of it as the detective's voice droned on. "About what happened to Mr. Forrester—"

Nori gasped, covered her mouth with both hands.

Nick tore his eyes away from the stain on the detective's shirt long enough to make eye contact with her.

"Börne." The word spilled from his mouth like broken teeth. "He's dead, Nori. Börne's dead. He was…" Nick's features suddenly sagged, as if his plug had just been pulled and all of his air was leaking out.

Nori's reaction was instantaneous. Her eyes welled up as she slowly worked her head back and forth. When she finally dropped her hands from her mouth, they revealed a quivering chin.

And for some reason, all of this surprised Nick. He expected Nori's reaction to be more professional, less personal. She was a reporter, after all. But, what did he know?

Nothing, that's what. Nick didn't know shit at the moment. Nor did he have any answers for the detective, who stood over him tapping his ink pen against the underside of his chin. Somehow, not having the answers made Nick feel even worse. He owed Börne more than that. Owed him way more. More of an explanation as to why he was being rolled out of The Chamberlain under a white sheet instead of walking out on his own two feet.

"Mr. Fallon? Did you hear me?"

He hadn't. Nick didn't realize the questions were still coming. When he met the man's stare, the detective gave him a frown. Turning away, the man called out to one of the lingering paramedics. The black bag she brought with her was the size of a small suitcase, and Nick immediately started a mental list of all the things she might be carrying inside.

"Hey, Marie," the detective said. "Can you give Mr. Fallon here a once over for me. I don't think he's entirely with us."

Act Three

THIRTY-SEVEN

It had been a week since tragedy at The Chamberlain had once again brought news vans to Angler Bay. A week since Mayor Blackwood left a letter of resignation on his desk and fled in the middle of the night. And a week since the theater itself was officially shut down, probably for good this time. Nick stood to lose his ass. It wasn't that the property wouldn't sell. The realtor who had brokered his purchase of the theater in the first place assured Nick that even murder houses sometimes sell before the new paint has dried. The problem was that even if the right buyer did happen along, they wouldn't have to open their wallet very far. Haunted buildings, after all, were a buyer's market by nature. There simply wasn't much competition. They were the cars on the lot with salvaged titles: they still ran fine, but were considered damaged goods. Name the price and it's yours.

Still, things were returning to normal all around him. Angler Bay was savoring what remained of its summer, the news crews had packed up and left town, and framed photos of the Deputy Mayor's family now sat on the desk where Blackwood's once had.

Yet, The Chamberlain remained shuttered.

And as Nick sat at his kitchen table surrounded by what amounted to a lifetime supply of Raisinets, Sno-Caps, and bags of unpopped popcorn, his theater wasn't the loss he mourned most.

The secret room had been investigated, wrapped in a bow of yellow police tape and ceremoniously forgotten by everyone. Everyone, it seemed, but Nick. He couldn't forget if he tried. And he did try. The images were still too vivid, the sounds too clamorous. The feeling of guilt, too damn oppressive. Peaceful slumber had become a forgotten luxury. Hence, the half-empty bottle of Kentucky bourbon also sitting on the table. His third of the week. Dulling the senses seemed the perfect antidote for what ailed him, pairing perfectly with his "pissed at the world" song playlist. He played them loud. Too loud. He was sure his neighbors despised him, wished he would just leave, but he gave no shits. Why should they be different than anyone else in town?

With his laptop open in front of him, the beginning of PJ Harvey's "Long Snake Moan" blistered from its speakers. The scratchy guitar chords. The steady, pulse-pounding drums. The visceral lyrics, painfully delivered. It was the perfect song to drown out the sound of Börne's gut-wrenching death. Which was the whole point. Sure, he could have turned the volume off on the video, but that somehow felt wrong. Like a slight to Börne's tragedy. The thought process didn't necessarily make sense, but what did anymore? The images meant more than the sound anyway.

Nick opened a box of Raisinets and hit play on the video again.

Twenty. That's how many times he'd watched the footage over the past week. At least that many. After handing it over to the police, he'd immediately requested a copy for himself. It was difficult to watch. The angle was off. The room was poorly lit. At the time of the accident, Nick's back had been to Börne, the camera down at his side. Which meant everything the camera recorded was upside down. The footage of that fateful moment was only partially caught in the frame. The fact the camera had caught anything at all could only be chalked up to luck.

As if anything about that morning could somehow be considered lucky.

As his speakers fell silent and he waited for the next song to start, Nick sipped from his glass. When the next song started with the wail of guitar feedback, he didn't recognize it. It must have been one of those "because you listen to…" selections the streaming service was always dropping in whether you wanted them to or not. As the drums kicked in and searing vocals started talking about caution tape and security gates, Nick found himself bobbing his head up and down.

"Who the hell is this?" he asked the empty kitchen. Nick pulled up the streaming window and checked to see what song was currently playing.

BROKEN BRICKS by The White Stripes

"Hmmm." Nick collapsed the window. "Might have to add this one to the playlist permanently." Nick took another sip of bourbon, leaned back and watched more upside-down footage on his laptop.

And then he saw it.

Well, he had always seen it. It was right there in front of him. If it had been Harvey's Long Snake, it would have bitten him.

It had just taken until now for it to click.

Nick tapped his laptop's mute key, abruptly cutting off Jack White's shouting. He leaned in toward the screen. "Holy shit."

It was so obvious.

*   *   *

"Why are all of the walls concrete except one?"

Nori pulled her cell away from her ear and checked the time. It was nearly midnight. On a Wednesday. Hadn't Nick spent the day at The Chamberlain clearing out his personal belongings? Shouldn't he be exhausted, both physically and emotionally? Yet, he sounded wide awake on the phone. And energized.

The same couldn't be said of Nori. "I'm sorry?" she asked, rubbing fresh sleep from her eyes. She'd been up nearly thirty hours straight working on a story, and had only recently fallen into bed.

"The secret room," Nick continued. "In The Chamberlain. All of the walls down there are concrete block except one. The wall where the shelving stood. It's brick. Why is that?"

Nori gave it only a few second's thought. How the hell was she supposed to know?

"Nick, my friend, do you know what time it is?"

"I do."

"And do you know how long I've been up?"

"I do not. But—"

Nori closed her eyes and laid her head back. There was always a 'but.' Nick had obviously been at it again. Probably watched the video for the hundredth time. And if she knew Nick's mental state—and she liked to think she did—a bottle of bourbon was most likely fueling him.

She worried about him. Nick was obsessive. Nobody blamed him for Börne's death. Not the police. Not Claudia. That didn't stop him from shouldering as much guilt as those close to him would allow.

Nori had taken it upon herself to question the investigators personally. There was speculation that the sudden change in humidity could have toppled the old shelving unit, the secret room having been sealed off for decades. Another thought was that the shifting of weight from Börne pulling out and replacing bottles was the cause. Perhaps he'd unknowingly triggered the collapse.

Neither explanation suited Nick. Nori wasn't sold, either. How heavy was a bottle of gin anyway? But they were biased, she knew. Nick, of all people, expected answers. More than anyone, save maybe Claudia. But when it came to answers, or anything resembling proof, there was a glaring lack of it. All anyone seemed willing to offer was speculation. Nobody wanted to put their neck on the line to contradict what appeared to be, by anyone's standard, nothing more than a very freak and very tragic accident.

Nori sat up in bed, put her cell on speaker, and reached for the bottle of water she kept on her nightstand.

"Okay, Nick," she said lifting the bottle to her lips. "The walls. Let's hear it."

Nori listened while Nick explained how he'd come to question the brick wall in The Chamberlain's secret room. How the change in building materials pointed to that one wall having been constructed long after the rest of the room. Why, or for what purpose, Nick couldn't offer an opinion. Nor could Nori. What a brick wall—regardless of how out of place it might seem—had to do with the accident, she was equally unsure. It was just a wall. Walls didn't kill people.

"I'm heading over there," Nick said, his words and breaths both coming in short bursts.

It sounded to Nori like he was in the process of either getting dressed or putting on shoes. She exhaled. She needed sleep. She was so tired, she could hardly think straight. She also wasn't about to let Nick go down into that room alone. And by the sounds of it, Nick wasn't in the market for excuses why they shouldn't.

Nori sighed. "Meet you there in thirty," she said, and tapped the screen to end the call.

THIRTY-EIGHT

Hunched under The Chamberlain's darkened marquee, Nick fumbled with his keys. He wished he hadn't turned off the exterior lights when he'd left that afternoon, but he'd had no reason not to. He couldn't afford the added electricity any more than he could afford the lease. Or the water. Or any other expense the theater brought with it. Besides, for all he'd known, he wouldn't be returning to The Chamberlain until it was ready to be sold. And who knew when that might be?

Yet, here he was.

His furlough from the theater had lasted all of four hours.

The first thing Nick did once the door was closed and locked behind them was to flip on the lobby's lights. Not just one or two. *All* of the lights. He could blame it on habit, but there was more to it than that, if he were honest. Ducking behind the concession stand, Nick brought the thermostat to life as well. Deep inside the theater, the furnace rumbled to life for the first time since Spring.

"Should only take a few minutes," Nick said, rubbing his hands together. "Get the chill out of the air."

It wasn't just cold inside The Chamberlain. It felt lifeless, void of a soul. Like its personality had been stripped away, leaving only an empty shell to speak of the grandeur it once possessed. Framed movie posters no longer lined the walls. They now lay stacked against the wall in Nick's spare bedroom, seen by no one. He'd donated the fake palm trees with their gold, ornate pots, to the Angler Bay public library. Even the concession counter and its glass display case had been stripped bare of anything more than dust.

In a matter of days, The Chamberlain Theater had been reduced to nothing more than a sterile, blank slate. A stark reminder that Nick's list of failed business ventures had yet another entrant.

"Is…" Nori started, turning to look toward the hallway. "Are we sure it's even safe? I mean…"

She didn't have to explain herself. Nick knew why she was asking.

"Should be," he answered. "The room's empty. Door's been removed. We won't be down there long. Just wanna get a look at it."

Nori wasn't wrong to be concerned though. With everything he'd seen over the last month, Nick would have thought the theater had nothing left with which to frighten him. But things were different now. Someone had died. The ante had been raised.

Now he knew what Floyd Cropper and The Chamberlain were capable of.

"Wouldn't happen to remember Claudia's prayer, would ya? I mean, just in case?"

Nori shook her head. "Didn't pay much attention. Usually when she was reciting it, I was thinking to myself how stupid I was for even putting myself in a situation where I needed a prayer of protection."

Nick nodded. He understood all too well. Even now, as eager as he was to check out that wall, his feet were reluctant.

"You okay?" Nori reached up and took Nick's arm.

And for the first time since hearing that White Stripes song and connecting the dots, Nick considered it. Was he okay with it? Was he okay with delving back down into the belly of the beast to try and find out why a vengeful spirit had caused the death of a man that he himself had invited? He wasn't. But that didn't matter. He owed it to Claudia, and to a greater degree, Börne, to help find out. He only wished he could channel some of Börne's vast courage.

Nick offered a slight smile and nodded. "I'm good. Let's go."

From the moment it had gone up, the police tape had seemed unnecessary. With the door having been removed, the gaping hole was a scar on the otherwise blank storage room wall; the yellow strips of plastic an ineffective bandage. The Chamberlain's doors were kept locked at all times. Nobody other than Nick ever came and went. Nobody other than Nick wanted to, and even he had grown wary. Most in town believed The Chamberlain was cursed. No one came near. On one occasion, Nick even witnessed an elderly couple cross the street, taking a wide berth around the property so as not to get too close on their Sunday stroll.

"Sorry."

Nick rushed over to the wall and began ripping down the tape. If he'd known Nori would be following him back here, he would have removed the tape earlier. It seemed, 'if he'd only known' was a regret he was becoming all too familiar with lately. One by one, the strips came away, and one by one, Nick fashioned them into a growing ball of yellow. When he was done, he looked around. Like everything else from the storage room, the trashcan now sat in his apartment. With nowhere to dispose of it, Nick simply tossed the ball of tape into a corner. A parting gift for the next owner.

Nori observed the barren storage room from just inside its doorway.

"I like what you've done with the place."

Nick broke into a full-on chuckle. Nori joined him, apparently thankful her icebreaker had landed as intended. The empty room soon echoed with the sound of levity for the first time in who knew how long. It wasn't, however, destined to last. As they turned their gaze to the opening in the wall, their laughter died a slow death.

Nori took an audible deep breath and let it out. "So that's it, huh?"

Nick knew what she was thinking: while they'd been talking in his office that evening, The Chamberlain's best kept secret sat a mere ten feet away.

Nodding, Nick stepped toward the door. "Come on."

Finding the pull string for the lights took only seconds this time. When Nick pulled it, the dreary room flooded with a brilliant white. The original yellow bulb, along with its two burnt out siblings, had been replaced with all new LED bulbs during the course of the accident investigation. The room was much brighter now. Not for the first time, Nick wondered if things might have gone differently that morning had there been this much light to see by. He doubted it. The lack of proper illumination didn't seem to have been a contributing factor. Still, with so many unanswered questions remaining, nothing was off the table when it came to 'what ifs.'

At least all morbid reminders of the accident had been cleared away. The wooden shelves and shattered crates were long gone. Blades of glass no longer littered the floor. The copious amount of blood they had drawn, along with what amounted to many gallons of decades-old liquor, had been mopped up by the cleaning crew he'd hired. What remained was an unnaturally clean spot in the middle of the otherwise grimy and dust-covered floor. It stood out like a bruised thumb that had been caught in a car door. A glaring reminder. In its own way, it spoke almost as much to Börne's violent end as the blood and debris would have.

Almost.

It was still better than the actual blood and debris.

Nori stared at the floor. Nick could see her mind directing a short film on how the accident might have played out. She would undoubtedly get the details wrong, but the conclusion would be the same. And just as damning. He scrambled for a way to draw her attention away from the floor. The best he could come up with was to simply move things along.

"This is it."

Nick approached the brick wall. He raised a hand to it, but stopped short of touching it outright. He remained there for a moment, trying to feel any sort of energy coming from the wall. It was stupid, he knew. He wasn't Claudia.

He placed his hand on the wall. The brick was cool to the touch, the mortar separating it, rough and sloppy. Nick traced his finger along the vertical and horizontal lines.

Behind him, Nori inspected one of the concrete walls, then another. Returning to inspect the brick wall, she said, "It's also the only wall without a trace of ash or soot on it."

It dawned on Nick now why the room had always seemed oddly-shaped. *The brick wall.* It appeared to cut off one of the room's pre-existing corners at a strange angle. He ran his hand over the brick. "I'd say that someone, at some point, sealed off part of this room."

"Why?"

"Million-dollar question."

"What's on the other side of it?"

"Even better question."

Nori locked eyes with Nick. "So, basically, the secret room…"

Nick nodded. "Is hiding a secret of its own."

Nori started to say something more, but stopped. "Do you hear that?" she asked, craning her neck. "Is that…"

"It is." Nick gestured toward the wall that separated them from the auditorium and its silver screen. "It's happened before."

Though the sounds were muffled by the concrete wall, soft music could be heard playing through the auditorium speakers. Calliope music. The low drone of the narrator's voice layered on top told the audience to sit back and enjoy the ride.

"I've come into work a couple times," Nick continued, "and the movie's already playing. Always that particular one. The matinee for the kids."

Nori turned to Nick. "Thought the theater was completely shut down, though?"

Concern suddenly clouded Nick's face. "It is."

Nori's earlobe found itself being tugged on. "And the control room?"

"Disassembled."

"Then how—"

Nick shook his head, bewildered that the film was even capable of being played since all of the equipment had been unplugged. Bewildered, but not surprised.

"Because, somehow, the energy isn't coming from inside the auditorium. Or even the control room. Börne showed me that much. The source of everything we've seen and experienced at The Chamberlain, its very lifeblood, originates from right here."

Nick rested his hand on the brick wall. "More specifically, behind here."

"But…" Shaking her head slowly, Nori backed away from the wall. "I'm sorry," she said, her voice picking up a slight tremble. "I just…I can't…" Nori turned and swiftly made her way through the open doorway.

The rising fear in Nori's eyes sent a chill rippling through Nick. Partly because he wanted to check on her, and partly because he suddenly didn't want to be in there alone, Nick hurried from the room.

He caught up with her as she made her way up the hallway toward the lobby.

"Hey," he said, taking Nori's arm, "you okay?"

Nori nodded and wiped at her cheek. "I'm fine. It's…it's probably stupid. I just…that music? Playing by itself? Son of a…shit, Nick! All while we stood in the very spot that Börne… It was just too much."

"I know," Nick said. "I know."

When they reached the end of the hallway and spilled into the lobby's harsh light, Nick let go of Nori's arm. "Let me check the control room real quick," he said. "I'll meet you back here."

Nori grabbed onto his hand before it could drop away. "Be careful," she said.

Nick held Nori's gaze briefly, then nodded and turned away.

He didn't hesitate at the control room's red door. He thrust it inward and stepped up into the room. There was no one there to surprise. No one to catch red-handed. The tiny room was as empty as he'd left it that afternoon.

Still, the film played on the screen at the front of the auditorium.

Its music played through the speakers.

"How the fuck?"

Nick looked under the projection console with the light from his cell, intent on finding the plug and cord the way he'd left it: snaking lifeless on the floor. It wasn't, and he gasped. The plug had been placed back into the electrical outlet. By who or what, he had no idea. Yet, somehow, surprise didn't register.

"You're not gonna believe this," Nick said, entering the lobby and finding Nori perched atop the concession counter.

And yet, even as he said it, he knew she would believe it. When it came to The Chamberlain, nothing seemed to cross the line into disbelief anymore. They'd seen too much. "Damn thing was plugged back in."

"I believe it."

Nick chuckled. "Knew you would."

"Which makes up my mind even more." Nori folded her arms across her chest.

"What do you mean?"

"Maybe we should get Claudia back in here," Nori suggested. "Maybe even before we go any further."

Initially, Nick was offended. On the surface. Deep down, however, he knew Nori was right. Claudia was better equipped to deal with anything they might encounter.

"Okay," Nick said, rubbing his hands up and down Nori's arms. "But do we even know if she'd step foot in here again?"

"She will."

"And how can you be so sure?"

"Because I called her on my way over here," Nori said. "She was up. Seems none of us are getting much sleep lately."

*   *   *

Claudia tossed her cell phone onto the bed and returned to her happy place. Photos of Börne surrounded her, spread out all over the bed. It was as happy a place as she'd been the past week.

The photos were all she had left, the photos. Some were of Börne alone; many showed the both of them together. Sure, she still had hundreds of hours of raw footage they'd gathered from investigations, but with the exception of a brief appearance here or there, the videos contained more footage of the places than Börne himself. And then there was the horrifying video of that fateful morning. For obvious reasons, watching that one didn't fill her with the same loving nostalgia as the others.

She still watched it. For a different reason than nostalgia.

Among the ones spread out on her duvet were photos from their wedding, their many ski trips in Mittenwald, Oktoberfests in Munich, and ultimately, when they'd arrived in Boston and had spent their first day on a duck boat tour soaking up some of their new country's history. Since then, it had been mostly work and little play. Sadly, there were very few photos of them from the past ten years. A regret that was slowly settling in.

Perhaps the past was all anyone truly had left.

With a deep intake of breath and long, drawn out exhale, Claudia began gathering the photos and placing them back in the old shoebox.

"I'll see you again real soon, *meine Liebe*." Bringing it to her lips, she kissed the wedding photo of Börne kissing her on the forehead. If she had to choose, it was probably her favorite. "I've got work to do."

When the last of the photos had been gathered and tucked away, Claudia placed the lid back on the shoebox and swung her feet off the bed. She carried the box back to the closet she and Börne had shared in their tiny house. It took rising up on her toes to slide the shoebox back into the open slot on the top shelf.

With the photos returned to their proper place, Claudia's focus shifted. Nostalgia can be a wonderful place to visit, but you can't live there. Clearing away some of the ornate gowns she often wore for work, she found what she'd been looking for. She grabbed the handle of the black soft-sided suitcase and pulled it out of the closet.

"It's time to finish what we started."

Claudia closed the closet door.

THIRTY-NINE

Lightning cracked the night sky. A low rumble followed. Cold rain found its way inside Nick's collar as he fumbled with his keys for the second time in as many nights. Rainwater ran down his neck and inside his shirt. This time, he'd left The Chamberlain's marquee lights on, electric bill be damned. And even though it had helped him unlock the door in record time, the damage had already been done. Nick was soaked through to his unmentionables.

Nick went behind the concession counter where he'd left a modest collection of cleaning supplies. A stack of folded, white rags sat on one of the shelves and he grabbed one off the top. After shaking it from its folded state, Nick brought it to his face.

A whoosh at the front door.

A gust of wind through the lobby.

For the first time in over a week, Claudia Forrester stood just inside The Chamberlain's lobby. The torrential rain had flattened her fiery red mane. Streaks of black trailed from her eyes. A stream of water sloped down her nose before plummeting onto her waterlogged black trench coat.

An equally miserable-looking Nori Park entered behind her.

Nick grabbed the last two rags from the stack and rushed

them over. "Sorry. Best I've got."

They both thanked Nick for the rags and proceeded to rid themselves of the evening's rainfall.

As Claudia ruffled her damp hair with the rag, Nick found it difficult to meet her gaze. He had, after all, been the last person to see her husband alive. He was part of the reason she was a widow. Guilt had kept him from making the trip north for the funeral. Which, in turn, made the weight of his guilt even heavier. It was a vicious cycle.

"Nice to see you, Nick." Claudia smiled weakly and began looking around the lobby.

Nick looked to Nori, raised his eyebrows.

"Yeah, um, Claudia. Great seeing you." Nick looked again to Nori and shrugged. Her soft smile and encouraging nod eased his sudden tension.

"Can't say I like what you've done with the place," Claudia said. "But I get it. And I'm sorry."

It was the first time Nick had heard Claudia speak since the day after Börne died. The day she'd packed up what remained of F.A.U.S.T. and followed Börne's body home to Chicago. Her voice was timid now, understandably softened by loss and sadness.

"Claudia, I'm...*I'm* sorry. I can't—"

Claudia raised her hand. "It wasn't your fault, Nick. Truly it wasn't. Börne was always... hazardous to his health. Fearless. Didn't always make the best choices for his own well-being. It was a side of him that both inspired and scared the hell out of me. I've watched the footage you shot that night. Several times, actually." Her eyes were on Nick, but as far as he could tell, she was looking *through* him more than at him. "I kept trying to see something. Anything that might explain what happened."

Suddenly, the thought of a grieving Claudia sitting alone in her empty home watching that footage over and over ground

Nick's heart to nothing, a cigarette butt under a boot heel.

Somewhere outside, thunder stole silence from the night.

He cleared his throat.

"It simply tips over," Nick said, recalling the video. "The shelving unit. It doesn't appear to be pushed or shoved or anything. It just…topples."

Claudia nodded her head. And for the first time since the conversation started, Claudia and Nick's eyes met. "Even using Börne's sophisticated equipment to enhance the video," she said, "I couldn't find anything that might have caused it to move. No shadows, no sudden glitches in the footage. Nothing earthly, at least."

Earthly.

Nick understood what Claudia meant. There were two worlds to consider. Even for him, it was too late in the spirit game to start questioning the existence of the paranormal.

As he took the damp towel from her, Claudia excused herself abruptly and turned for the ladies' room. A moment later, she disappeared through its swinging door without another word.

Nick approached Nori, who also handed him a damp towel.

"So," he said, nodding toward the restroom door, "what do you make of that?"

Nori took a moment to think on her answer.

"I think it's just being here," she said. "Remember, she never came inside that day. The police kept her out. This is the first time she's stepped foot in here since Börne…" Her voice trailed off. She didn't have to finish the sentence. Nick knew where she was going with it. He'd been there, after all.

Nick blew hot air into his hands. "So, are we sure this is even a good idea? Her being here? Maybe we should have just done this ourselves."

Nori eyed Nick for a second, then looked to the restroom door. When she turned back, Nick could see her wheels turning.

Though he knew her well enough at this point to know they weren't necessarily turning in his favor.

"Do you want to tell her?" Nori's eyebrows arched as she tilted her forehead toward him. "Do you want to be the one to tell Claudia that she shouldn't look any further into why her husband might be dead right now?"

Put that way, of course he didn't.

Claudia emerged from the restroom, hair now tied back, face free of smear.

Nick breathed a little easier. Apparently, Claudia wasn't as upset as he'd feared. She hadn't run to the restroom in distress. She'd simply needed some minor upkeep.

"And yes," Claudia said as she approached. "I'm seeing this through. Don't even think about asking me to walk away now. I didn't spend all day driving here just to turn back."

Nori and Nick stopped and exchanged a look. Had their voices really travelled that far? Or was mental telepathy another sense that the spiritual Mrs. Forrester possessed?

"Okay," Nick said.

"Okay," Claudia repeated, calmer and more collected than Nick would have guessed; more than he would have been in her shoes. "So, are you gonna show me this room, or what?"

"We should say the prayer," Nick said. "Just to be safe. We didn't say it that morning. And…well, we should say it now."

Claudia nodded, reached out her hands.

As the three of them clasped one another's hand, they closed their eyes. A moment later, the prayer of protection had been said and everyone dropped their hands.

"And the pendants?" Nick asked, pulling his own necklace from his pocket and slipping it over his head. "Everyone have theirs?"

Claudia reached into the front of her blouse and produced the black tourmaline that hung by a leather cord around her neck. "Always."

Nori pulled her pendant from the collar of her blouse as well.

Then Nick caught a nearly concealed grin from Nori. She looked to be doing her best to hide it, but the grin wasn't having it.

He lost his train of thought. "What?"

Instantly, Nori disposed of the evidence, and with a straight face, said, "Nothing. Never mind."

Nick held her gaze for a few seconds more before finally letting it go. "So," he said, taking the first step in the direction of the hallway. "Shall we?"

Claudia turned to Nori, smiled briefly, shelved it, then followed Nick.

A moment later, Nori did the same.

* * *

Standing in the middle of the empty storage room, Nick cast a sidelong glance at Claudia. He couldn't imagine what it must be like for her. She was about to enter the room where her husband had taken his last breath. And a grisly last breath it had been. Nick was wary of entering himself. Each time he did, he felt like he was playing a dangerous game of Russian Roulette. Claudia, as he should have expected, was handling it with her usual poise.

Awkward silence reigned. Nick wanted to give Claudia time, wanted her to go at her own pace. At the same time, he could feel himself growing anxious. The nest of hornets in his stomach were agitated. They'd delayed long enough.

"Anyone else notice how quiet it is in here?" Still damp and visibly shivering, Nori shoved her hands into her jean's pockets. "I mean, it's coming down in buckets outside, and we can't hear a thing."

Nick nodded. A movie theater, by nature, is designed for optimal acoustics. That included a good amount of soundproofing. Not to mention the fact that The Chamberlain was old. Buildings built back then were more solid, more structurally sound. Which made The Chamberlain not only the perfect place for a speakeasy, but for any other activities deemed necessary to hide from the outside world.

"Well," Claudia shrugged, "we could stand here all night, but that wall's not going to investigate itself."

That was all of the prodding Nick needed. He took the lead and disappeared through the darkened doorway. A shiver rattled his shoulders as he entered the adjoining room. He was already damp, but he could still feel the unmistakable chill in the air.

Nick turned on the lights and wasted no time making his way to the wall where the shelving unit had once stood. He'd hoped to move Claudia swiftly past the gleaming spot on the floor. It had caught Nori's attention the night before. He hoped it wouldn't catch Claudia's.

Quite possibly with the same intent, Nori appeared immediately at his side.

Claudia soon followed.

Nick stepped to the side, allowing her full access. While she slowly ran her hands along the wall's rough façade, he inventoried the barren room. The thing about completely clearing out a room and leaving it barren, is that it then tends to have very little in it. Nick silently cursed himself. What he needed was some kind of tool. A big, heavy one. He'd come as woefully unprepared as last night. He'd been in a rush. He was nervous about seeing Claudia, unsure as to what her wishes would be, how she would want to proceed. Now, having laid eyes on the wall a second time in as many days, there was obviously only one option: they needed to bust through it. After all, it was brick. There were no secret doors to discover this time.

Only problem was, Nick had nothing at his disposal worthy of creating a hole in a brick wall.

"What you need is a sledgehammer."

Nick chuckled at Nori's ability to read his mind. "What *I* need?"

"Your theater." Nori grinned. "Your wall."

Nick found it difficult to argue either point. It was his theater, and what he needed was indeed a sledgehammer. "Wouldn't have one in your pocket, would ya?"

"Sorry," Nori said with a shake of her head. "Left mine at home."

"Same." Claudia hugged herself, rubbed her arms. "You?"

Nick chuckled. "Do I look like a guy who owns a sledgehammer?"

"So," Claudia said, "where would someone find a sledgehammer this time of night?"

Nori and Nick exchanged a look.

"City council still battling on how to pay for the sand dune restoration project?" Nick asked.

Nori shook her head. "It's all been worked out. Project's almost done."

"Almost, huh?"

Nori nodded.

Nick smiled. "Then I guess I know where we can get a sledgehammer."

FORTY

Thirty minutes later, Nick was in possession of a shiny new twelve-pound sledgehammer, and the construction company rebuilding the retaining wall along the beach possessed one less. Leaving a trailer full of expensive tools unattended at night seemed like a bad business practice, even in a town the size of Angler Bay. If there was any question before, Nick had proved it so. He reasoned that was what insurance was for. He only wished there was a policy covering the loss of revenue due to vengeful spirits.

"Here we go." Nick wiped his hands on his jeans and approached the wall. He lifted the sledgehammer. The lights flickered. They didn't go out. Nick stood, sledgehammer poised over his shoulder, and waited. He exchanged a look with Claudia.

"New bulbs, right?" she asked.

He nodded.

Claudia returned it. "He's here," she said, and Nick thought she was referring to Floyd. Then Claudia smiled. When she said, "Börne is with us," a tear ran out of her eye and down her cheek.

A chill ran down Nick's spine.

The first strike rang out like a church bell. The impact of the forged steel hammerhead against the brick reverberated throughout the room. The walls shook, freeing themselves of years of dust and ash and soot. The floor vibrated beneath their feet. The echo of the blow pinged around the room. It took several seconds for the clamor to die out. All in all, it spoke to a much greater strength than Nick possessed.

"Wow," Nori said. "Now there's an argument for having the right tool for the job if I ever saw one."

Nick glanced around the room, wide-eyed. "Right tool or not, no way that was all me."

A chunk of brick and mortar the size of a shot glass lay at the base of the wall. A substantial crack now zigzagged a good eighteen inches down through the mortared seams. The fracture nearly reached the floor. One blow, and Nick couldn't be happier with the immediate results. If the brick wall had truly been entrusted to keep a secret, its tenure was about to end.

The second strike of the hammer chipped more brick, cracked more mortar. Once again, the ground and walls shook out of proportion with Nick's strength. This time, the rumble took a good ten seconds to fade out. What continued in its absence was a sound all-too familiar to Nick.

"Beautiful," Claudia muttered. "What is it?"

"Children's matinee," Nick said. "Must be playing in the auditorium. Happens sometimes." The sound they were hearing was the opening scene of the film. The narrator was welcoming everyone aboard the submarine that would soon dive down and show all its passengers a world they had probably never seen before. The film, and their adventure, was only just beginning.

"Interesting," Claudia said, eyes to the sky, but closed.

Nori followed suit. "Creepy is what it is."

Claudia held her pose and breathed in and out deeply.

Nick could only imagine what was going through her mind. The spirit that had most likely caused the accident that claimed her husband's life was making an appearance. And if Floyd hadn't caused the accident outright, he was at least somehow responsible. Bizarre as it might sound, no other theory made sense. One way or another, Nick was certain Floyd Cropper was as much responsible for Börne's death as Nick.

With the muffled sounds of inspirational music playing in the background, Nick took a deep breath and swung the hammer a third time. A solid strike that again rocked the entire room. The brick wall now displayed a deep crater. A ragged blemish on its façade.

Tiring, Nick drew a couple of deep breaths and wiped sweat from his hands. "One more might do it," he said, and hefted the sledgehammer. Drawing it back, he brought it around like Babe Ruth. The next time the steel head connected with red brick, steel won the battle hands down.

Like the release of a redlined pressure valve, a canon blast of air, white ash, and what sounded like the screams of a hundred children erupted from the newly-formed hole. All three light bulbs shattered, plunging the room into utter darkness. The burst of wind was like a freight train, knocking everyone off of their feet. Nick, Claudia, and Nori all hit the floor in a tumble as hands rushed to cover ears.

Anguished wails spewed from the hole in the wall, like the cries of tormented banshees. Their pain and sorrow filled the room. High-pitched screams swirled above the three like a tornado unleashed, threatening eardrums. The bits of brick and ash it carried peppered their faces and arms. It stung their skin.

As the tornado slowly lost strength, so did the cries. A moment later, they'd faded completely. Only soft music and a narrator describing how coral reefs were formed disturbed the silence.

A light sprang up in the darkness, thanks to a quick-acting Nori. She shined her cell phone on Claudia first. Blanketed from head to toe in white and grey, the investigator used her hands to fluff ash from her hair, appearing otherwise unharmed. Nori turned her cell light on Nick next. Sitting dumbfounded on his backside, sledgehammer between his outstretched legs, he wore the same thin layer of snow-like ash.

The overwhelming reek of burnt wood and old smoke filled the air.

No one said a word. Everyone quietly climbed to their feet and commenced with brushing themselves off. Eventually, it was Nori who broke the silence. The question she asked was the same question running through Nick's mind.

"What...the fuck...was that?"

As was his usual response, Nick looked to Claudia. She had already retrieved her cell phone and was using its light to closely inspect a small mound of ash in her hand. She swirled a pinky through it. She smelled it.

"What's the saying," she said, dropping the mound of ash and brushing her hand on her slacks, "I'm no rocket scientist, but I'd say there was a fire on the other side of that wall at one time."

"And those screams?" Nori asked. "What does your Spidey sense tell you about those?"

After taking a moment to think it over, the only answer Claudia could offer was a subtle shake of her head.

"Awesome," Nick muttered. "Just great."

After pulling out his own cell phone and bringing up the screen, he trained its faint glow on the hole in the wall. Within a matter of seconds, the light from Nori and Claudia's cell phones had joined the party. The crater surrounding the hole was fairly large, but the hole itself was roughly the size of a fist. Nothing but pitch black could be seen on the other side of the wall.

Nick's ears were ringing. His heart rate was going, in Börne's words, apeshit. He half expected something to emerge from the hole at any moment. A rat. A snake. A damn hand. Anything that probably shouldn't be there.

When Nori cleared her throat beside him, Nick almost pissed himself.

"So, who wants to take one for the team?" Nori turned her light away from the hole long enough to question Nick and Claudia with it.

"What do you mean?" Claudia asked. "Take one for the team?"

"She's asking," Nick chimed, "who wants to be the first to look in the hole. Because anything we find through there was probably meant to be hidden. So, probably not anything good or pleasant."

"At some point in time," Nori added, "something far worse than drinking and gambling took place in here."

In The Chamberlain's bowels, Nick thought.

"Well, then," Claudia said, "let's keep going. No one's getting in through that little hole."

The sledgehammer made a sound like fingernails on a chalkboard as Nick drug it across the ash-covered floor toward the wall. Two blows later and the hole had doubled in size. Roughly the size of a basketball, it was now large enough for someone to poke his or her head through. Nobody rushed forward to do so. A scene from the movie *Jaws* flashed in Nick's mind: Ben Gardner's severed head appearing at the hole in his sunken boat's hull. He envisioned a similar scenario playing out with the brick wall, and even though he quickly struck the image from his mind, its residue lingered.

After a few more swings, the hole had once again grown. First doubling in size, then tripling. Unfortunately for Nick, the weight of the sledgehammer had also grown. His shoulders screamed. His back muscles were raising the white flag. He didn't envy those who made their living swinging sledgehammers all day long. Or hammers of any kind, for that matter. Despite the chill in the room, beads of sweat ran down both sides of his face.

Nick dropped the hammer to the floor and shook the sting from his hands.

He stepped back from the wall.

The three stared at the opening.

The opening stared back. Its gaping maw awaited the bravest among them.

What awaited them on the other side of the wall? The possibilities were endless. And not all good. The rest of the room? A chasm? A tunnel leading to an underground sewer system filled with skulls and bones like the catacombs in France?

Nick took the brunt of a shiver.

As possibilities filtered through his imagination, each one increasingly more diabolical, Nick's courage struggled to keep up. It dragged its heels. He wondered if Nori and Claudia were as nervous. He also wondered which of the three of them had balls enough to climb through the opening first.

The fact that it was Claudia didn't surprise him.

"So," she said, echoing Börne's own words, "rock, paper, scissors?"

FORTY-ONE

"God, it smells."

Even from ten feet behind her, in the middle of the darkened room, Nori and Nick knew what Claudia was referring to. The acrid stench of rot, stale smoke, and charred wood oozed from the opening like a sewage leak. Even when Nick started thinking the smell couldn't possibly get any worse, the thick, nauseating odor somehow grew more overpowering. Within seconds, it had infected the entire room.

Nick gagged, pulled the collar of his shirt up over his nose.

"Damn," Nori said, waving her hand in front of her face. "Smells like something crawled in there, caught on fire, and died." The second the words left her mouth, she grimaced. Turning to Nick, she mouthed the word 'sorry.'

Claudia pulled back from the hole. If she'd heard Nori's comment, she showed no sign of it. "Probably should've checked that trailer for some portable lighting, too."

They huddled around the light from their cell phones like homeless folks around a barrel fire.

Nick looked skyward, where the rain assuredly still fell outside. "Wanna go back out there?"

"Not really." Claudia turned her cell phone back to the hole. "Not entirely excited about going in there with nothing but these, either."

"Guys," Nori interrupted, her eyes darting around the darkness. "You hear that?"

A moment later, Nick nodded. "Feel it, too."

The music had stopped. A new sound had replaced it altogether.

The air didn't just hum, it buzzed. The static energy of an electric substation surrounded them. The hair on Nick's arms and neck tingled. The energy slowly grew. It was as if a dial was being turned. What had started out as nothing more than a low, barely perceptible murmur only seconds ago, was quickly intensifying into something more tangible.

In the dark, Claudia's silhouette nodded toward the opening in the brick wall. "The answers we seek lie in there."

Nick swallowed hard. "About Börne's accident?"

"About everything," she said. "All of the activity you've been experiencing here at The Chamberlain. This is where the energy is the strongest." Claudia shined her light on Nick's face. "Vengeance was born behind that wall."

Once the initial shock had faded, Nick's brow furrowed. "Wait a second. Floyd. He, you know...out on the front steps."

Claudia turned her light from Nick to Nori, then trained it on the opening in the wall. "I'm not so sure the spirits here at your theater have anything to do with Floyd anymore."

A chill ran through Nick, top to bottom. His stomach churned lava rocks. "But—"

Before he could question further, Claudia ducked through the opening and disappeared into the darkness.

"Well, alright then." Nick took a deep breath of stale air, then let it out slowly. He looked to Nori, gestured with his hand. "Ladies first, I guess."

Nori snickered, placed a hand on his chest. "How very chivalrous—"

A gasp came from the other side of the wall. It was Claudia's, and it was abrupt.

"Shit." Without hesitating, Nick ducked through the opening. Inside the awaiting darkness, the buzzing was stronger. The energy, more palpable. Even in the pitch, the walls inside the cavernous space seemed somehow darker.

Oppressively so.

"Watch your step." Claudia instructed. "There's…I don't even know what you'd call it."

Joining them in shining her light across the floor of the tiny space, Nori was the next to suck in a sharp intake of air. "I'm not a cop," she said, "but I'd call it evidence."

FORTY-TWO

Scattered in and out of their faint light were items not normally found in the basement of a theater. Or a speakeasy for that matter. All burnt, all destroyed, all horrifically out of place.

Nick could hardly believe his eyes.

Balled up just inside the opening, were the remnants of a light blue shirt. By the size of the only remaining sleeve, it looked to be a child's shirt. The layer of grey ash covering it, and the fact that most of the shirt was burnt away, made it difficult to tell for sure. A neatly stacked, but scorched pile of clothing sat beside it. A pair of dinner plates with two mugs beside them. The handle to one of the mugs had been broken off, leaving only a jagged stump. A toy building set and numerous miniature cars, all metal, all the ones he himself had played with as a kid, lay scattered about. Spines and partial covers from countless books littered the floor. Most of the pages were missing, assumedly accounting for much of the ash covering everything. Where ash hadn't settled, black soot coated the surfaces.

One after another, long-hidden objects revealed themselves at the behest of cell phone screens.

Nick hung just inside the opening, a swirling cloud of disturbed ash engulfing his shoes. He couldn't yet bring himself to venture further. Nor was there much room to do so. He turned and investigated the wall from which he had just entered. He drew his finger across the stone. It came away clean. The entire wall was absent of ash, soot, or anything else a fire leaves behind. By the looks of the two others, it was the only one of the three unmarred by the black substance.

Static electricity continued to hum at full strength.

"Guess we know which came first," Nick said, shouting over the din. "The fire or the wall."

Claudia appeared beside him. When she cast her own light on the adjoining concrete wall, she sucked in a sharp gasp.

Nick swung his cell around.

Nori's light made three. She yelped for the memory of whoever had occupied the room before them.

Handprints, small and clearly defined, spread themselves all over the blackened concrete wall. Desperate scratches. Anguished claw marks. All carved through the soot and stone.

Nick lightly traced the gouges with his fingertips. A tragic realization dropped Nick's jaw like a sucker punch. "Someone was in here when it happened."

Claudia's eyes filled with tears. "And trying to get out," she said, her voice somber.

Nori slid her hand inside Nick's arm and took hold of his hand. "My God," she whispered. "Can you imagine?"

"No," said Claudia. "If only God were there."

The beams from three cell phones slowly converged on the next most logical artifact: the charred remains of a wooden rowboat wedged in the nook of the two far walls. A small, lightweight type, big enough for two at most. The pointed bow had been burned away, leaving the rest of the tiny boat intact, but covered in black soot.

Trailing her light up and over the watercraft brought another cry of distress from Nori.

Nick swallowed hard, pulling her in tighter.

Claudia clamped a hand over her mouth as The Chamberlain continued to lay bare its secrets.

Among an array of blackened blankets and pillows sat an unmistakable lump nestled on the floor of the boat's hull. Covering the lump were the charred ruins of what looked to have once been a sleeping bag. The huddled lump was roughly the size of a human being. Maybe two, if small.

Whispers flowed from Claudia on a string, "No, no, no, no, no…"

Fighting back his own rising fear, Nick put his hand on her shoulder. "Claudia?"

She shook her head back and forth, eyes closed, mumbling through trembling lips. Nick quickly realized that her words were no longer pleas, but a softly recited prayer. He could feel her body tremble beneath his hand.

Nick looked to Nori. Wide eyes greeted him. She made no move, offered no words. Shock was keeping her from registering any more of a response.

It was up to him.

And with the icy hand of utter dread gripping his soul, Nick turned back to the boat.

He had to step over what had most likely been the remains of someone's last meal—scorched plates, forks, and what appeared to be a smattering of small chicken bones—on his way to the vessel.

The closer Nick drew, the sharper the buzzing in his ears became. It was painful now. A mini electrical storm brewed inside his head. Pressing against his temple offered no relief. Cupping his hand over his ear did nothing. The sensation of something trickling from his ear and down his cheek was very real.

At the edge of the rowboat, Nick knelt and cast a glance behind him. Nori looked on with hands clasped over her ears.

Claudia's eyes remained closed. Tears now streamed from them. Her lips worked feverishly.

He turned back to the boat and breathed deep. As he reached for the singed edge of the sleeping bag, the buzzing hit a crescendo. The floor vibrated, causing the forks to dance and rattle on the stacked plates. The walls shook. The ceiling rumbled. Light ash fell like soft snow.

Nick grabbed a fistful of nylon.

His heart threatened to rip free of his chest.

The room threatened to rip itself apart.

He couldn't stop now. His only path out of this was forward. One, he counted. Two. Nick tore away the sleeping bag.

An explosion of ash filled the air.

All other excitement in the room ceased.

The trembling stilled. The buzzing fell silent. The crescendo of ash billowed down as The Chamberlain laid bare its most heinous secret.

Nick stumbled backward, landing on his backside among the cups and plates and half-burned books.

Nori screamed in despair.

And as Claudia slowly opened her tearful eyes, a satisfied smile crept across her face. "It's okay, little ones," she said, turning toward the tiny boat. "You're free now."

FORTY-THREE

For the second time in just over a week, Nick leaned against the concession counter answering a detective's questions as a body made its way through The Chamberlain's lobby on a stretcher. It was a time too many. What made this time worse, was the additional body bag that followed close behind the first. It would be a few days before positive identifications could be made. Dental records would be required. The general consensus, however, was that the identities of the two small skeletons were already known.

It appeared as if the Blackwood brothers, Stephen and Mitchel, hadn't been lost at sea after all.

"I just don't get it." Nick massaged both temples once the detective had taken her leave.

"It actually explains so much," Claudia said, sipping from a cup of freshly made coffee. "The two sets of hands coming through the screen. The times you'd come in and find the movie playing. The *kids'* movie."

"And why they didn't lash out when the students were here," Nori added.

Nick nodded in agreement. "They must have been thrilled to have other kids around to watch the movie with. Why act up and potentially scare them all away?"

The three fell silent, reflecting. Despite the discovery, Nick still had more questions than answers. Or, perhaps because of it. What happened? Why were the boys down there in the first place? Had Floyd hidden them when they ran away? Had he kidnapped them? Is that why they'd reacted so violently toward their father, the mayor? Nick would have to be content with the fact that most of his questions would probably never be answered. There was one, however...

"The smell of smoke in the auditorium. What do you guys think..."

"When the smell was the strongest..." Nori added.

Claudia grinned maternally, winked at the two of them. "That's when the boys were the closest."

EPILOGUE

It was determined over the following week that the two young brothers most likely died of smoke inhalation. The fire itself was probably a very small one, limited by the lack of oxygen in the room. Small, but deadly enough. It was also determined that Floyd Cropper had chosen to simply entomb the bodies where they lay instead of risking discovery by disposing of them outside The Chamberlain.

What couldn't be determined, and never would be, was the motive. Why was the old man hiding the brothers away in the first place?

Regardless, Floyd's good standing among some in the community, at least that of his memory, sank faster than a storm ravaged ship with a breached hull. They couldn't distance themselves from past associations fast enough. Others stood by their claims of him being a good, decent man. All over town, debates took place over whether or not an actual crime had been committed. Was he a saint for helping them escape their abusive father? Or, was he a sinner who'd never had kids of his own and couldn't resist the temptation when coming across two young boys out on their own at night?

"If he'd only had children of his own."

"That's no damn excuse!"

"What if he was trying to help those boys?"

"Doesn't matter. Hope he's enjoying his time in hell."

It seemed there were only two things the town could agree on: that the whole ordeal was a horrible tragedy; and that The Chamberlain's doors should never reopen.

"If it were up to me," the scruffy cashier told Nick as he counted out change, "I'd finish the job. Burn the whole damn place to the ground." The man, somewhere around sixty years of age, spit on the floor behind the counter.

Nick was becoming all too familiar with the sentiment. Over the past few weeks, he'd heard it put both more civilly and expressed far harsher. The sentiment itself, however, was always the same. He could only offer a nod and wry grin as he stuffed his change in his pocket and retrieved the two paper cups from the countertop. "Have a nice day."

And as Nick Fallon exited the coffee shop and stepped out into the first cool morning of an early autumn, he turned his focus to the fifteen-hour drive ahead of them.

"What did they have to do, roast the beans?" Nori asked from the passenger seat. "I told Claudia we'd be in Chicago by nightfall."

Nick climbed up into the cab of the rental truck, which held most of his and Nori's worldly possessions, at least the items they'd deemed necessary for a new start, and handed her one of the cups.

"Guy had no idea what a skinny chai latte was. Looked at me like I was from another planet."

"Geez," Nori said, taking a sip from her steaming cup, "things are gonna be so much different in the big city."

Nick considered the reality of her statement as he pulled onto a street that would put Angler Bay behind them. "That's the hope."

About the Author

Tim McWhorter was born under a waning crescent moon, and while he has no idea what the significance is, he thinks it sounds like a very horror writer thing to say. A graduate of Otterbein College, he is the author of several horror-thrillers and lives just outside of Columbus, OH, with his wife, a dwindling number of children and a few obligatory 'family' pets that have somehow become solely his responsibility. He is currently hard at work on one of several ongoing projects and relies on interaction with readers for those much-needed breaks...

Website:
www.timmcwhorter.com

Email:
tm5to1@live.com

FB Author Page:
www.facebook.com/pages/Tim-Mcwhorter-author

Twitter:
https://twitter.com/Tim_McWhorter

Instagram:
https://www.instagram.com/tim_mcwhorter

More by This Author

Shadows Remain

Bone White

Blackened

Let There Be Dark

The Winding Down Hours

CPSIA information can be obtained
at www.ICGtesting.com
Printed in the USA
LVHW021716040521
686471LV00018B/1108